TRUE BLUE

A CASH NELSON MYSTERY

NATHAN BIRR

Copyright © 2026 Nathan Birr

All rights reserved. No part of this book may be used or reproduced by any means, graphic, electronic, or mechanical, including photocopying, recording, taping, or by any information storage retrieval system, without the written permission of the author except in the case of brief quotations embodied in critical articles and reviews.

Published by Nathan Birr

Cover image generated by AI

ISBN: 979-8-9931371-0-0 (hc)
ISBN: 979-8-9931371-1-7 (sc)

This novel is a work of fiction. Names, characters, businesses, places, events, and incidents are either the products of the author's imagination or used in a fictitious manner. Any resemblance to actual persons, living or dead, or actual events is purely coincidental.

www.nathanbirr.com

Also by Nathan Birr

The Douglas Files

Overnight Delivery
Three's a Crowd
All an Illusion
Shot List
Chasing the Wind
Blood and Treasure
One Life to Lose
Golden Key
Mine to Avenge
Nine Lives

Douglas Files Shorts

Black Male
WinterKill
Short Sail
As Good As Dead

Non-Fiction

Rights or Wrong? Examining the Declaration of Independence in the Light of Scripture

The Last Resort Series

Fire & Ice
Broken Trust
The Fountain
Backs Against the Wall

Standalone Stories

God, Girls, Golf & the Gridiron (Not Always in That Order) . . . A Love Story

The Book of Levi

All is Calm?

Augusta Whispers

Final Rest

Shades

www.nathanbirr.com

In loving memory of Don and Flo Essink—Grandpa and Grandma—
who always made "the good life" that much better

One

DESPITE the early morning heat, I took a swig of coffee from the lid of my old Stanley coffee thermos before stepping out of my truck. I hadn't had a chance to grab breakfast, and I wanted something—a taste, a smell—to hold onto as a counter to whatever my senses were about to experience. This was, after all, my first homicide.

The pink sun against a hazy orange sky was barely over the tasseled corn that edged the park, but already the air was hot—not warm; hot—and sticky. Without even thinking, I'd thrown on a long-sleeve button-down Lee County Sheriff's Department shirt instead of a cotton polo, and now spent a moment folding up the sleeves. I craned my neck, looking at the tops of the ash and maple and oak trees that shaded much of the six-acre park, then at the town's white, double ellipsoidal water tower peeking over them. For some reason, water towers always struck me as ominous, and now, tinged orange by the morning sun, it did too.

I exhaled and concluded I couldn't stall any longer. I shoved the door of my pickup shut and walked to where two of my deputies waited by the curb at the edge of the parking lot. William "Bill" Murtaugh wore a shirt just like mine, sleeves not folded up, and a traditional campaign style hat. His hands were on his hips, his mouth thin and tight. He nodded as he greeted me with a quiet, "Sheriff."

"Bill."

Cheryl Johnson stood six inches shorter than him, her brown hair threaded through a navy LCSD baseball cap, identical to the one I was wearing. She had smartly opted for the polo with the department crest emblazoned on the breast, and wore her badge clipped on her belt. She forced a smile as she said, "Morning, Cash."

"What do we got?" I asked. The call that had come in to our dispatcher, Bonnie, had only said there was a dead body in the park, and it looked like she'd been shot. That had been fifteen minutes ago, two minutes before Bonnie had given me my Monday morning wake-up call.

Before either of them could answer, we all turned as the sound of tires on the pavement signaled the arrival of a third LCSD vehicle, this one a navy-blue Crown Vic, the oldest of our fleet.

"Wally," Cheryl said.

Brett Wallace, known to just about everyone as Wally, parked at an angle over the lines and practically jumped out. No hat, Ray-bans to combat the sun, and a tight button-down with sleeves all the way up over the elbow, about to cut off circulation. He joined us, and we said quick greetings, and then I repeated my question. "What do we got?"

"Body's over here," Bill said, pointing over his shoulder with his thumb. "Jenny Paszkiewicz found her. She's sitting at the table over there." This time he nodded left. "Thought you might want to talk to her."

"She was jogging?"

Bill nodded. "I've seen her several mornings in the park or around the area."

Jenny was a teacher at Lee County High School, a mom of two girls. They sold me Girl Scout cookies every winter. "Cheryl, you want to get her statement?"

"Sure thing."

"Wally, cordon off the area before we get any other joggers or dog-walkers."

He touched two fingers to the edge of his forehead in an informal salute and turned back to his car.

"All right, Bill," I said. "Let's go."

Bill turned and strode purposefully through grass due for a cut, and I followed half a pace behind. Fifty feet from the parking lot and just over the faintest of rises we stopped. The cornfield was no more than a first down to our left, and there was nothing but grass for a hundred feet right or ahead. Nothing, that is, except for the teenage girl prostrate in the dew. Her head was pointed north, toward the parking lot, and we came around to look at her upside right.

Exact age was hard to tell, but I guessed her to be seventeen or eighteen. She had a pretty face, marred only by the pallor of death. Lifeless blue eyes stared straight up into the sky. Roughly shoulder-length, blond hair was splayed in curls around her head. She wore a silky, cobalt blue, twist-neck blouse. The top left portion was stained with purplish crimson that was turning brown. There were two primary splotches corresponding with a pair of tears in the fabric that I presumed were bullet holes. More blood had run out the top of her blouse and onto her shoulder and upper arm, where it had dried. Another rivulet had trickled down the right side of her neck, getting sidetracked by the thin gold chain of a necklace that was askew, the pendant resting just above the right underarm. She wore a black miniskirt—leather, it appeared. Neither the blouse nor the skirt showed any indication of having been modified by anyone. She had long legs, straight out, as were her arms at her side. Preliminary analysis: she'd been shot twice—double-tapped, in fact—and had fallen straight back, dead before she hit the ground.

I swallowed hard, trying to taste the coffee. I got bile instead. I took a deep breath, trying for the smell of the corn or the scent from a pair of spruce trees at its edge or even Bill's aftershave. Nothing.

I swallowed again. "You know her?" I asked.

"Looks familiar, but no."

Bill was in his fifties, married, two grown sons, one of whom lived in Omaha and one out in the western part of the state. I doubted he had a lot of affiliation with the town's teenage population. But then again, Lee wasn't that big. The fact that neither of us knew who she was struck me as unusual, but not to the point of suspicion. If neither Cheryl nor Wally had a clue . . .

I turned my eyes back to the body. There was a black purse next to her left thigh, tipped on its side. A small purse, at least compared to the one my wife lugged around. It would likely contain an ID, but first things first.

I took a few steps around the right side of the body, then crouched down. I was grateful for a whiff of perfume, something floral. I looked at her face again. It was a very pretty face, the skin nearly flawless. She wore scant makeup, just enough to notice, except for lipstick. It was red, turning plum as her lips turned blue. I looked down her arms to her fingers. Matching reddish nail polish, a fairly new coat. Instinctively my eyes flicked to her toes, where there was no polish. Then I frowned, looking around.

Bill sensed something. "What is it?"

"Why's she barefoot?"

He shrugged. "Lots of girls go barefoot."

"In the park?"

He shrugged again.

I looked back at her face and hair. It lay mostly on top of the grass, but the ends of some of the curls and strands had fallen beneath the top of the blades. I looked around the edge of her neck, shoulders, and arms. Her skin was wet where it touched the grass, but I didn't see any moisture on top of the body or clothes.

I stood again. "You have any idea when the dew fell last night?"

"Can't say as I do."

"It didn't form on her," I said.

"So she was killed after the dew."

I nodded, then walked around her head and knelt again, this time looking for blood beside the body. I didn't see any in the grass and presumed it had pooled under her. Then I looked back at the purse. It had a half-moon shape, may have been the same material as her skirt. A strap was coiled randomly around it.

"She wasn't wearing the purse when she was shot," I said. "Or it would still be over her shoulder."

"Maybe the killer took advantage of her looking in her purse to surprise her?"

I exhaled.

"Or removed it postmortem to search it, then just left it here?"

"Possible," I said, wiping my hand across the back of my neck, which was already sweating.

"Sheriff, check this out," Bill said, crouching down beside her right leg, and I came over and did as well. He extended his finger over her right knee and pointed at the inside of her left knee. "There's some kind of substance here."

"Blood?"

"I don't know."

I braced myself with my hand and leaned in closer. The substance was mid-tone brown, semitransparent, and almost appeared to have been smeared in a small streak on her knee. It may have been accompanied by the faintest of scrapes, but there was just enough shadow on that part of her leg that I couldn't be sure, and I wasn't ready to move her.

"Little more right here," Bill said, and I pushed off the ground with my hand to get back into a regular crouch. I followed his finger to her right calf, where a tiny dab of the same substance clung to her skin like a smear of dried glue. "She spilled," he speculated, "was looking in her purse for something to wipe it off with . . . ?"

"Maybe."

We both stood. I had circled the body once and did so again, looking not at it but at the grass around it. Other than ours, there were no footprints leading to the body or away from it, but that wasn't a surprise if she had been there for several hours or more. I saw nothing that didn't belong. Particularly, as I stood at her feet, then backed up and made another circle, I didn't see any shell casings. There would be time for a more thorough search later.

I rejoined Bill as Cheryl came around the spruces from where she had been interviewing Jenny Paszkiewicz. She stopped beside Bill and looked down at the body, then away to the left. She took a moment to compose herself, then faced us.

"Jenny left her house over on Goldenrod about six and jogged into the park on the main drive. She turned into the parking lot because apparently she's computed her route down to the foot, and this helps her get to exactly five kilometers."

Bill and I just looked at her, waiting for her to continue.

"She said something caught her eye, so she went to investigate and found the body. At first, she thought she was alive, until she got closer and realized what she had found. She said she didn't touch anything, but immediately called 9-1-1, then waited for us to arrive. She didn't see anyone or anything else."

"That it?" I asked when she was done.

"She didn't have much else to offer."

"She happen to say if she recognized the girl?" Bill asked.

"You guys don't?"

"No, do you?" I asked.

"No." Cheryl frowned. Then added a furrowed brow. "She's not wearing any shoes."

"We noticed," Bill said.

Cheryl shrugged. "I could see the appeal of a barefoot walk in the grass at night."

"Dressed like this?"

"Maybe she was out on a date, out with friends, and stopped to take a walk."

"Then where did she leave her shoes?"

"In the car?"

"Where's the car?" I said, looking at the empty parking lot—empty except for my pickup, Wally's Crown Vic, and the CR-V Bill and Cheryl had come in.

"Hmm."

"She didn't come alone," Bill said.

"We're getting ahead of ourselves," I said, "but if that's the case, it means she very likely knew her killer."

"Or he stole her car afterward. Or she."

"We're getting *way* ahead of ourselves," I said.

"I'm going to send Jenny back home," Cheryl said.

I nodded. "Offer her a ride. She's had a rough morning."

Cheryl nodded and turned to go.

I looked back down at the body. "And she's not the only one."

Two

WALLY finished stringing yellow barricade tape around the clearing and the section of the parking lot where we had parked, then walked over to Bill and me. He stopped, removed his sunglasses, and looked down at the girl. Then he swore.

He lifted his eyes. "Uh, sorry."

I nodded. I thought it important that law enforcement officers conduct themselves above reproach, meaning no profanity, no getting drunk while off-duty, no crude behavior—anything that might give the department a black eye in the community. But neither was I a den mother, especially when it came to Wally. He'd run against me two years ago and had expected to be the new sheriff after my predecessor retired. There had been a few rough spots between us since, but he was a good cop, and I didn't want to do anything that would seem antagonistic toward him.

"You know her, Brett?" Bill asked. He was the only one on the force who didn't call him by his nickname.

"I think it's Pat and Molly's niece. Caitlin?"

My sigh this time was almost a groan. Pat and Molly Erickson had taken in their niece from Lincoln when her parents had been killed in a horrific traffic accident on Highway 77. That had been back in the spring, and I'd only seen the niece—pretty sure her name was Caitlin—once from a distance, but I'd thought she'd had brown hair. Not that such a thing was permanent.

"Purse will have ID," Wally said. "I can confirm."

"I want to get photos first," I said.

As if having read my mind, Cheryl trekked our way from the parking lot, a Canon EOS Rebel camera on a lanyard around her neck. "Jenny opted to jog home," she said, then raised the camera. "I figured you'd want pictures?"

I nodded, then instructed Bill and Wally to comb the clearing for any possible evidence that might have been left by the killer. There wasn't anything to dust for prints, except the purse, and maybe the skirt. But first I let Cheryl take pictures from a variety of angles while I looked over the girl's body again, looking for anything in her "posture" or on the body that might provide another clue. I directed Cheryl to the two smudges on her legs. She crouched on the ground to get close-ups of the bullet holes, her necklace, a pair of small hoop earrings. When she was done, I touched my first dead body, using the palm of my hand to close her eyelids. Then I looked up at Bill and Wally, who had returned.

"Nothing," Bill said.

I nodded. "You got her purse?" I asked Cheryl.

"Yes."

"Wally, you got the fingerprint kit?"

"Yeah."

"See if there happen to be any prints on it, or her skirt."

He knelt down, and I looked at the cornfield. The sun was now a bright yellow ball, its intensity turning the tassels white. Something about the corn bugged me, but I couldn't place it. Then I looked around the park. Thankfully, our location was blocked from either Jefferson Avenue or Main Street by trees, and, other than the occasional jogger or dog-walker, no one else visited the park this early.

"A few partials," Wally reported a minute later.

"Let's see what's inside it."

"Me?" Cheryl asked when I made no move toward it, and Bill and Wally just looked at her.

"You have more experience with purses than any of us. You'd know better if anything's out of order."

She nodded, then lifted the camera strap over her head and handed the camera to Bill before kneeling beside the purse. It was on its side, and she tipped it upright, then finished unzipping it. As if it might be booby-trapped, she gently pulled it open.

"A wallet," she said, lifting out a zip-up wallet with her thumb and forefinger. She handed it to me, and I opened it as she continued.

"Small compact, tube of lipstick, mini tin of Altoids. A single key on a ring."

I opened the wallet, which had a folded-up twenty-dollar bill but no credit cards. A driver's license and student ID both had photos that matched the face of the dead girl, albeit both with brown hair. Her name was Caitlin Thomas, and I tipped the wallet to Wally on my right.

"It her?" Cheryl asked.

"Caitlin Thomas."

Bill pursed his lips and turned away. It wasn't as if a dead girl without a name wasn't repulsive, but somehow knowing who she was—and whose she was—made it hit home.

There was also a library card and a pair of gift cards, one for Runza and one for Chick-fil-A. Lee had a Runza as of a few years ago, but the nearest Chick-fil-A was in Lincoln, thirty-some-odd miles east.

"Anything else in the purse?"

"Small pack of tissues," Cheryl said, holding it up, "and . . . a photo wallet." She set down the purse and stood, opening the small vinyl pages. "Only one picture, a man and a woman together."

"Her late parents," Wally said.

"No cell phone?" I asked.

"No," Cheryl said, frowning.

I knelt down and looked closely at her skirt. It had no pockets. I didn't want to move her body before the county coroner had a chance to inspect it, which reminded me that I should call him soon. Caitlin's body wasn't giving off an odor yet, but after too long in the heat, it would.

Without disturbing her, I felt my hand under her waist. Then I shook my head.

"How many teenage girls go out without a cell phone?" Wally asked.

"None," Cheryl said.

"Maybe whoever shot her took it."

"He didn't take her cash," Bill said.

"It's twenty bucks."

"He didn't kill her for her phone," I said. "He took it because it would incriminate him."

"She *did* know her killer," Cheryl said.

"It's a theory." I reached into my pocket. "I'm going to call George. You guys want to take a peek in the first few rows of corn over there, see if there's any sign that someone entered or exited?"

"You think the killer was lurking and waiting and stepped out like Ray Liotta?" Wally asked.

"I think if I'd just left a dead body in a public park, I'd want to get out of sight as quickly as possible."

"We're on it," Bill said.

"Cheryl, there's a trashcan by the corner of the parking lot and another one amidst the picnic tables. I doubt he tossed the gun there, but you want to take a look?"

"Trade you corn for garbage duty?" she said, looking at Wally.

"You're immune to bees, you've said it yourself."

I gave her a sympathetic I-told-you-so look, then alerted our county coroner that his week was off to a lousy start too. While I waited for him to arrive, I took another look at Caitlin's body. The light had already changed since my first inspection of her, and I spotted another tiny smudge on her left forearm, similar to the two on her legs. I didn't dare touch it to contaminate a possible sample, but I did observe that three smudges on her skin and none on her clothes was a little odd. Had they been obtained before she dressed?

George Hendricks arrived in his navy cargo van just as Cheryl returned and reported nothing but trash in the trashcans. Stinky trash, she insisted. But no bee stings.

George was in his seventies, maybe close to eighty, and had been the Lee County Coroner and town barber for as long as I had known. He had a triangle-shaped face, white unkempt hair and bushy sideburns to match, and was always a day behind on a shave. I remembered going to him to get my hair cut as a kid, and he'd looked exactly the same then as he did now. He was deliberate in everything, from his "Nebraska drawl" to trimming the hair over one's ear to his work as a coroner. His pace was also deliberate, and Cheryl and I stood and watched him walk to us from the parking lot.

"Morning, George," Cheryl said.

"Gonna be a hot one," he answered.

"Gonna?" I asked.

"Mmm."

I briefly explained what we'd observed so far, then stepped back and let him work. While he did, Bill and Wally came back and explained there were no visible footprints at the edge of the cornfield, no broken or bent stalks or torn leaves. Not even deer tracks. And certainly no gun dispatched a few rows in.

I pursed my lips. "Not surprising."

"Whoever did this seems like a pro," Wally said.

"What would a professional killer be doing in Lee County?" Bill asked.

"Let's not get ahead of ourselves," I said.

"You don't think it's the work of a pro?" Wally asked. "No shell casings, no fingerprints unless he was a young boy or a woman based on their size, no evidence of any kind. And she was double-tapped, Cash."

"I know. It looks that way. But I'd rather go slowly down that road."

"One thing strikes me as odd with that," Bill said, then took off his hat and wiped his arm across his forehead, removing a sheen of perspiration.

"What's that?" Wally asked.

Bill replaced his hat. "Why leave the body right here, where anybody could come across it?"

"Moving a body's a lot of work."

"If we are dealing with a 'pro,' and I'll admit it *looks* like it, a killer who would police his brass and take a cell phone that could incriminate him and so forth, why not carry or drag the body a few dozen feet and hide it in the cornfield?"

I turned and looked at the rows upon rows of mature field corn. That's what had been bothering my subconscious.

"Good chance that corn isn't going anywhere till the end of the month," Bill continued. "Maybe longer. Could be an animal gets to the body and leaves evidence out in the open, or the smell attracts the curious. But there's an equally good chance nobody finds the body till they take the corn down, if even then. Seems like a pretty easy way to dispose of the body."

I pursed my lips again.

"She's a local, so she'd be noticed missing," Wally said.

"Missing girl's a long way from a dead body the police are investigating already the next morning."

"Maybe he didn't have time. Heard something, saw something, got spooked."

"Maybe," Bill said.

I looked at the corn some more. Then swept my eyes around the park. Caitlin had been facing away from the parking lot, unless she had spun around upon being shot, which didn't seem to fit her posture. Then again, an arm or leg could have been posed, so no such assumptions were certain. But it seemed she had been facing south, meaning her killer had been facing north. He had been waiting for her, but hadn't come or gone through the cornfield, based on the lack of footprints. It spoke to a deliberate, intentional killing—a premeditated murder. That was chilling. Those things happened in big cities, not in Lee, Nebraska, population just under a thousand. Unless Caitlin had brought something with her from Lincoln, the "big city." But I hated to delve into speculation. I hated even to make too much of her body having been left where it was, where it would be discovered, as opposed to being dragged into the field. And yet, all these observations and points of speculation had to be considered.

George stood. "Preliminary assessment, as I'm sure you guessed, is the victim died of a pair of gunshots to the chest. Holes are small, I'd guess nine millimeter or under, but I'll know once I get her on the table—assuming the bullets didn't go through her body. If they did," he said, turning and looking back toward the parking lot.

"They could be anywhere," Cheryl finished for him.

George nodded. "There are no signs of stippling on her blouse, so she wasn't shot at a particularly close range, but that doesn't tell you much."

"Rough idea on the time of death?" I asked.

"Based on lividity of the body, initial onset of rigor in her face and extremities, I'd say between six and eight hours ago."

We all looked at our watches or phones. It was quarter after seven. That put death between eleven and one-thirty, giving for fifteen minutes' leeway. That time caused me to frown.

"Something wrong?" George asked.

"There was no dew on her body."

"No, there wasn't," he said, as if he hadn't noticed previously. "But, that doesn't mean anything." He looked at me and shrugged. "There was already dew on my car when I went to move it back into the driveway last night, a little after ten."

"So she could have been killed here as early as eleven o'clock and laid in the grass all night," I said. "That wouldn't contradict what you've observed?"

"I'd be surprised if it was as early as eleven. I'd put it closer to midnight or one, but no, that wouldn't contradict what I've observed."

I nodded.

"If there isn't anything else, I'm ready to load the body and get her out of this heat."

"I'll help you," Bill said. George nodded, and they headed to his van to get a gurney. They loaded Caitlin's body, and George departed. Blood had pooled under her and soiled the grass and dirt. But the removal of her body didn't reveal anything else, other than the lack of exit wounds from the bullets. I dispatched Bill and Wally to canvass the houses north of Jefferson Avenue that would have had a view to the entrance of the park. I asked them not to say why yet—not until I'd had a chance to speak to Pat and Molly Erickson—but to simply ask if anyone had seen anything between ten and two the night before.

Then Cheryl and I walked back to the parking lot. The morning was eerily quiet, with only the distant chirping of cardinals and an occasional passing car making any noise. I turned and looked back across the clearing to where trees separated it from a ballfield on the far side of the park. Off to the right, across the entrance road, an old-fashioned bandstand sat in a grove of trees, and beyond it were a playground, the city pool, and a larger parking lot. In just a few hours, screams and shrieks of kids cooling off on a hot, summer day would resound across the park. The kids would all be blissfully unaware of what had occurred overnight just a few hundred feet away.

"Cash," Cheryl said, drawing me back to the moment.

I turned and saw her walking toward the corn. She stopped at the last parking spot on our side of the lot and dropped to a crouch. In front of her, a roughly circular dark splotch covered the ground. Its surface was shimmering with rainbow colors, and it appeared tacky if not wet altogether.

Bill had taken the camera, but Cheryl drew her cell phone and snapped a few pictures of the spot. I crouched down and dabbed my finger in the substance and rubbed it between my finger and thumb. It was slimy, and a quick sniff confirmed it was what I suspected.

"Oil?" Cheryl asked.

I nodded.

"Wally parked over there," she said with a nod.

"This is fresh," I said.

"Fresh as in somebody was here early this morning or fresh as in the killer parked the getaway vehicle here?"

I looked at her but said nothing.

She looked around at the faded yellow parking lines, then the curb. "He backed in. Or she."

"That's quite a bit of oil."

"He was sitting here a while. Dismisses the idea that the killer was rushed and thus didn't have time to hide the body."

I shrugged. "Could have been waiting a while for Caitlin to show. And we don't *know* this was the killer's vehicle. Could have been some kids parking or someone giving their dog a late run."

"I suppose," she said with a sigh. "But if it was the killer, that means he or she and Caitlin arrived together, or one of them came on foot and the killer left in the car."

"Let's scour the lot quick," I said, "see if they happened to leave anything else behind."

We weren't lucky enough to find an ID that had fallen from a pocket or a cigarette butt flicked out the window and covered in DNA, but we did find a tire print in a muddy pothole roughly in line with where a vehicle parked over the oil slick would have had to drive to exit the lot. There was no guarantee the same vehicle that had leaked oil had also made the print, but it had rained the previous afternoon, pretty heavily for a brief period, meaning any tire print left prior to that would have been erased by the rain. Cheryl took a couple pictures of the print, and we collected a few samples of dirt that were quite a bit darker than the rest. It was likely as not they meant nothing, but they *could* have come off the tires.

There was nothing else to find in the lot, and Cheryl said she would get the samples of dirt to George to send to the state crime lab in Lincoln along with whatever other evidence he collected and then work on the pictures she'd taken.

"Actually," I said, "I was hoping you'd come with me. It might be helpful to have a woman present."

Her countenance fell, but then she nodded dutifully.

"You can ride with me," I said, and we got into my truck to go inform Pat and Molly that another tragedy had befallen their family.

Three

PAT and Molly Erickson lived on a cul-de-sac in a subdivision on the northeast edge of town. Like City Park—and like the whole town, really—it was rimmed by cornfields. Their house was a two-story with dormers over a front porch and a double garage with a basketball hoop mounted over the door. Old Glory hung listlessly from a flagpole beside the driveway, and the walk to the front door was lined with multicolored flowers. The Erickson house was a postcard of the Midwest. Pat and Molly were staples of the community, he a CPA and a fixture at town meetings and beer-league softball games and she a part-time secretary for his firm and a well-known volunteer for a handful of causes. Their son had been a star wide receiver for the Lee County Longhorns and now ran a bar and grill somewhere in Texas, and their daughter had married and moved to western Iowa, but both were the kind of people who got hugs and handshakes when they returned to town. The Ericksons were an All-American family and had garnered the sympathy of the whole county when tragedy had befallen Molly's sister and brother-in-law in the spring. A drunk driver going the wrong way on a four-lane highway had plowed into their crossover at seventy-five miles per hour and sent them to eternity, leaving their teenage daughter an orphan. Pat and Molly had come to the rescue, and the community had rallied around them. As I parked the truck at the curb and unbuckled my seatbelt, I wanted to puke.

The air felt as if it had grown more humid on the two-minute drive over. Because of that, or because of the task at hand, sweat beaded on my forehead beneath the brim of my cap as Cheryl and I walked up to the front door. The neighborhood was quiet, still before eight in the morning on a Monday, but there was no telling how many nosy faces were concealed by sunlight reflecting off windows.

The Ericksons had a video doorbell, and I wondered if already their hearts were sinking as they checked some or other device to see who was on their doorstep. After all, there wasn't a good reason for the sheriff and deputy to visit, especially this early in the day. But when the front door drew back and I saw Molly through the wide-framed screen door, a look of confusion flashed across her face.

"Good morning, Sheriff," she quickly covered. "Deputy."

"Ma'am," Cheryl said with a slight tip of her cap.

"Molly, I'm sorry to bother you," I said. "May we come in?"

"Of course," she said with a furrowed brow, then pushed the lever and extended the screen door to us. I removed my cap and let Cheryl enter ahead of me, and we followed Molly toward the base of a stairway straight in from the door. "Pat," she called. "Sheriff Nelson and Deputy Johnson are here." She turned to us, the look on her face impossible to discern. Something between confusion, fear, and down-home hospitality. "Would you have a seat?"

She ushered us into the living room, and we sat down in a pair of armchairs flanking a table in front of the window. A moment later, we stood again as Pat Erickson descended the stairs. He wore a nicely starched shirt and tie, and his face had just as much dissonance as his wife's. We exchanged quick greetings and handshakes and, at his insistence, sat down again. He and Molly sat side by side on the couch.

"To what do we owe the pleasure?" Pat asked.

I had delivered bad news on a few occasions before, including news of an unexpected death, and found myself wanting to ease into it, as if dumping the bad news on someone would ruin their day and beating around the bush wouldn't. But I knew there was no undoing this, that their lives were about to change irreparably for the worse, and nothing I did could soften the hammer that was about to fall.

"I'm sorry, but I have some bad news."

They exchanged a quick glance, and Molly grabbed for Pat's hand. He clasped it in his, holding it against his thigh.

I licked my lips and took a breath. "We found Caitlin's body in the park this morning. She had been shot twice in the chest."

I watched their faces drain of color. Pat's expression faded, whereas Molly's eyes went wide, and her face contorted as if she was about to wail. Instead, she raised her free hand to her mouth. "N-no," she said. "No."

Pat's eyes finally focused. "You're sure?"

"She had her ID in her purse. It's her."

"You said she was shot?"

I nodded with a soft, "Yes."

Words caught in his throat as his eyes misted over. Molly let out a soft whimper, then louder sobs as she buried her face in his shoulder. Pat embraced and held his wife for several minutes as she cried, and Cheryl and I sat silently, unable to do a thing about it.

Finally, when it seemed appropriate, I interjected. "When was the last time you saw her?"

Molly separated from her husband. "Last night," she said, before reaching for a tissue from a box on the coffee table. She dabbed her eyes, then spoke through more tears. "She came home just before eleven. She liked to push curfew, so I . . ." She started crying again, dabbed, blew her nose. "I'm sorry."

"Don't be," Cheryl said. "Take your time."

Molly sniffed, clenched her husband's hand a little tighter. "I had a cup of tea and made sure she was home. She went up to bed and I thought she was still there until you came," she said, just getting it out before falling into her husband's shoulder again.

"She sleeps late in the summer," he said.

"I need to check," Molly said, suddenly pulling away. She got up. "I need to see for myself."

"Molly," he said, but she had already stepped past him and swept toward and up the steps. I nodded at Cheryl, and she followed. Pat and I remained seated.

He swallowed back his emotion and cleared his throat. "Sheriff, where did you find her?"

"City Park, just south of the north parking lot," I said softly.

"Shot?" he asked again.

I nodded. "Twice in the chest."

"She was murdered?"

"It appears that way."

He looked away, wiping his hand over his mouth. "Who . . ."

I gave him a moment. "I know this is a strange question to ask regarding a teenage girl, but is there anyone you know of who might . . . have a reason for wanting her dead?"

"No, of course not," he said, looking back at me.

I nodded.

"If you'd have said—"

Molly returned with a shriek and buried herself in her husband again, and he as much as possible back in her. Cheryl and I stood there, me fumbling with the brim of my cap, giving them space. After several minutes, they composed themselves and sat back down on the couch, now on opposite sides as before.

"I'm sure there's questions you need to ask," Pat said.

"There are, but we also want to respect your grief," I said. "We can come back later if you would prefer."

"No. The sooner you get answers, the sooner you can find out who did this, right?"

I nodded.

He swallowed hard again. "What do you need to know?"

I wanted to follow up on what he had been about to say before Molly returned, but decided that maybe should wait until I had a moment alone with him. So I picked up where Molly had left off.

"You said Caitlin returned a little before eleven?"

She nodded. "Just a couple minutes."

"Where had she been?"

"I don't know."

"Caitlin took things very hard after her parents' death, obviously," Pat said. "Staying with us, being in a small town, was quite an adjustment, on top of everything that . . . goes with losing someone you love," he said with a gasp. He willed the emotion away. "We imposed some basic rules but gave her some leeway in terms of what she did, where she went. She was a good kid, Sheriff, and we trusted her enough to give her that space."

"I understand." I gave it a moment and turned to Molly. "Did you speak with her?"

"We said hello and goodnight, nothing else. She went to her room, and I went up to bed a few minutes later."

I looked to Pat.

"I was already asleep. Never heard her come back."

"Did you observe anything in your brief interaction last night that suggested she was in trouble?" I asked. "That she might be going out again or have plans?"

Molly shook her head at both questions.

"What about throughout the day, or in recent days?"

More shaking of heads, from both of them.

"Had you noticed any behavioral changes recently, any signs that maybe something was bothering her or she was stressed in some way?"

"She was stressed since she arrived in late March," Pat said. "And she was a teenage girl," he said with a thin smile. "There were mood swings, crying, sullen behavior, anger—all to be expected—but I can't say it was different lately."

"No," Molly said with another sniff.

"Before she went out, what was she doing yesterday?" I asked.

Molly sat back a little. "We all went to mass in the morning, then had lunch. She went for a run in the afternoon, before the rain, and then left before dinner."

"Does she have a car?"

"No, but she drives our Nissan," Pat said.

"Did she drive it last night?"

"Yes."

"I know this is silly, but did she return in it too?"

Molly frowned. "She came in through the garage. And, yes, I heard the garage door open and close behind her."

"Why do you ask, Sheriff?"

"There were no vehicles at the park."

"Well, it sounds like she snuck out after curfew, so it would make sense she wouldn't risk opening the garage door to get the car out again."

"It does," I said. "Your Nissan doesn't happen to leak oil, does it?"

Pat shook his head.

"Have you noticed her sneaking out before?" Cheryl asked.

They looked at each other.

"Once, back in spring," Pat answered. "We eased up on the curfew a little, and . . ."

We waited.

"We think she snuck out a few times recently, but never confirmed it," Molly said. She shook her head. "We should have pushed. We should have—"

"This isn't your fault," Cheryl said.

"How recently?" I asked after a moment.

"Last week or two," Pat said.

"Not before that?"

"Nothing that made us suspicious."

"Did she have a boyfriend?" Cheryl asked.

"Not that we know of," Pat answered.

"I kind of suspected she might," Molly answered, looking down. "Little things, you know, like doodling with a faraway look in her eye and then turning the page when I walked in, dressing a little nicer to go out some nights than others. But I didn't push—I figured she'd tell me if she wanted to."

"I know this sounds like hands-off parenting," Pat said, "but you have to understand, we weren't her parents. We tried to walk a fine line and . . ."

"No one's judging you," I said.

Cheryl caught my eye, as if she had another line of questioning, and I nodded.

"What was Caitlin wearing last night?"

Molly squinted. "Let me think . . . She changed after her run and a shower . . . I think it was a white Huskers tee and a pair of shorts. And she took along a sweatshirt but . . . I don't remember her wearing it when she came back."

"You're sure on the tee and shorts?"

"Yeah," Molly said.

Pat nodded as well. "Why?"

I took a breath. "She was wearing something different when we found her, a dressier blouse and a black leather skirt."

"She did have a boyfriend," Molly said with a look out the window. Her eyelids fell.

"It's a possibility," I said.

"Meaning it's possible he's the one who killed her, too," Pat said.

"That's possible, but only speculation."

"We found her barefoot," Cheryl said. "Is that unusual, for her to go without shoes?"

"Around the house, no, or in the backyard," Molly answered. "But I wouldn't think she'd leave home without shoes."

"What about a phone?" I asked. "Did she have a smartphone?"

Pat nodded.

"We didn't find one on her or in her purse," I said. "Might she have left it here?"

"I doubt it. She was on it all the time, like most kids."

"Would you mind checking in her room to see if it's there?" I asked.

"Of course," Pat said, rising. "You want to come along, take a look?"

I stood, and Cheryl and Molly followed me as I followed Pat slowly up the stairs, then to the right down the hall to the back right bedroom. Two windows looked out, one facing west, one north. The latter let in light filtered through a tree, shining on an unslept-in bed. The room lacked the typical teenage girl frills I would have expected, either because Caitlin wasn't frilly or because the room wasn't hers but hers at her aunt and uncle's house. Or because my expectations of teenage girls' living quarters were flawed.

There was a poster on the wall of a woman in Team USA gear playing soccer, a couple more of actors or musicians, presumably. No one I knew. There were also a couple photo collages on the walls, and more framed photos of places and people—Caitlin with her parents, just her parents, Caitlin with a handful of girls. There were no boys, with or without her, but if she was keeping a boyfriend a secret from her aunt and uncle, that made sense. The room was mostly clean, other than for a gray sweatshirt on the floor behind a small office chair at a desk against the west wall.

"I don't see her phone," Pat said, "but I also don't know where she might have kept it or hidden it if she didn't take it with her. Feel free to look around," he added before again consoling his wife. Cheryl and I entered the room, looking first with just our eyes. Nothing jumped out at me as being out of place.

"Is this the sweatshirt she was wearing last night?" Cheryl asked, nodding at the one on the floor.

Molly nodded with a sob.

I opened her closet. A few boxes were stacked on a top shelf beside some folded sweaters. Blouses, dresses, skirts all hung above a shoe rack that was full of shoes. More were wedged under the hanging clothes on top of the rack, and even more were in front or beside it. Sneakers, flip-flops and casual sandals, an assortment of dressier shoes and sandals, a pair of cleats. There was also a soccer ball in the back corner. I stepped back.

"Caitlin played soccer?"

Pat and Molly both smiled. "She loved soccer," Molly said. "It was one of the few times when she came alive, talking about it or playing or practicing or training or anything. It was her escape."

"She's go—" Pat swallowed. "She *was* going to UNL in the fall on a soccer scholarship."

"Do you mind if I look in the dresser?" Cheryl asked.

Molly shook her head, and while Cheryl dug around through socks, underwear, and pajamas, I looked at the desk. Caitlin's laptop was closed, revealing several stickers on the top—a Team USA Soccer logo, a red N with "Huskers" scrawled atop it in black, what I assumed was the name of a band, a Scooter's Coffee logo. I touched the lid. "May I?" I asked.

"Whatever you need," Pat said.

"Any idea what her password is?" I asked when stopped at the login screen a moment later.

He shook his head.

"I might be able to crack it," Cheryl said as she closed the top dresser drawer. "No phone, no diary."

"You check under the pillow?"

She nodded and turned toward the bed.

The desk had a few more photo frames, which in itself was old-fashioned. As far as I knew, pretty much everyone had gone away from actual photos to digital collections on their phones. There were also a couple of pens and pencils and a small notepad, but nothing of relevance.

I circled the room again, then stopped at the north-facing window. The window was unlatched.

"Did Caitlin have many visitors in her room?"

"No," Molly said.

"We had a rule about boys, which may not have mattered," Pat said. "But she usually went out instead of having friends over. Why?"

"The window's unlocked," I said, turning the latch. "And there's no screen," I added as I lifted the window.

"That's odd," Pat said. He walked over beside me. "I remember removing the storm and putting on the screen this spring, after Caitlin moved in."

I crouched down and looked through the opening—an opening big enough for a human to fit through—at a very sturdy branch of the maple tree filtering the morning sunlight. I tried putting myself in a teenage girl's shoes—or perhaps lack thereof—and imagined myself crawling onto that branch, then shimmying down to where it connected to the trunk about eight feet off the ground. It wouldn't be easy to get up or down via the branch, but for someone accustomed to climbing trees—or for a good athlete—it would certainly be doable. But not likely in the sort of shoes one might wear with a twist-neck blouse and a leather skirt.

"You think she climbed out?" Pat asked.

"I do."

"It would explain the substance and scrapes," Cheryl said, and I quickly explained we had found what might have been sap and a few scrapes on Caitlin's skin.

"I don't believe this," Pat said. "Sneaking out to meet some boy and now . . . If her parents knew . . ."

I put a hand on his shoulder. "Pat, we don't know anything yet. But this is not your fault. I know you, and Caitlin's parents knew you and Molly, and they would know that you did everything you could for their daughter."

Holding back tears, he nodded.

I shut the window with a mental note to take a look around outside after we were done in Caitlin's bedroom. And we almost were. With Pat and Molly's permission, I grabbed the laptop to take back to the office where Cheryl could try to get past the password to see if it contained any secrets. We asked about friends and got a few names, although Caitlin didn't have a lot of friends in town, which made sense given her recent arrival. Pat and Molly knew nothing of her social media presence, so I made another mental note to task Cheryl to that as well. Then, as we all started down, I asked Molly if she would mind taking a quick look through Caitlin's shoes to see if she recognized any that were missing. She said she doubted she would but was willing to check. Cheryl remained with her, and Pat and I went downstairs.

Standing alone with him in the living room, I said, "Earlier you were about to say something when I asked if you knew of anyone who might want to harm Caitlin."

He rubbed his hand over his forehead and blew out a breath. "I was going to say, if she'd been shot once in the head, I might consider suicide. Please don't say anything to Molly, as I don't want even the thought to upset her."

"You think Caitlin was suicidal?"

"I don't," he said firmly. "I would have done . . . I don't know what—something—if I had thought so. And yet . . . I'm not sure it would have surprised me either given everything she's been through."

I placed a hand on his shoulder again. "Pat, we're going to do everything we can to find out who did this and bring them to justice. You have my word on that."

"I know it, Sheriff."

We shook hands as the women came downstairs. Cheryl and I said our goodbyes, then left the Ericksons to their renewed grief.

Four

ORANGE and white signage blocked my path and reminded me why I had been dreading this Monday morning. Main Street, a.k.a. Highway 28, runs south past the school and then City Park, before making a gradual turn west and heading through downtown before exiting town and continuing west to the next county. At least, it did. But as of this morning, I remembered, the three blocks that roughly comprised downtown were closed for repaving and some civil engineering upgrades. That made getting through town difficult and getting to certain downtown businesses—including the Lee County Sheriff's Department—almost impossible. And somehow, with all that had gone on that morning, I had missed the detour signs and found myself putting my truck in reverse to make a Y-turn on Main Street while a young woman in an orange hardhat, neon yellow vest, and hot pink work boots arranged barricades on the sidewalks.

I had planned on cruising through downtown to the West Street Diner to grab some breakfast to go, but opted to get a cup of coffee and a box of donuts from Casey's instead. I retreated a block north and approached downtown via 5th Street, using the alley and back entrance to the parking lot that served both the sheriff's department and the courthouse/jail. It had been enlarged a year or two ago, paving over the remains and foundation of an old, demolished Victorian house, and the blacktop was still dark black, absorbing the heat of the sun well enough to make my boots feel as if they were sticking to it as I walked to the side entrance.

Cheryl, who I had dropped off at the park so she could bring the CR-V back, met me before I made it to the bullpen at the end of the hallway. "You have a visitor," she said, nodding back at the open door to my office.

I narrowed my eyes.

"Mayor O'Reilly."

"He know?"

She nodded.

"How?"

She shrugged. "Word travels fast."

I nodded, then handed her the donut box. "Save me one."

"No promises."

I took a gulp of coffee, then a deep breath, before turning the corner into my office.

The four-term mayor of Lee, Nebraska, was not sitting at one of the two chairs facing my desk, but rather immediately around the corner at a chair under the window that looked into the bullpen. Ron O'Reilly was in his sixties—maybe seventies by now—but wore his age with the distinguished demeanor of a politician. The crisp, collared dress shirt, slightly loosened tie, and gold bracelet on one wrist to match the gold watch on the other added to an air of authority. The truth was, O'Reilly was as down to earth as they come, a lifelong Lee County resident who knew how to play the political game but also did a more than fair job of representing the people of Lee and their rural, blue-collar, conservative way of life.

"Mayor," I said, extending my hand.

He stood and shook it. "Cash. How are you this morning?"

"Been better, to be honest with you."

O'Reilly's face quickly sobered. "It's a tragedy, isn't it?"

I nodded. "That why you're here?"

He reciprocated the nod. "I know your head must be spinning, but I was hoping for just a few minutes."

I gestured at one of the chairs facing my desk, shut the door, and took a seat opposite him in my chair. "How'd you find out about the murder?"

"So it is a murder? Not a suicide, not an accidental death?"

"Double tap to the chest, no shell casings. Yeah, it was a murder."

He shook his head and sighed. "You spoken to Pat and Molly yet?"

"They're taking it rough, as you'd imagine."

"After what that family went through in the spring . . . Sometimes I have to question how the Man Upstairs dispenses hardship."

Now was not the time to get into a theological discussion on why God allowed pain and suffering, so I let the mayor's remark pass. And I waited, having known him as long as I had. He would ask his questions but eventually get to answering mine.

"A tragedy," he muttered again, then licked his lips. "I was at West Street Diner this morning and Roger Marion mentioned that a body had been found in the park. I called Greg McDonald and he thought it was Caitlin Thomas. Deputy Johnson confirmed as much when I got here a few minutes ago."

"What time were you at the diner?" I asked.

"Mmm, got there a little after eight."

I did a little math. That was about the time we'd gotten to Pat and Molly's, meaning the only people who had known Caitlin was dead at that time had been those of us in the department, Jenny Paszkiewicz, and the killer. But if Jenny had said something to her husband who had said something to someone, or Bill and Wally had said something to someone who had seen something the night before, or one of Pat and Molly's neighbors had seen the police car at their place . . . Word indeed traveled fast in a small town, as Cheryl had said, but this fast? At any rate, I highly doubted eighty-year-old Roger Marion or Greg McDonald were suspects, nor that the killer had spread word around town. I chalked it up to gossip spreading fast.

"Anyhow," O'Reilly said, "the reason I stopped by is to ask that you keep me in the loop. Something like this is going to reverberate through town, and with everything else going on . . . well, I'd like to be up to speed."

"I'll keep you updated," I said.

"I know you will, Cash. I didn't mean to imply otherwise, but . . ."

"But?"

He looked toward the door, as if it might have come ajar. "This sounds awful, but it is an election year. Not that I want the killer brought to justice any more than any other year, but I really don't want to be blindsided by anything."

"I'll keep you in the loop."

He nodded, clapping his hands down on the arms of his chair. "You got any leads?"

"Not really." I weighed how much to say, balancing keeping the mayor in the loop without telling him too much. Mayor O'Reilly was trustworthy, but he was also a politician, and information was a commodity. So I didn't tell him we were pretty sure based on the unlocked window, removed screen, and nearby tree limb that Caitlin had snuck out after curfew, potentially to meet the killer. It was all conjecture anyhow, even after Cheryl and I found what could have been the imprint of the heel in the dirt at the base of the tree—say a stiletto that would go with a twist-neck blouse and leather skirt, a shoe that had been dropped out the window before Caitlin had climbed down the tree barefoot and then stepped into said shoe. Beyond conjecture, really, and still didn't explain what had happened to the shoes. Nor did I mention the oil spot in the parking lot because, as of yet, it didn't mean anything one way or the other. I did mention the missing cell phone and our suspicion that the killer had taken it, and the believed time of death, somewhere around midnight.

"Anything I can do to help?" O'Reilly asked.

"I'll let you know."

He nodded. "I'll let you get to it. And I shouldn't be too far from the office too long."

"Something going on?"

"It's an election year, and now with the construction . . ."

"Yeah, I suspect your office may field a few calls."

"Oh, we've been fielding them already. I know it's a hassle, but so were the potholes and cracks you could lose a small child in. The downtown economy will thrive with new paved streets, new sidewalks, new landscaping . . ."

Like I said, politician. I let him give his spiel.

"And the economy of the county is benefitting now with all the construction and engineering contracts. My granddaughter Shelby even got a job working on one of the road crews. It's sure nice to have her back in town."

"And so the true motive for the project comes out," I said, tongue planted just a little more firmly in cheek to make sure the mayor knew I was joking.

He waved me off. "You make me sound like a Democrat."

I smiled. "She happen to wear pink boots?"

O'Reilly smiled, then shrugged. "She's a woman, and you know women."

I pursed my lips.

"Come on, Cash, I didn't mean anything. It's just women love their shoes. My wife must have twenty pairs."

"I know what you mean. Jessi has close to that many. So did Caitlin."

Now he frowned.

"We found her barefoot in the park, but dressed like she was going out."

"Odd," the mayor said.

"It is, and maybe nothing more than that. But oddities stick out to me."

He slapped his hands down on the arms of the chair again. "Well, I'll leave you to the oddities," he said, and we stood. He extended a hand. "Keep me posted, and let me know if I can do anything."

"I will, Mayor. Thanks."

I walked him to my office door, closing it again behind him. I spent just a moment pondering pink work boots, stiletto imprints (maybe) in the dirt, and barefoot murder victims. Then I decided to quit mulling with furrowed brow and do some actual policework.

Five

HALFWAY through Cheryl's briefing—and halfway through my chocolate covered, unfilled long john—Bill returned to the office. He pulled up a chair—and a long john of his own—and listened as she explained that she had called Caitlin's cell phone provider, learned by a call to the Ericksons, to try to ping the location of her phone. It had not pinged, and unlike on TV, they couldn't turn it on remotely to ping it. I figured if the killer had taken it because it incriminated him or her, it and its SIM card were likely smashed and/or burned and/or at the bottom of a pond somewhere.

"Can they get records of who she called or texted?" Bill asked before taking a bite of his donut.

"Not without a warrant."

"Call Judge Felix and get one," I said.

"Will do."

I turned to Bill. "Find anyone who saw anything?"

He swallowed. "No. Nothing. Wally and Lake are now canvassing the entire subdivision, since we figured she had to get from her house to the park somehow."

I nodded. Lake Ryan was my other deputy, and he had worked the night shift, but apparently murder made up for lack of sleep. I then explained what Cheryl and I had learned at the Erickson home and our theory Caitlin had snuck out.

"There aren't any security cameras in the park, are there?" Cheryl asked when I was done.

"No."

"What about along Jefferson?"

"Not that I'm aware of," I said as Bill shook his head.

He swallowed another bite of donut. "We had one house facing the park on Sunrise that had a doorbell camera, but they said it didn't record. I can have Wally and Lake check for any as they go."

I stood and walked to the wall beside the break room, where there was a large map of the entire town. Each building was outlined on it, with the address. I looked at the subdivision on the northwest intersection of Main Street and Jefferson Avenue. Sunrise Avenue made a looping journey from Main to Jefferson, with four other streets branching off from it, each ending in a cul-de-sac. The map didn't have trees, bushes, or fences on it, so if Caitlin had snuck out and tried to remain inconspicuous on her way to the park, it was hard to tell which route she would have taken.

"They're going to every house?"

Bill nodded.

"Yeah, tell them to ask if anyone has security footage or a doorbell camera or anything that was filming between eleven and one last night. Maybe somebody caught something."

"I'm on it," he said, already moving for his phone.

"And you might want to join them. There's quite a few homes in the whole subdivision."

"Roger that."

"Where are you headed?" Cheryl asked as I deposited the remainder of the long john in my mouth.

"I'm going to visit Caitlin's friends."

"You want a woman along?"

"I'd rather you get that warrant and pursue it. Then see if you can make any headway on the laptop."

She nodded.

Before heading out, I used the restroom, and when I came out, Bonnie Klein, our dispatcher/secretary was waiting for me. Bonnie looks

Indian—from India, not the Native Americans we call Indians—even though she's not, with raven black hair usually messily piled on top of or behind her head, and with penetrating dark eyes. She's divorced and her kids have grown and moved away, so we at the department benefit from all her cooking now—two or three times a week she brings in homemade pastries, chips and dips or crackers and cheese spreads, or leftover—and sometimes not leftover—casseroles. She is fastidious when it comes to administration—she says it's her OCD—and it comes out in chitchat that can take up fifteen minutes in no time. So I was dreading a delay, but Bonnie was all business.

"Jim Vander Zee is here to see you," she said.

"In my office?"

"Out front."

"He say what it's about?"

"I believe his exact words were 'infernal racket.' The construction."

"You didn't redirect him to the mayor's office?"

"I tried," she said with a smile, "but he wanted to talk to you."

"Okay, thanks."

Jim was a partially disabled Vietnam vet. I say partially because while he had limped ever since coming back from "the jungle" and would tell anyone who would listen about the shrapnel in his knee and thigh, he had also worked an assortment of odd and part-time jobs around town until recently. Now he spent most of his time milling around town, swapping stories at West Street Diner with the other aging Baby Boomers, drinking free coffee at Al's True Value, and sitting on benches and chatting up passersby. I considered Jim something of a fixture in a small town, even if he could be a little irascible at times. That may have been old age setting in or may have also been attributed to the jungle. No one really knew.

A large counter separates the bullpen from the lobby of the department, but instead of talking to Jim over the counter, I pushed through a door on the left and out into the lobby. South-facing windows let in plenty of morning sunlight, and west-facing windows the sunlight's reflection off a dump truck idling on 4th Street. Jim stood off to the side, reading a labor law poster beside the public restroom.

"Morning, Jim," I said, and he turned. He wore a corduroy jacket over a white V-neck, even though it had to be pushing ninety degrees by now. He held a John Deere baseball cap in his hands, revealing a bald spot surrounded by wisps of ever-thinning hair. I never could tell if he hadn't shaved in a while or never shaved and his beard just didn't come in. His face was perpetually a little crooked, and his mouth formed a triangular grin as I approached. Old enough to be my grandpa, his hand was still like a vice.

"Sheriff, thanks for the time."

"What's on your mind?"

"Did you give permission to rip up the whole cottonpickin' town?"

"Afraid it's not my permission they need."

"Then whose is it?"

"Town council, county board, maybe even the state since Main Street is also a state highway."

He mumbled under his breath and tried to wad up his cap.

"They had public information hearings back in the spring."

"I remember, I remember. My memory didn't go with my hair."

I nodded.

"But, Sheriff, have you heard the racket they're making? Clangin' and bangin' and trucks rumblin' all the time," he said, jerking his thumb sideways toward the dump truck on 4th. "And barely waited for the sun to come up to get started."

That reminded me of standing beside a cornfield as the sun had come up, and standing over a dead body. I remembered the silence, not the clangin' and bangin' and rumblin' from several blocks away. But I'd learned that arguing with Jim was usually pointless.

"Can't you do something about it? Ain't there an ordinance or something they're violating?"

"Maybe if they were working at night," I said, shaking my head. "But construction is going to be loud." I stopped just short of reiterating a few of the mayor's talking points about how nice downtown would be once construction was finished—they were, after all, the mayor's talking points, not mine.

"I don't know," he muttered, looking down, twisting his cap some more. "I don't know."

The age-old lines of someone who was licked but didn't want to admit it.

He looked back up. "Ain't there nothing you can do?"

The devilish streak in me made an appearance. "Have you talked to Mayor O'Reilly?" I asked, knowing how much Jim grated on his nerves. "I'm sure he'd value your input. It is an election year."

I reaped what I sewed with that last remark, as Jim went on a ten-minute harangue about politics, hitting everything from Vietnam-era peaceniks to Communism infiltrating our schools to drugs coming over the border with illegal immigrants. I stopped him when he got to theories about the government salting the sky to influence the weather. I thanked him for stopping by but told him I had some police business I had to tend to, and even mollified him by saying I'd put in a word with the mayor. It seemed to do the trick enough that he left peacefully.

"The government is controlling the weather?" Bonnie asked with a raised eyebrow as I came back through the door to the bullpen, where her desk is closest to the front counter.

"You heard that?"

"Who do I vote for to get a break from this heat wave?"

"You'll have to ask the mayor," I said. "Politics are his domain."

At least for another two years, until it was time to elect a sheriff again.

Six

RYLIE Kučera lived with her parents in a ranch house a mile southwest of town. Hers was the third name Pat and Molly had given me when I'd asked for friends of Caitlin's I could speak to. Ashlee Blaine's mom had told me she was at work but should be back around noon, and no one answered at Ti'Ana Parker's house. Ashlee and Ti'Ana were the only really close friends Pat and Molly knew Caitlin had. Rylie, on the other hand, was a teammate on the Lee County High School girls soccer team and a frequent training partner.

A thirty-something woman with a purse over her shoulder opened the door just as I was about to ring the doorbell. She startled and took a step back, almost coming out of her flip-flop.

"Good morning, ma'am," I said. "Sorry to startle you."

"No, it's fine . . . Sheriff," she said after squinting to see my badge.

"I'm hoping to speak with Rylie Kučera. Is she here?"

The woman's face blanched. "Is she in trouble?"

"No," I said with a quick shake of my head. "No, but I do have some bad news about a teammate of hers."

"Oh dear, I just knew it would finally happen here."

I frowned. "What's that?"

"Fentanyl, right? I hear so much on the news about accidental overdoses and—"

"It wasn't an overdose, ma'am. But there was a shooting."

Her eyes turned into dinner plates. "A shooting? My goodness, is Rylie okay?"

"I have no reason to think otherwise. I was hoping to ask her some questions about the victim."

"Is she a suspect?"

"No, ma'am. I just want to talk to her. Is she here?"

"No," she said after a brief hesitation, I assumed because she was trying to figure out if there was any other way her daughter—I also was still assuming might be in trouble. "No, she's up at the school training, actually."

"All right, I'll try to catch her there. She is a minor, so you're welcome to come along."

"You say she's not in any trouble?"

"No."

Well, unless it turned out she'd killed her teammate, but there was no reason to even think that, much less say it.

"She's with her aunt. Maybe I'll text her and give her a heads up."

"That's fine," I said, then thanked her and headed back to my truck. I drove back into town, detoured around all the "infernal racket," and passed the west entrance to City Park on my way to the school. Lee and the surrounding county are small enough that there is only one public school to service the entire county, and the elementary, middle, and high school are all combined in one rambling, added onto and re-added onto edifice. The school is surrounded more or less on three sides by parking lot, at the north end of which are the baseball and football fields, the latter encircled by an eight-lane synthetic rubber track. Fly balls and touchdown passes soar and spiral toward cornfields just across the highway, making for an incredibly bucolic scene on summer afternoons or fall evenings. On hot, muggy, August mornings, the fields are usually empty. Today, someone was cutting grass on the baseball outfield while two females were at the far end of the football field that doubled as a soccer pitch. I pulled my truck up to just short of the bleachers and small press box on the west side of the field and drained the last of my lukewarm coffee from my thermos before getting out. The thermometer on my dash read 93.

As I started across the track, one of the two females broke off and headed to intercept me. The other continued "dribbling" a soccer ball around cones set up in the end zone. I concluded the female approaching me was Rylie's aunt, a conclusion I doubled down on when she was close enough that I could see she was not a teenager. She was dressed oddly for soccer, in a heather gray T-shirt with an unfamiliar bird logo on the front and a black miniskirt. Athletic shoes. Dark hair was bundled on top of a Nike visor. The visor kept me from recognizing her until we were just a few yards apart.

"Sheriff Nelson," she said. "Rayanne texted me that you were coming."

"Miss Ives. I didn't realize you were Rylie's aunt."

"Kassondra, please. How do you know Rylie?"

"I guess I don't."

Truth was, I didn't really know Kassondra Ives, the Democratic challenger to Mayor O'Reilly. I'd run into her a few times before, and everyone in town knew *of* her since the fall when she'd announced her candidacy. She had been hard to miss with signs and flyers, radio spots, informal meet-and-greets when she would walk in to anywhere from the grocery store to the library to the hair salon to engage her constituents, and her presence at every civil function throughout the summer. To be fair, it would take an epic grass roots, populist campaign to unseat an incumbent as entrenched as O'Reilly. And from the little I knew of Ives, she didn't fit the demographic particularly well. Lee was a rural, working class, largely conservative community. Ives' mayoral platform was about equity and justice and reform, things that all sounded good but likely meant different things to her than to most of the town's citizens who considered "welfare" to be a dirty word and DEI a Trojan Horse for Marxism. Working in her favor were youth—she was at most thirty-five—and good looks, and, so she claimed, the fact that she wasn't a lifelong resident of Lee and could "think outside the box." It was enough to make things interesting in November, but I expected a landslide reelection.

"Rayanne said there had been a shooting, of Rylie's teammate?"

"Caitlin Thomas," I said. "Pat and Molly Erickson's niece. She was found dead in the park this morning."

Kassondra covered her mouth with her hand. "How awful," she said through her fingers, then dropped her hand. "You don't think Rylie's involved?"

"I do not. Caitlin's aunt and uncle said she didn't have a lot of close friends, but that she worked and trained with Rylie. I'm hoping she might know something that would point us in the right direction."

Kassondra nodded. "I haven't said anything to her yet. Do you mind if I'm present while you question her?"

I didn't correct the perceived tone that this was an interrogation. Instead, I said, "Not at all," and we set off toward the end zone.

Rylie was dressed like a soccer player—short-sleeve jersey, bright red shorts, tall white socks, cleats. Dark brown hair was in a ponytail and partially covered by a headband that failed to keep sweat from pouring down her reddened face. She came around the far cone, deftly passing the ball from foot to foot, then with an impressive suddenness ripping off a left-footed shot that sliced like a banana and entered the soccer goal under the football goalpost just beneath the crossbar. She picked up a towel and a water bottle from beside the cones and trotted toward us.

"Rylie? I'm Sheriff Nelson."

She nodded. "Yeah, I recognize you. Is something wrong?" she asked before squirting a stream of water from her bottle into her mouth.

"I'm afraid I have some bad news," I said.

"Is it my mom?"

"No, she's fine. I actually just spoke to her."

Relief briefly passed over her face.

"It's Caitlin Thomas," I said. "She was found dead this morning in City Park."

Rylie's face went blank.

"I'm sorry."

She blinked a couple times, then wiped the towel across her face.

"Are you okay, Ry?" Kassondra asked.

"Wh-wh-wh . . ." She swallowed. "What happened?"

"She was shot twice."

"Somebody murdered her?"

I nodded.

"Who . . . who would kill Caitlin?"

"Do you mind if I ask you a few questions about her? Pat and Molly, her aunt and uncle, said the two of you trained together?"

"Yeah." She wiped a tear from her eye. "Um, yeah, go ahead," she said, then wiped her face with the towel again.

"When was the last time you saw Caitlin?"

"Saturday afternoon. We went for a run, grabbed a smoothie afterward."

"How did she seem to you?"

Rylie shrugged. "Fine, I guess."

"Was that the last time you spoke to her, texted her?"

"She sent me a text Sunday afternoon to see if I wanted to go for another run, but we were in Hastings visiting my grandma."

"The last few weeks, did she seem different? Did she seem bothered by anything, scared, frustrated? Did she confide anything that was wrong?"

"No," Rylie said, having been shaking her head all along. "If anything, I thought she was maybe a little happier the last few weeks. She talked a lot about college in the fall, playing soccer at UNL. It seemed to give her hope," she said, then took another drink. She squirted a little more water on her face and wiped it with the towel yet again.

"Did her text yesterday say anything about her plans last night, or did she say anything Saturday?"

"She said something Saturday about seeing Scott."

"Scott?"

"Her boyfriend, Scott Cooper."

"She had a boyfriend?"

"Yeah. Her aunt and uncle didn't tell you?"

"I don't think she told them."

Rylie's eyes widened a little. "They'd been dating for a while. She didn't say it was a secret or anything."

"How long's a while?"

Rylie shrugged. "Maybe a couple months?" Another shrug. "Maybe only a month."

"Does Scott go to LCHS?" I asked. The name was vaguely familiar, but I didn't have the entire town census memorized.

"He graduated in the spring."

"Her aunt said she came home a little before eleven, but she then changed clothes and went out again afterward. Do you think that would have been to see Scott?"

"I really don't know. I wouldn't think so, but I don't know. She didn't talk a lot about what they did or when."

"Or where?" I asked.

Rylie frowned.

"Sorry. Do you know if they made a habit of meeting in the park, or if she often hung out there?"

"No, I don't think so. We jogged through it once or twice, but the park's kind of a hangout for little kids. I can't imagine her hanging out or meeting someone there."

"Do you know if she routinely snuck out after curfew?"

Rylie shook her head. "She got along with her aunt and uncle okay, but it just wasn't home. The accident that killed her parents really haunted her and made it hard with them."

I nodded, having gleaned the same from Pat and Molly. It was understandable.

"Do you know of anyone who had anything against her, might have had motive to be angry, jealous, anything like that?"

"No. She kept to herself a lot, even once she joined the soccer team." Rylie winced.

"What is it?"

She wiped sweat off her brow one more time. "She was way better than everybody else on the team. I'm one of the best players, and I'm nowhere in Caitlin's league. I kind of got the impression she cared less about the team winning and more about making sure her status as one of the top players in the state didn't get tarnished. That sounds awful to say."

"Was there friction between her and her teammates?"

"No. We had our best year ever, and it was because of her."

I nodded and thought about follow-up questions. But I doubted that a teammate who got less playing time or her disgruntled parents would have taken to murder, especially months after the high school soccer season ended. Then again, petty jealousies could fester and grow over a summer. So I asked, "Nobody had any problems with her, with her taking over, playing style, anything?"

"No, not that I ever saw or heard."

I thanked Rylie for her time and gave her my business card, asking her to call if she thought of anything else. I thanked Kassondra as well, and, because she was a politician, she shook my hand. Then I headed back to my truck, thinking that a secret boyfriend was a long way from a motive for murder, but it was the closest thing to a lead I had.

Seven

LEE sits about seven miles south of Interstate 80, connected to the major east-west thoroughfare by Nebraska Highway 28, which also runs north of the interstate to small towns no one outside of central Nebraska has ever heard of. We get a fair amount of traffic passing through town on 28, which makes the stretch of highway through farmland a good place for my deputies to sit and look for speeders. I'm not real big on speed traps or trying to catch out-of-towners, but it is part of the job. And the vast majority of people ticketed on 28 are non-residents, because locals know we occasionally hang out there. That also means you can pretty much bank on a seven-minute drive from I-80 to town. So it was no surprise that Ashlee Blaine, whose morning shift at the Philipps 66 at Exit 363 ended at 11:30, pulled into the driveway of her home on Arbor Court at precisely 11:42—factoring a few minutes to punch out and get to her car.

Per my agreement with Ashlee's mom, I waited in my truck as Ashlee got out and walked to the front door. Laura Blaine wanted to break the news about Caitlin to Ashlee herself, so I had said I'd give her several minutes. I studied the quiet, peaceful neighborhood, a new subdivision that had been cut into the farm fields northwest of the school within the last dozen years. Arbor Court was so named for the trees planted by the city in the breezeway, all of which were about fifteen to twenty feet high but would one day shade the stub of a road and the cul-de-sac at its end.

Now, they still let in plenty of haze-filtered sunlight, so I let my truck idle and the air-conditioning run.

Back when I'd been in high school, we'd had a classmate killed when he rolled his dad's Camaro doing ninety on a country road. He had been a classmate, nothing more, so his death had been sobering but hadn't really affected me. I didn't know what sort of bond Ashlee and Caitlin had formed in the four-plus months since Caitlin had moved to Lee, so I wasn't sure how long to give her. I settled on what was likely a very cold ten minutes, then left the sanctuary of my truck and trudged dutifully to the front door. Laura Blaine opened it almost before I knocked.

"Come in, Sheriff," she said, her eyes red. She led me into the living room of their two-story house, similar in style to Pat and Molly's, where a teenage girl was sitting on the ottoman of an armchair. Curly brown hair hung around her face and the collar of a red, Philipps 66 polo shirt. "Ashlee, this is Sheriff Nelson," Laura said.

Ashlee looked up, her eyes also red, and wiped tears from one side of her face with her palm.

"I'm very sorry for your loss," I said.

She uttered a soft, "Thank you," as Laura motioned for me to sit down. I took a second armchair, no ottoman, facing Ashlee.

"Can I get you something to drink, Sheriff?" Laura asked.

"No thank you."

"Honey?"

"No," Ashlee said in barely more than a whisper.

"Let me know if you need anything," Laura said, then withdrew to the kitchen.

As delicately as possible, I recounted the necessary points of Caitlin's death and asked basically the same questions I had asked Rylie. Caitlin had hung out at Ashlee's house Saturday evening and seemed fine. They had watched a movie and talked about college, with Caitlin headed to Lincoln in the fall and Ashlee set to attend Doane University in nearby

Crete. She said for various reasons neither of them had a lot of friends locally, but had formed a quick friendship, one they had expected to continue post high school. "I thought Caitlin would be one of those friends you always have," she said, "that you introduce your kids to one day."

Through tears and with a few pauses to blow her nose, Ashlee said she had no reason to think anyone would harm Caitlin, nor had she observed anything suspicious regarding Caitlin's recent behavior or moods. I was about to chalk Ashlee up as a dead end, nothing more than grief-stricken best friend, until I said almost in passing, "I assume you know her boyfriend?"

Ashlee looked down.

I waited.

When she raised her head, her bottom lip was pinched between her teeth. She flicked her eyes toward the doorway through which Laura had exited previously, then focused them back on me. She swallowed. "Caitlin told me she was seeing an older guy," she said softly. "She swore me to secrecy."

"An older guy," I said. "Not Scott Cooper?"

Ashlee shook her curls back and forth. "Scott was her boyfriend, but she was seeing this other guy too. She didn't tell me his name."

"What did she tell you about him?"

"Not much." She swallowed again. "She said he was a man, though, compared to all the boys at school. We talked a lot about how immature and dorky most of the guys at Lee are."

"Including Scott?"

"I think Scott was kind of a rebound for her." She shrugged. "He's nice, but a typical immature guy."

"And this new boyfriend wasn't."

"No." She looked down again. Her eyes slowly came up. "Caitlin was almost eighteen, in just a few weeks, and I don't know that they were even sleeping together. She didn't talk about him much, but it sounded like he treated her like an adult, like someone who had a future and not just a horrible past. He was someone to have mature conversations with, about life, not high-school life."

"Did anyone else know about this?"

"I don't think so," she said with another shake of her head.

"Do you know how long she'd been seeing him?"

"Just a couple of weeks. At least that's when she mentioned it."

"Do you know anything else about him, who he is, where she met him?"

Ashlee shook her head.

"Do you think she might have snuck out after curfew to meet him?"

It was the sort of question that would get struck down by any reasonable attorney in a court of law, since it led to speculating on Ashlee's part. But if anyone was qualified to speculate on this mysterious, older boyfriend, it would be the one person in whom Caitlin had confided. And frankly, a seventeen-year-old girl coming home just before curfew, then changing into more "adult" attire and sneaking out to go to the park fit with having an older boyfriend.

"I don't know," Ashlee answered. "Maybe. She didn't talk much about him."

A few other standard questions revealed nothing new, so I thanked Ashlee for her time and offered my condolences again. Like I had Rylie, I gave her my business card and then went on my way. A boyfriend and a secret, older boyfriend. I was a long way from knowing what had happened to Caitlin, but potential motives were starting to surface.

I called Jessi as I drove back to the office to let her know I wouldn't be coming home for lunch. She had assumed as much, given my earlier text about a murder, and we talked until I was back in the parking lot listening to jackhammers in the distance. I promised her I'd be home for dinner and headed inside. All four deputies were huddled around Cheryl's desk, looking at her dual computer monitors.

"You all better not be setting up a Fantasy Football League again," I said.

"Hey, Boss," Lake said turning to me first. At just twenty-seven, Lake is our youngest deputy, a Gen-Zer by definition and the department's liaison to the younger demographic. He's also our tactical expert, a weapons aficionado, but not the gung-ho "gun nut" stereotype. Slow to speak, eager to learn, the only real knock on Lake is that he's originally from Wausau, Wisconsin, and is thus a Badgers fan.

"Lake, thanks for coming in."

"Day like today, all hands on deck, right?"

I nodded. "You find anything canvassing?"

"Nothing," Bill said. "Four homes had some sort of security camera footage, but we've gone through it all," he said with a nod at Cheryl's screens, "and there's nothing but a racoon."

"We also doubled back to the houses where we got no answer earlier," Wally added. "No new info."

"So we've got an unlocked window by a tree and maybe sap smears on Caitlin's legs to suggest she snuck out and walked to the park, but nothing to corroborate?"

"And nothing as far as a lead on who was there with her."

"I may have something on that," I said, but first looked to Cheryl. "Where are we with a warrant and cell phone records?"

She oriented her right monitor so I could see a list of names, numbers, and dates. "She's a teen, so there are a million texts and a few calls. I've been cross-referencing names and numbers, and there's two things of interest."

"Okay," I said, edging in closer.

"There are all the expected contacts—her aunt and uncle, the friends you mentioned, her soccer coach at Nebraska, some one-offs that all make logical sense for a teenage girl's phone. And no sudden pattern changes or numbers that just popped up except one I'll mention. There are a lot of texts and calls between her and a Scott Cooper over the last month and a half."

"Boyfriend," I said.

Four sets of eyes turned my way.

"According to Rylie Kučera and Ashlee Blaine."

"Well, that would make sense."

"When was the last contact with Scott?"

"Sunday at . . . six-oh-four. A text."

That fit with Pat and Molly's account that she had left before dinner—she had texted Scott to say she was leaving, theoretically.

"What's the second thing of interest?"

"This number," Cheryl said with a click, highlighting about a dozen rows in her list on the screen.

"No name?"

"It's a burner, four-oh-two area code, so local-ish, but that's it."

"Mostly texts?"

"All texts."

"Both ways?"

Cheryl nodded.

"Last one . . ."

"Two, back and forth, a little after five on Sunday."

"Do we have access to the actual messages?"

"No."

"Need another warrant?"

"No, they're encrypted and even the provider doesn't have access."

"How many total to that number?"

"Let's see . . . twenty-seven."

"Starting when?"

Cheryl scrolled. "Just about two weeks ago."

"That fits," I said, then shared Ashlee's news that Caitlin had a secret boyfriend as of the last few weeks.

"Boyfriend finds out about secret boyfriend . . ." Wally said. "Or vice versa."

"Wouldn't that be more likely to leave the secret boyfriend dead than Caitlin?" Bill asked.

"Your girl cheats on you, you go after her or the other guy?" Wally asked.

"The other guy," Bill said. "If I loved my girl."

"I don't know, bro," Lake said. He tipped his head to the side. "My girl was cheating on me, I might be inclined to double tap her . . . Hypothetically speaking," he said, looking up at me.

"Cheryl, pull up everything with Scott."

She did her computer magic and isolated just the calls and texts to and from Scott Cooper. There were 131, spanning seven weeks, back to early June.

"A lot at first, then a slow dwindling," she said.

"The last two weeks?" Wally asked.

"Maybe a little, but especially the last month."

"That fits," Lake said. "I had a girlfriend in college. We texted forty or fifty times a day the first couple weeks. After a month, it was a couple times a day."

"Bill, how many times a day you call your wife when you were dating?" I asked.

"Until the tin cans and string wore out," he said with a grin.

"I don't want to jump to any conclusions, but this is the closest thing we have to a lead. I'm going to try to visit Scott. Cheryl, if you can do anything to find out who owns that burner, do it."

She nodded.

I turned to the other three. "Any of you have anything pressing?"

"I have some paperwork I should tend to," Bill said.

Wally and Lake shook their heads.

"See if you can get a list of Caitlin's teachers from the spring, her soccer coach, anybody else who might be able to give you any insight into what was going on in her life. Pat and Molly said they all went to mass, so let's find out where, see if she confided in a priest or a counselor or something there. It seems she's been pretty guarded, not even giving her best friend many details about this mystery boyfriend, but I'm guessing she told someone."

"Maybe a digital diary," Cheryl said. "I'll work on cracking the laptop password too."

"Good. Anybody hearing anything from outside these walls?"

"I'm sure the town's talking, but I haven't heard anything," Bill said. The others echoed him.

"Okay. Sooner or later, expect it. People will want answers, and we'll want to give them some, but until we know anything, 'the investigation is ongoing.'"

They all nodded, so did I, and then I grabbed another donut for lunch and headed back out into the heat.

Eight

AFTER again getting no answer and seeing no signs of life at the Parker home, I drove south almost to the county line to where Scott Cooper was registered as still living with his single mother. Jackie Cooper practically forced me to sit down at the kitchen counter and have a glass of lemonade while she busied herself cutting a variety of fruit for a snack for her afternoon book club. I gathered she was also making a homemade caramel dip, and fully expected samples before I left.

Scott was at work all day, she said, at Loehr's Cattle Company. When I asked if he was dating Caitlin Thomas, she confirmed it but said she thought it was pretty casual. Caitlin was going away in the fall, and he wasn't, and they both realized there wasn't much of a future to it. In some ways, she thought, they were more good friends than a couple.

"Why are you asking about Scott and Caitlin?" she asked as she set down a knife now that a pineapple had been neatly cubed. She wiped her hands on a dish towel.

"I'm afraid Caitlin was found dead last night."

Jackie stepped back, bracing herself on the counter with one hand and covering her mouth with the other. "Oh, no. Oh . . . Is that why you're asking about Scott?" she said with suddenly wide eyes. "Do you think he's involved? Is that why you're here?"

"I don't think anything, Ms. Cooper. I'm just trying to piece together last night."

"My Scott would never kill anyone."

"I'm not saying he did."

She gave me something of an evil eye, then turned to the refrigerator and pulled out two clamshell containers of strawberries. "Scott didn't kill her," she said again, then grabbed a smaller knife and began removing the stems and slicing the strawberries.

"Do you know if he saw her last night?"

Jackie gave me the evil eye again before saying, "Yes. They went out."

"Do you know where?"

"He said something about going to Clay Center."

I frowned. Clay Center was a small town—smaller even than Lee—about forty miles southwest. And not to diminish the fine people of Clay County, but I couldn't think of any reason for a couple of teenagers to drive there—any more than there'd be a reason for Clay Center residents to come to Lee.

Jackie responded to the frown. "Somehow they found an ice cream shop out there, and they liked to bum through the backroads on a summer night."

I mulled. That made sense, in theory, for a couple that was more friends than lovers, but also made a convenient cover story for pretty much anything else.

"I can't believe she's dead," she said, staring off into space. "What happened?"

"She was shot," I said.

Jackie shook her head.

"Do you know who drove?" I asked.

"I assume Scott," she said, resuming slicing her strawberries. "He took his truck."

I frowned again. Scott had driven and so had Caitlin. Why would they drive and meet somewhere and drive from there to another location? Because Caitlin didn't want her aunt and uncle to see her boyfriend pick her up?

"He was back a little before eleven," she said, then looked up. "When was Caitlin killed?"

"Likely after eleven," I said.

"So you don't suspect him?"

"I don't suspect anyone yet," I said, mostly truthfully, since the secret older boyfriend wasn't yet anyone. "Did he say anything about the evening?"

"I was in bed when he came home. I heard the door, then heard him in the kitchen."

"What about this morning?"

"He had a bowl of cereal and a muffin and didn't say much. That's pretty normal." She sliced through more berries, her knife clacking on the cutting board with each stroke.

I didn't gather anything else from Jackie Cooper, other than when Scott's shift ended and when he was likely to return. That and the fact that she'd only met Caitlin once or twice. I thanked her for her time, and the lemonade, and was just getting back in my truck when Wally called.

"Tell me you've got something," I said.

"Between Lake and I, we talked to every teacher she had. General consensus is she was quiet, withdrawn, but not a loner, not a problem child. I've got a sit-down with the school psychologist at three, and Lake's chasing down leads at her church."

"Which church?" I asked.

"St. Pete's."

Moderate-sized Catholic church on 6th and Lincoln. A third of the church-going town attended St. Peter's.

"Anything else?" I asked.

"Lake had an idea," he said, in a way that made me think he didn't think much of the idea. I waited for him to continue. "Maybe there is no motive," he said at last.

"Like a serial killer?"

"Yeah. But serial killers don't double tap their vics in the chest."

"Not usually," I said.

"They knife them or strangle them or worse things."

There was an unspoken "But" in the air, and I left it hanging.

"Thing is, the shoes."

"Yeah," I said, switching my phone to the other ear. "What about them?"

"Bill said something about thinking it was weird she was barefoot in the park, and I don't disagree. What if . . . what if the killer took her shoes, as some kind of weird trophy?"

"A trophy?"

"You know, they cut off a lock of hair or a piece of clothing or a finger or something? What if the guy who killed her had a thing for shoes of his victims?"

"That's a weird thing to have."

"Well, if we're talking serial killers . . ."

"Point made." I sighed. "I don't think we can rule anything out, but a serial killer coming to Lee County to take teenage girls' shoes after he shoots them in the park . . ."

"That's what I told Lake."

"The school psychologist is at three?"

"Yeah."

"Patti Davis?"

"That's her."

I'd consulted with Patti before. As far as a public-school psychologist went, she was pretty sound. "Okay, keep me posted."

"Will do, Cash."

I shook my head and then, as I backed out of the Coopers' driveway and headed back to town, I chased from my brain the image of a dingy basement occupied by a stringy-haired serial killer who kept women's pumps and flats in a glass display case under the stairs.

Nine

FOR reasons I've never understood, the Lee County Coroner's Office is not in Lee proper but four miles north and a mile east on Pioneers Road. George Harrington called as I was almost back to town, so I again detoured around downtown and pulled into Casey's for the second time today, this time to fill up my nearly empty gas tank. My donuts, coffee, and lemonade were not holding me over, so after filling up, I went inside to buy something to munch on. I got in line at the register behind Caleb Tucker, who owns a small construction company in Lee, but who is better known for mashing homeruns down the left field line in beer league softball games.

"Cash, how is it?" he asked as we shook hands. His other held a pair of microwaved sandwiches, a bag of chips, and a one-liter of Pepsi.

"It is," I answered.

"Construction messing with you too?" he asked. "I've been back and forth about five times, and if this goes on till the snow flies . . ."

"Ha," said a voice emerging from the candy aisle. I didn't recognize him, but he wore a Tucker Construction long-sleeved shirt over dirty jeans. "We'll be lucky if they finish by the time the snow flies."

"Cash, you met my cousin Danny?"

I had not, and we shook hands.

"He's working for me this summer and just loves our small town."

Danny huffed.

"Ya'll think construction's bad," another voice sounded from the next register over. A potbellied man with a cap pitched back on his head and a toothpick in his mouth turned with a plastic sack of items to face us. Cal Hunter was a third-generation farmer from a little west of town, and never short of opinions. I started to think I might be delayed in getting to the coroner's office.

"Try getting farm equipment through town." He moved the toothpick around with his tongue and shuffled closer. "I lease a field from Dennis Hall east on Denton Road, and you can't hardly get there from here any longer."

"Maybe O'Reilly wants to make the election interesting," Caleb said, nodding for his cousin to go ahead and pay first.

"Shoot," Cal said with a drawl. "Gon' take a lot more than ripping up half the town to lose to a liberal woman. You know she wants to legalize marijuana and other recreational drugs, allow kids to take puberty blockers at school. She'll turn Lee into Little San Fran before a term's up."

"She doesn't stand a chance," Caleb said under his breath, almost as if embarrassed to be openly discussing politics in line at the convenience store. "Unless she can pave the streets quietly," he added with a chuckle.

"Yeah, well . . ." Cal said, then waved and headed out.

I asked the Tucker cousins where they were working this afternoon, then paid for my bag of Combos and bag of jerky. At least the road construction was giving people something else to talk about besides murder, and maybe making for a harder week for Mayor O'Reilly than me.

The heat of midday had intensified as I parked on the cracked asphalt lot in front of the building that served as the Lee County Coroner's Office and also the office for the county veterinarian. It was much cooler in the lab where I found George. He was in a lab coat over a button-down shirt and slacks, a paisley tie loose around his neck. We shook hands and he led me into the autopsy room where Caitlin's pale body lay rigid on a stainless-steel table. Her hair had been washed and fell straight into a basin beneath her head. A light blue sheet covered her body from below her knees to her shoulders, providing modesty but not hiding the Y-cut George had used to open her chest cavity. The sterility of death was overwhelming.

"I confirmed the cause of death as two nine-millimeter bullets to the chest," he said, referencing the contents of a manila folder attached to a clipboard as he spoke. "One entered just above the left breast, chipping her third rib and perforating her lung. The second was just below it to the right." He looked up. "Straight in the heart."

"Did you recover the slugs?"

"Yes. There were trace elements on each of them, which I sent along with the bullets to the lab in Lincoln."

"Trace elements?"

"One was a fiber of some sort, maybe a hair."

"Hers?"

"Too small to tell."

"So it could have belonged to the killer?"

"Could have, but whoever he or she was, he or she left no DNA on the body. None."

I nodded. "Does that confirm no sexual assault?"

"It does."

That wasn't a surprise—rapists usually didn't shoot their victims before or after the assault, and there had been no outward signs of a sexual assault at the park—but it was still a relief.

"There was some very minor bruising on her elbows, one shoulder, her buttocks, and the back of her head, all likely results of falling after being shot. No other signs of a struggle or any other injuries on her body. No scratches or bruising on her hands, nothing under her nails, no indication of any altercation before the shooting."

"What about dirt?" I asked, walking around to the foot of the table—and her still bare feet sticking up into the air.

"There was a small brown smudge on her right heel," he said. "Why?"

"Any sign that she had walked barefoot for a quarter mile?"

"No, but depending on the surface, there may not be much sign."

"Dirt, grass stains on the bottom of her feet?"

"No."

"Where the heck are her shoes?" I asked, apparently out loud.

"That reminds me, I do have her personal effects here," he said, pointing to a small clear container on a stand beside the table. "Do you need any of them for evidence?"

I took the container from him. Two small hoop earrings and the pendant on a thin gold chain, slightly stained with blood. No rings, which was unusual for teenage girls in my limited experience.

"Her clothes," he said as my eyes settled on a small pouch also on the stand. "Including her shirt, which was a mess with bullet holes and bloodstains. I put it in a separate pouch inside."

"What about the substance on her legs?" I asked.

"Yes," he said, looking back at his notes. "There was also a small trace on her skirt. It's sap."

"Tree sap?"

He nodded.

"Any idea what species?"

"I sent a sample to the lab, just to be positive, so they can maybe tell you, but I'm sure it's sap. Does that mean anything?"

"Our theory is she climbed out a second-floor window to meet someone in the park. If the sap matches the tree outside, that would help confirm that theory. If it's from a different species of tree, well, that would add another piece to the puzzle."

"I'll be sure to let you know as soon as I hear back from the lab."

"Appreciate it. Anything else of note?"

"Yes. I'm confident the time of death was between eleven p.m. and midnight."

"That's precise."

I did some quick math. Caitlin had come home just a few minutes before her eleven o'clock curfew. Five minutes to change. Five minutes to add jewelry, perfume . . . "Was she wearing perfume?" I asked. "I thought I smelled it this morning."

"Yes, as a matter of fact. I found strong traces on her neck of a fruity scent. And some blush and lip gloss, for what it's worth."

Five minutes and five minutes, plus another five to climb out the window and down the tree. Then, depending if she walked straight or stuck to the shadows, ten to fifteen minutes to get to the park. That put it at eleven-twenty at the earliest. I made a note to pin down with Molly Erickson the exact time she had gone to bed, assuming Caitlin would have waited until her aunt was no longer in the kitchen to sneak out. I also wanted to check with her on how Caitlin's hair had been styled when she'd returned just before eleven, as time may have been needed to curl and style it the way we'd found it in the park. I blamed not asking these questions earlier on it being my first murder investigation—and on the fact that there was no reason then to think they mattered. Maybe they wouldn't anyhow.

George had nothing further, so I thanked him and left. I stopped in the parking lot, wishing for just a hint of breeze as I reached for my phone and called Lake. "What's up, Boss?"

"You were an athlete in high school, weren't you?"

"Yeah. Basketball, football, baseball my freshman year."

"Dumb question."

"Okay."

"How far do you think you could throw a pistol?"

"Why?"

"If you're free, I could use your help at City Park."

"When?"

"As soon as you can get there."

Ten

MY hat, shirt, jeans, socks, and underwear were all soaked with sweat as I pulled into my driveway a few minutes before five. Lake and I had spent ninety minutes beating through row upon row upon row of the cornfield east of City Park on the off chance the killer had disposed of the gun by heaving it into the corn. It was unlikely that a pro—or as much of a pro as Caitlin's killer was—would have just chucked the gun. But it was possible, as it was that he or she had used the field as a means of egress and left some evidence deeper in the field than Bill and Wally had searched earlier. We had left a lot of sweat behind and gained a lot of scrapes and scratches from the corn leaves and found no gun or other evidence. But given the extent of our search, I felt confident in putting a red X through the field as far as a source of clues. That was something.

Jessi was in the kitchen when I entered our three-bedroom ranch on 2nd Street. The very picture of petite, Jessi is a good nine inches shorter than me—a few less when she wears her blond hair on top of her head like in this case. Wide blue eyes give her a youthful look—even more youthful than her thirty years. Along with her eyes, a small Greek nose and dimpled cheeks had helped make her Homecoming Queen the year after I graduated and Miss Lee County of the County Fair a year later—a title she had sought only for the meager scholarship money it provided. I had known Jessi Randall in high school, but didn't fall for her until a "chance" meeting arranged by mutual friends after we graduated.

"Hi, Hon," she said, looking up from the island sink. Her brow furrowed. "You're all wet."

"You're cute," I said, noting the lavender sundress that failed to conceal her baby bump, also petite despite her being seven months and change into her first pregnancy. I leaned down to peck her neck beside a loose strand of hair. "Smells good," I said as a I straightened up. "What are we having?"

"Pizza casserole," she said, shaking out a colander of mixed greens. "You smell like . . . a cornfield?"

"I have time for a shower?"

"Mmm-hmm. Should be ready about five-thirty."

I quickly showered and put on a clean LCSD shirt—a polo this time—and sat down at the table a few minutes before Jessi served dinner. I had long ago learned she didn't want help with prep—I just got in the way. Cleanup and dishes afterward were a different story.

"How was your Monday?" I asked as I prepared to sip from a tall glass of iced tea.

"Fine, other than for trying to get to the bank," she said, bringing a stack of plates, napkins, silverware, and a precariously balanced salad bowl to the table. "I forgot about the road construction starting today."

"You and everyone else," I said, taking the bowl off the top.

She set the plates down. "How long is this supposed to last? Quite a while, I assume?"

"All questions regarding downtown construction are hereby referred to the mayor's office," I said, then took another drink.

"Aha," she said and retreated to the refrigerator. "Ranch, Caesar, French?"

"Whatever you're having."

"I'm having balsamic vinaigrette."

"Ranch," I said.

She brought back two bottles.

"How's Junior?" I asked, eyeing her abdomen.

"*She* has been kicking like a mule today," Jessi answered. "Like *her* daddy."

Although it went against our mutual desire to plan ahead and be prepared, we had decided to be surprised by our first baby's gender, but it didn't stop either of us from having our druthers and lobbying for them. I wanted a little boy I could teach to play ball and go hunting with and she wanted a little girl to dress up and take shopping. Besides, if we had found out the gender ahead of time, we'd have had to have a "reveal" party with colored cupcake frosting or exploding confetti in balloons or something that I wasn't sure I could put up with. Then again, settling on neutral paint colors for the bedroom-turned-nursery hadn't been real easy either.

Jessi did something with the casserole—sprinkling cheese on top, maybe—while I found myself lost in thought about the possibility of a baby girl. A baby that would grow up into a teenager someday, then have boyfriends. I suppose it was every father's subconscious fear—that something awful would happen to his little girl. But having seen a dead blond teenager in the park that morning drove home the fragility of life. A part of me didn't want him or her to ever come out of the safety of Jessi's womb.

Pizza casserole is a long-running Randall supper staple. Essentially lasagna with pepperoni, sausage, and mushrooms or olives to taste, it hits the spot—especially when the spot has had nothing but donuts and Combos all day. I served us each heaping, serving-spoon-sized helpings, and, as we dressed our salads, Jessi said, "Okay, tell me what's going on in town with the murder."

"You haven't heard anything?"

"Other than the bank, and a quick stop at the market, I've been here all day."

Jessi taught at the First Baptist Church of Lee Elementary School, and thus had summers off. She kept herself busy gardening, reading copiously, and participating in several ladies Bible studies, prayer groups, and maybe even a book discussion group. I lost track of which group met when.

I briefed her on Caitlin's body being found in the park, a few of the details provided by George's autopsy, and the mostly empty questioning of her friends and teachers. That included Wally's conversation with Patti

Davis, the school psychologist, and Lake's questions at St. Peter's Catholic Church. He'd told me, while traipsing through the corn, that he'd spoken with Father Holmes and the church's secretary, both of whom knew Caitlin but hadn't had any formal conversations with her.

"You think it's one of the boyfriends?" she asked when I was done with my casserole. Eating for two, she had plowed through most of her dinner and scooped out a second serving.

"Not necessarily, but it's the only place the evidence points as of yet."

"Maybe something followed her from Lincoln."

I held a forkful of casserole in front of my mouth. "Could be," I said, then ingested the bite. "Problem is," I said, gulping it down, "is that's a pretty wide-open door."

"Well, they don't give you the biggest and shiniest star for nothing," she teased.

"Thing is, a jealous boyfriend or something of that level wouldn't look like this."

Jessi set down her fork. "How do you mean?"

I spent a moment weighing my words. I had no qualms about sharing department work with Jessi because she was trustworthy and knew where the lines were, and because sometimes a women's intuition—or just another perspective—helped me see things from a different angle. Even so, there were limits to how much I should bring home, or how much I wanted to. Seeing Caitlin's lifeless eyes, watching her aunt's body shake as she cried, getting a glimpse into the evil behind murder they were all things I'd rather shield my wife from if possible.

"The killer left no evidence," I said. "No DNA that George found, no shell casings, no witnesses. That's a pro move. Cheryl made no headway finding out who owned the burner phone that Caitlin was texting the last few weeks. It may or may not be the killer, but whoever it is, they covered their tracks well."

"And that doesn't match with a high-school love triangle gone bad."

"Not likely. Not unless one of the high schoolers is also special ops."

"Or watches every episode of *NCIS* like some people . . ."

"I get your point, but there's a difference in knowing how to be discreet from watching TV and actually doing it in real time."

"I suppose."

I stabbed my salad, sending crumbs of crouton flying everywhere.

"So why were you soaked when you came home?"

"Lake and I walked through the cornfield, looking for a gun or some other piece of evidence."

"You think the killer tossed the gun into the cornfield?" she asked with raised eyebrows.

"It's not a ridiculous idea."

"No, unless he was a pro . . ." she said and took to gazing out the sliding glass door at the backyard. I wasn't sure if that was indicative of there being something on her mind or if my amateur ornithologist of a wife had been distracted by a particularly bright cardinal. So I crunched on mixed greens and waited.

"You didn't find anything?" she said, turning back.

"Not so much as a footprint or a bent stalk."

"Hmm."

"What?" I asked, then waited as she took a bite of casserole.

"If the killer was a pro, or something like it, why did he leave the body in plain sight?"

"Instead of dragging it into the corn?"

"Yeah."

"That's exactly what Bill said this morning. And Lake this afternoon."

"And?"

"And . . ." I said, "I have no idea. Just like I have no suspect and no motive and nothing to tell Pat and Molly about who killed their niece."

Eleven

WHILE I washed up a few of the dishes, Jessi put away leftovers and asked about Pat and Molly and how they had taken the news. She asked if I'd heard of any sort of support system for them—meals, help with funeral arrangements, the like. I hadn't, and said so, and she took that as her cue to lead such efforts. She had the right blend of compassion and tact to handle it, so I left it in her hands and headed out to do a little more policework.

Jackie Cooper had told me Scott worked until five-thirty or six most days. I timed my arrival to their place near the county line to six-thirty, and found Scott in the driveway, on a creeper under his truck. He heard me approach and rolled out, then sat up. "Sheriff. My ma said you might be coming out."

"Scott," I said, then extended a hand to help him up.

He looked down as he withdrew his hand, dirty from who knew what under his truck. "Uh, sorry."

"Don't worry about it."

He wiped his hands on his jeans, which didn't do much for either of them. A sleeveless red Kansas City Chiefs tee was equally dirty, but neither held a candle to a sweat-stained LCHS ball cap that was turned backward over dark, unkempt hair. "Patching an exhaust pipe," he said. "Wouldn't want the Law pulling me over for disturbing the peace or something," he said with a grin and a wink.

"Do you have a few minutes to talk?" I asked.

Scott nodded, wiped his hands again, and retreated into the garage. He came back with two five-gallon buckets which he turned upside down in the driveway and nodded for me to have a seat. Good as anything.

"You said your mom mentioned I might be coming. Did she tell you why?"

He looked right at me. "Caitlin."

I nodded. "I'm sorry."

"Yeah. Me too."

I waited a beat. "How long had the two of you been seeing each other?"

"June 14. Flag Day. Don't ask me why I remember that."

"Your mom thought things were pretty casual between the two of you?"

He shrugged. "I guess. It was temporary. She was going to UNL in the fall, then bigger and better things. I'm stuck here in Lee County."

"What sort of things?"

"I dunno. I just meant, I didn't think she was coming back here, you know?"

I nodded.

"I can't tell you why, but we clicked. Like that song, 'Girls Love Country Boys.'"

It was "Ladies Love Country Boys," by Trace Adkins, I knew because it used to thump through my pickup truck when I drove around the county. But that didn't seem relevant at the moment.

"Were the two of you together last night?" I asked.

He nodded.

"You mind walking me through the evening?"

Scott rubbed his hands together. "Not much to walk. We drove around for a while, got some ice cream. Parked and talked for a while."

"What'd you talk about?"

"Nothing." He stopped rubbing his hands and looked up. He shrugged. "Little stuff, nothing important."

"How did she seem to you last night?"

"How do you mean?"

"Was she preoccupied or distracted, anxious, fearful, mad—was she different than normal?"

"Mmm, not really. Maybe a little distracted. It was kind of hard to tell with Caitlin, you know? She was always a little distracted, I think because of what happened back home."

"The accident?"

"Yeah."

I gave the conversation another beat. Then asked, "Whose car did you take last night?"

"Mine."

"Her aunt said she left the house in their car."

"I picked her up at the clinic."

"Why's that?"

"Empty parking lot," he said with a shrug. "She said her aunt and uncle were strict and it was best they didn't know we were dating." He shrugged again.

"That was okay with you?"

"Wasn't like I was asking for her hand in marriage or something. And they were her aunt and uncle, not parents."

There was a certain logic there, at least, whether or not I agreed with it. But that was beside the point anyhow.

"What time did you get back?"

"Uh . . . dropped her off at her car at quarter to eleven . . . ish, and was back home by eleven."

"Did the two of you spend much time with her friends or yours?"

"No." He looked down and rubbed his hands again. "Truth is, Sheriff, I think she might have been a little embarrassed to be dating a nobody like me. Caitlin came from an upper-middle-class family, her aunt and uncle had big bucks the way she talked, and I'm trying to fit a tin can around the exhaust pipe of my decades' old F-150."

"That didn't bother you, her not wanting others to know about you?"

"It was just for the summer," he said. "We were friends, little more than that."

"But you were dating?"

He shrugged. "We hung out together a lot, went on 'dates,' so, yeah, I guess we were dating."

I nodded. "I have an awkward question."

"You mean as opposed to all the other ones so far?"

I exhaled a grin. I kind of liked this guy. "Yeah. Is there any chance she was also seeing someone else?"

"Why? You think she was?"

"Covering all bases, Scott."

He shrugged. "Anything's possible, but I don't think so. Why would she still hang out with me if she had another boyfriend, you know?"

"Yeah," I said. "You remember what she was wearing last night?"

"White Huskers tee and jean shorts. Had a hoodie with her too."

"Shoes?"

"Flip-flops, I think. Yeah, she kicked them off as soon as we got in the truck."

"Did she put them back on when she left?"

"I assume so. She wouldn't have driven home without them. Why?"

"She was found barefoot in the park."

Scott got up off his bucket and walked to the passenger door of his truck. He opened it and looked inside. "No flip-flops."

I took his word for it with a nod.

Scott slowly retook his seat.

"Was she wearing perfume, makeup?"

He thought for a moment. "Perfume, yeah." He smiled. "Caitlin always smelled like when you peel a clementine." The smile faded. "Makeup . . . I dunno, maybe. She didn't wear much."

"Jewelry?"

Scott thought for a moment and exhaled. "No, I don't think so."

So she had changed into nicer clothes and put on jewelry before leaving the house again. The secret older boyfriend was looking like a good possibility.

"Scott, I know this will sound odd, but is there any reason you can think of why anyone would hurt Caitlin, or anyone who might have something against her?"

He looked down, rubbing his hands hard, for almost thirty seconds before answering with a croaky voice. "No." He swallowed. "Caitlin was a sweet girl, Sheriff. I can't imagine anyone would hurt her."

"All right. I'll let you get back to work." I stood. So did he. "If you think of anything else, your mom has my business card. Give me a call"

He nodded.

"I'm sorry for your loss, Scott," I said, and shook his hand again.

He nodded but said nothing, the lump in his throat too thick to get words past it.

Twelve

CLOUDS on the southwestern horizon indicated storms might be brewing, and also explained the breeze that had kicked up while I was sitting in the driveway with Scott. I drove back toward town with the windows in my truck down, enjoying the fresh air blowing across my face instead of the air conditioning.

I replayed my conversation with Scott as I drove. He had seemed sincerely moved, and yet also a little cold at times—cracking jokes and pushing back against my questions. I couldn't get a feel for whether his grief was affecting his behavior or if he was hiding something. There wasn't anything overt in what he'd said, but I just had a feeling. Maybe the way he rubbed his hands when he answered. Maybe the pauses in answering. Maybe nothing at all.

I also replayed everything we had learned—or not learned—since finding Caitlin's body that morning. No obvious motives had come to light. The closest thing to a suspect was the mysterious older boyfriend Ashlee knew of, and the evidence could fit Caitlin sneaking out of her room via the maple tree after her date with Scott to meet this other boyfriend in the park. But why would he have shot her twice in the chest? Did he know about Scott, and had that made him jealous? Was there some other motive eluding us? And who was this mysterious boyfriend?

My phone buzzed in my pocket. I took a glance at the dirt road in front of me, saw it was empty, and dug out my phone to see who had texted. No one. Rather, the National Weather Service had issued a severe thunderstorm watch for central Nebraska. I stuck my phone back in my pocket and craned my neck to look to the southwest. The sun was still a good ninety minutes from setting, but I judged it would disappear behind the rising sheet of light gray and purple clouds before falling behind the horizon. Severe weather—high winds, tornadoes, hail—was a part of life on the prairie, but one a person couldn't afford to take for granted. So I diverted back to the office.

Bonnie had gone home, but Bill and Cheryl were both there.

"You're putting in long days," I said.

"You get the weather alerts?" Cheryl asked.

"Alerts, plural?"

"Severe T-storm watch until one a.m., and there's a line firing up from Red Cloud down to Hays, Kansas. Already multiple warnings, including a tornado warning for Osborne County, Kansas."

"Who's on duty tonight?"

"Me until two," Bill said. "Then Lake's coming in."

"Wally said he'd patrol until the watch is over," Cheryl said. "And I'm going home, but only ever a call away."

"Have you alerted our spotters?"

"Yeah. All the usual alerts have gone out."

"Then it's a waiting game," I said. "Bill, how about some company?"

"Naw," he said. "You've had a crazy day, a lot on your mind, and a pregnant wife at home. Go home. I'll call you if I need anything."

"You sure?"

"Positive. Besides, the Lee Dome will come through again."

For years, storms moving up out of Kansas or sweeping east across the state had bombarded nearby towns and counties, but left Lee largely unscathed. There had never been significant damage in town while I'd lived there. Farmers swore lines of storms split before hitting Lee and then reconnected after, and supercells blew up right after or died out right before town. Damage reports and rain totals backed up their claims. Some attributed it to the protection of the Almighty, others to luck, and others to some combination of geographical and atmospheric conditions that insulated Lee from the worst weather and heaviest rain. Jim Vander Zee likely had his own theory about the workings of a shadow government on the weather. Whatever the case, I'd be happy for the Lee Dome to shield us again.

I briefed them both on my talk with Scott and where the case stood, and asked Bill if he and Wally and Lake had asked the people in the subdivision about noises—say a pair of gunshots or perhaps a loud truck in need of exhaust maintenance. Not specifically, he said, but their line of questioning would have led to it, he thought, if anyone had heard anything.

Then, after looking over Cheryl's shoulder at the radar and trying to will myself to see something meteorologists couldn't—namely, that the storms would miss us—I double-checked with Bill that he would be okay. Assured that he would, I bid them goodnight and headed home.

Jessi was picking beans in the garden, and I helped her for a few minutes while telling her about the impending storm. Fortunately, I had come late enough in the process that she was almost done, so I endured a few mosquito bites and only started to sweat again. Her face and arms were glistening, and she went to take a shower while I flipped on the TV. I alternated between a Royals game on ESPN and The Weather Channel. A few pop-up storms in Kansas didn't get much attention with a pair of tropical storms brewing in the Atlantic, and Kansas City was getting clubbed by Detroit, so I canned the TV and decided to rely on my phone for weather info. Looking out our west-facing window, my view of the sky above was largely blocked by a giant silver maple, but I could see the clouds building on the horizon over the houses across the street and the field behind them.

I stepped on the porch for a few minutes to get a better view, listen for thunder, and feel the electricity of an impending storm in the air. One of the neighbors was mowing his lawn quickly before darkness and rain set in, and the whine of the mower drove me back to the couch.

Absentmindedly at first, but then with intention, I began flipping through one of Jessi's women's magazines. The women were all beautiful, even if airbrushed to be so, with hair floating gently in the breeze, and most of their clothing a little trendier than what I saw at the Lee Market or West Street Diner or the Tuesday night softball games. One of them wore a twist-neck blouse similar to Caitlin's, but with jeans and not a leather skirt. The photo was cropped just below the knee.

The Randall line has a touch of Sioux Indian a few generations back, and Jessi walks like a brave hunting in the woods. I nearly jumped as she leaned over me from behind the couch, loosely wrapping her arms around my neck. "I take it the Royals are losing?"

"Would you believe I was getting a jump on Christmas shopping?"

"Not a chance," she said, patting my sternum, then loosening her grip. "What are you doing?"

"Trying to figure out what a young woman would wear with a twist-neck blouse and a leather skirt."

Jessi frowned for a second as she walked around the couch. "Is that what Caitlin was wearing?"

"Changed into it from a tee and shorts before going to the park."

She was still frowning as she sat down beside me. She smelled of indiscernible flowers, which reminded me of Scott talking about Caitlin always smelling like peeled clementines and George saying she'd been wearing a fruity scent.

"So what are you missing, an outer layer or something?"

"Shoes," I said. "She was barefoot."

"Hmm."

"Suppose it was you," I said.

"Wearing the twist-neck blouse and leather skirt?"

"Uh-huh. What kind of shoes would you wear?"

"Where am I going?"

"To the park."

"Why would I wear a twist-neck blouse and leather skirt to the park?"

"Presumably to look good for a guy, but that's conjecture."

"Hmm." She got up and walked around the couch, then down the hall. She came back a minute later carrying a pair of black sandals by the strap. They were glossy, with a block heel and several straps crisscrossing back and forth, leading to a buckle at the ankle.

I nodded.

"Not ideal for walking in the park, admittedly," she said.

"So what would you do?"

"Huh?"

"With the shoes."

"I'd probably chuck them in the cornfield," she said with a thin smirk.

"Funny."

"If I was going for a long walk in the park, I'd probably leave them behind and go without."

"Leave them behind as in at home?"

"No. In the car."

"What if you walked to the park?"

"Then I'd wear them until I got there and, I don't know, set them down to pick up later or carry them along. But if I was going for a walk in the park, I probably wouldn't wear the leather skirt, either."

I nodded in concession to her point.

She turned to go back to the bedroom.

"What if you had to climb down a tree?"

"I'd toss the shoes down, climb down, and then put them on."

"You wouldn't climb down the tree with them?"

"With these?" she asked, holding them up again.

"You think when you threw them down, one might make an imprint in the dirt?"

"Did you find an imprint in the dirt?"

"Maybe. Maybe from a heel, maybe nothing at all." I sighed. "I don't know. And I don't know how this all matters or if it even matters, but it's one of those things that keeps coming up in my head, like why didn't the killer hide the body in the cornfield. Like one of those loose ends Columbo always chased down."

"Worked for him," she said, then left me to think for a moment while she returned the sandals to her closet. When she came back, she said, "You know what all this talk of shoes has me thinking of?"

I sighed. "Let me guess, the pregnant lady would like a foot rub."

"Ooh, you're so perceptive. But then I'll get us some ice cream and we can sit here and wait for the storm to just miss us."

I sighed one more time, then patted the couch. "Deal."

Thirteen

HEAVY rain fell for about ten minutes just after Jessi and I finished moderate-sized bowls of rocky road ice cream. It was accompanied by a few flashes and booms, and more rumbles accompanied the gentle shower that fell for another twenty minutes. But that was it. A short-lasting severe thunderstorm warning was issued for the northwest part of the county, and a tornado briefly spun up to the southeast, near the state line, but the Lee Dome came through again.

Tuesday morning dawned clear and cooler, albeit with the forecast still calling for temps in the mid-eighties. I kissed Jessi goodbye a little after seven-thirty and headed not for the office but for the West Street Diner. It was far enough west to be out of the construction plaguing downtown, which I could hear rumbling in the distance as I walked to the front door. Booths line the windows facing Main Street on the right and those facing West Street on the left, and they, like the L-shaped counter, are usually half full most mornings. Today, there was hardly an empty seat, and the buzz of conversations drowned out the bell over the door as I entered.

I returned several waves and shouted hellos and found an empty stool at the stained Formica counter. Gwen Martin, who was eighty if she was a day and who had been waiting tables at the diner for as long as I could remember, had a steaming and dripping mug of coffee before me almost before I sat down. "A or B, Sheriff?" she asked.

Old-timers at diners like this were supposed to have a "usual," but I wavered between eggs, bacon, toast, and hash browns or a stack of pancakes with a side of sausage patties. "Mmm, surprise me," I said with a wink. Gwen smirked at me and jotted something down on her order pad.

I drank coffee and tried to pick up on a couple nearby conversations with no luck. So I did what I'd done in the shower that morning—rehashed everything from the day before to see if I could figure out what I was missing. As I had in the shower, I realized the answer was nothing. At least, not in the sense of being unable to put the pieces together. What I was missing was enough pieces.

Gwen set a stack of buttermilk pancakes and separate small plate with sausage in front of me just as Butch Hanrahan approached from the suddenly vacant seat on my left.

"Sheriff, we got a problem," he said while Gwen splashed some more coffee in the general vicinity of my mug.

"What's that, Butch?" I asked. Butch owned Buddy's Tavern at the corner of 5th and Main, and I had a sinking feeling I knew what the problem was. "Isn't it before your standard wake-up call?" I asked.

He ignored the jibe. "We were practically empty last night. I closed early because the bar was vacant."

"Construction?"

"And if that isn't bad enough, my glasses keep shattering, I've got stuff falling off the walls, and that fool running the backhoe dang-near swung the thing through my front window. My power was even flickering."

"Are you sure the weather didn't have something to do with power flickering and low patronage?" I asked, cutting into my pancakes.

"Aw, what weather? If people stayed home every time some fool said there was gonna be a storm, we'd be out of business."

I lifted the cut stack to my mouth and immediately winced. Dry. I'd forgotten syrup. I chased the pancakes with some coffee as I reached for the syrup dispenser. "Butch, there's nothing I can do about it," I said after swallowing. "It's an inconvenience, I know, but they aren't breaking any laws."

"What about noise ordinances? Jolene over at the antique store said she got a migraine yesterday."

"Technically, I think most lawnmowers violate the official noise ordinance, but it's got to be seventy or eighty years old." He made to object, but I cut him off. "Have you talked to Mayor O'Reilly?"

"What about?"

"Or one of the town council members? They're the ones who should field the complaints."

"Aw, Sheriff, are you passing the buck?"

"Trying to, Butch."

"Our tax dollars at work."

"Shut up, Butch," Gwen growled. "Let the man eat his flapjacks in peace."

"Yeah," a voice from a stool behind Butch said. "Sheriff's got enough to deal with right now."

Butch pawed the ground with his boot. "I'm sorry. I didn't mean to cause trouble, Cash."

"Look, Butch, I feel your pain. I do. But I'm telling you, there's nothing I can do. We all have to put up with the inconvenience for a while."

"What about the mayor? Is there anything he can do?"

"You mean like call off the project?" the guy from the stool asked. I recognized him, but a name was escaping me at the moment.

"Like maybe making 'em work quieter or gentler?"

"Maybe if you ask real nice, Butch," Gwen said.

"Else threaten to vote Democrat in November," the guy said. Billy or Willie, a salesman of some kind. Maybe insurance.

"That's a dang-fool thing to say," Butch said.

I swallowed another bite of pancakes. "Try embracing it," I said.

"Do what with it?"

I shrugged. "Run a construction special, drinks half off while the ground shakes, or invent a new drink and name it the Cement Mixer or the Big Dig or something."

Billy or Willie pointed at me.

"Hmm," Butch said. "Maybe." He stood there for a minute, then said "Maybe" a few more times as he shuffled away. I re-focused on my breakfast. Until Billy/Willie slid over to the adjacent stool.

"Sheriff, you making any progress on the Thomas murder?"

"Investigation's ongoing," I said, looking up. "How's that for noncommittal?"

He pointed with a smile. "Now *you* sound like the politician."

"What a dang-fool thing to say," I said with a return grin. "Seriously, we're working it."

"Well, best of luck, Sheriff."

I thanked him and started eating again before anyone else could bother me. Only Gwen, with even more coffee. "Whooda thought you'd need to be a psychiatrist too?"

I lifted my eyebrows in agreement, then drank some coffee. I polished off the breakfast, dropped a tip on the counter, and headed to work, knowing that breakfast was on my tab as always.

Cheryl and Lake were both at their desks when I walked into the office. "Hey, help us out," Lake said, sitting up straight.

"You got something?"

"If you hypnotize yourself, would it be impossible to ever come out of hypnosis?"

I stared incredulously.

"She thinks that's stupid," Lake said, pointing with his thumb at Cheryl.

"So do I," Bonnie called from her desk.

Lake leaned forward. "Think about it though, Boss. You're swinging your talisman or pocket watch or whatever it is," he said, making the motion with his hand, "and you fall under your own spell. Who's going to snap their fingers or give you the codeword while you're under to wake you up? You'd be stuck that way forever."

I looked at him for a moment, then cut my eyes to Cheryl.

"I told him I don't think you can actually hypnotize yourself."

"Or what if you get put under and the hypnotist has a heart attack or something before they can give you the right method to bring yourself out?"

"Somebody else could surely do it."

"If anyone knew you were hypnotized."

I looked at them both again. "How long has it been since our last drug screening?"

"I'm not wrong," Lake said.

"I must be under hypnosis now, because I could have sworn we have a murder investigation ongoing."

"We do," Cheryl said, "and I have news. I cracked the password on Caitlin's laptop."

"When, this morning?"

"I couldn't sleep. I've been here since four. I sent Wally home to get some sleep."

"Should have just hypnotized him," I said. "What'd you find?"

"Website history is all over the place, but nothing I found suspicious. Everything from ESPN to KOLN's weather page to beauty tips to exercise regimens to Amazon shoe orders. I made a list if you want to look it over."

"Shoot me an e-mail."

"Consider it done."

"What else?"

"I'm still trying to crack her e-mail password, using various algorithms now that I know her laptop password. She uses Gmail, and her computer login was local, not through Microsoft."

I nodded as if I knew what the heck she was talking about.

"She didn't have a lot of files on the computer—some homework from the spring, applications to colleges, apparently before she got her scholarship to Nebraska. She downloaded various school forms and a *ton* of music and a few podcasts, but her temporary files, downloads, and recycle bin were all relatively empty."

"Like she was covering her tracks?" Lake asked.

"Or trying to save space on her hard drive. She didn't have a lot of extra."

"Anything else?"

"Yeah. She played around with photo editing and was pretty good at it. Some really nice landscapes, some random artsy shots of stuff around town."

"Anything with people?"

"Yeah, some."

"Who?"

"These . . ." Cheryl said, opening a folder full of thumbnails. I leaned in to look through about a hundred images as she scrolled. She clicked on a few at my request, showing Caitlin's parents, Pat and Molly, a few friends, I presumed, including Ashlee Blaine. She had added filters to some of them, done something to make them look three-dimensional, made a photo of herself playing soccer into a cartoon. There were none of an unknown, "older" man.

"Also a few in her recycle bin," Cheryl said, and clicked up half a dozen more photos.

I leaned closer. "That's Scott Cooper."

"The boyfriend?"

I nodded. Leaning against his truck, the wind blowing his hair, the sunset behind him. Him squatting in front of his truck. Her laying on the hood of his truck, fully clothed, but a little seductively. Three of both of them sitting in various poses in the bed of the truck. Combined, they made a nice collage of the All American couple straight out of a cologne commercial.

I stood up. "In her recycle bin?"

Cheryl nodded.

"And you didn't find any like this anywhere else?"

"No."

"Hmm." I stroked my jaw. "When were they deleted?"

She clicked a few times. "Saturday afternoon."

"Saturday three days ago Saturday?"

She nodded again.

"Hmm."

"Nothing so far in terms of cracking her social media passwords, but Lake's been roving through Instagram and TikTok for any place she's tagged."

"Anything so far?"

"No," he said.

"Okay. Any word from Bill this morning?"

"Texted, said he'd be in around nine," Bonnie called. "Oh, and there's buffalo ranch dip in the break room."

I sent her a thumbs up and headed for my office. I spent twenty minutes going through e-mails before scanning the website list Cheryl had pulled from Caitlin's computer. Nothing stood out to me either . . . except maybe one thing. I stood and walked to the door. "Hey, Cheryl?"

"Yeah?"

"When you need a break from password cracking, would you run over to Pat and Molly's house?"

"What am I looking for?"

"External hard drives, flash drives, anything else that might contain more data than what was on her computer."

"Okay."

"And cross-reference the shoes she bought on Amazon with what's in her closet. If there's a pair she ordered that isn't there, they could have been what she was wearing."

"You're stuck on these shoes, huh?" Lake said.

"Something tells me it's important. And while you're there, pin down the exact time Molly went to bed Sunday night and if she recalls Caitlin's hairstyle when she got back."

"I'm on it," Cheryl said, making notes on a pad.

"Take some dip to go," Bonnie called, then answered a ringing phone that changed the course of my day.

Fourteen

NESSA worked at the state crime lab in Lincoln and had processed a variety of items George Harrington had sent her yesterday. She called to see if I had time for a video conference call to go over what she'd found. While I made a cup of coffee, Cheryl "cast" the video call to the flatscreen on my office wall, and at nine-thirty, Bill and I greeted Nessa virtually.

She wore a lab coat over a burnt orange V-neck blouse. Square-rimmed glasses covered brown eyes, and her dark curly hair was bound on top of her head in a ribbon that matched the blouse. Her smile was genuine, but she was all business. After introductions, she split her screen to bring up a lab report on the left side.

"I ran a tox screen on Miss Thomas and it came back negative for any standard drugs—opiates, barbiturates, benzodiazepines, etcetera. That's not a surprise given the cause of death, but I thought you'd want to know."

I nodded.

The screen blipped and, instead of the lab report, now showed four up-close images of the bullets George had pulled from Caitlin's chest cavity.

"These are the nine-millimeter slugs recovered from her body," Nessa said. "As you can see, there's a small scratch on the one in the upper . . . left corner."

"Ballistics able to match it to anything on file?" Bill asked.

"No, but I don't think this is a ballistic marking."

I frowned.

"Dr. Harrington said one of the bullets had creased the victim's ribcage, so I think that's what you see here."

I nodded.

"I did find a speck of what tested to be cement on one of the bullets," she said, doing something to enlarge one of the photos.

"Are you saying the bullet ricocheted off concrete?" Bill asked.

"Cement, and no. The speck *could* have come from a bullet ricocheting off a structure containing cement, but that seems unlikely given the details of the shooting." She shook her head. "This could have happened when the bullet was loaded or sometime prior when it was touched. It could have come from a person working construction, a person doing home repair, a person who sold cement or who bought a bag of it or even touched a bag at the store and had a speck on them before loading the weapon—any number of possibilities. It doesn't really tell us much, but it *was* there."

"Dr. Harrington also mentioned a fiber of some sort," I said.

"Yes, that one's more interesting," she said, enlarging a different photo. It was a close-up of the bullet, showing a very tiny fiber that almost seemed wrapped around it. Nessa clicked another photo beside it, showing just the fiber.

"Hair?" I asked.

"No. It's steel wool."

Bill and I looked at each other.

"Several possibilities," Nessa said. "Actually, I suppose innumerable. But the most likely are someone cleaned the bullet thoroughly before loading it, although I can't imagine why, or that someone used steel wool to make a homemade sound suppressor."

I had heard of homemade "silencers" composed of steel wool inside a water bottle. Someone suppressing the noise of the shot fit with no one reporting a gunshot in the late hours of Sunday, and with our theory that the killer was a pro. Although to that latter point, "pro" was a relative term, as a true professional killer wouldn't need to make a suppressor—he or she would have one. But then again, we were a long way from suspecting that an assassin or contract killer had taken out Caitlin.

"Dr. Harrington also sent me photos of tire prints," Nessa continued.

"Yes."

"They're fairly standard tires for pickup trucks. Cooper Discoverer Rugged Trek LT, to be precise. Common for trucks that do a fair amount of off-road driving, say, on a farm, for example."

I tried to picture the tires on Scott Cooper's F-150, but I hadn't been looking closely.

"An old truck?" I asked. "Say 'decades old'?"

"Possibly, yes. Multiple makes and models. Probably doesn't help a lot either, but I also looked at the dirt samples from the tire print. There were two different types present."

"Neither happened to be cement dust, I don't suppose?" Bill asked.

"No, both topsoil, although one did have trace elements of manure."

"So that doesn't narrow it down much," I said.

"It doesn't, I'm afraid."

"Anything else?"

"There was sap from a maple tree found in several places on her skin."

"We thought as much. We think she climbed out her window and down a maple tree."

"That would track. Beyond that . . . I have the brand of perfume she was wearing, nail polish, shampoo—Dr. Harrington was very thorough. But I'll send that all to you in my report. There's nothing else I deemed worth highlighting."

We thanked Nessa for her time and, between the two of us, managed to turn off the video call. With a look at Bill, I reached for the phone on my desk and pressed the intercom button for Cheryl's phone.

"Yeah?"

"Good, you're still here."

"Just about to head out."

"Before you do, can you send the photos of Scott's truck to my screen in here?"

"Give me two minutes."

"And the photos of the tire prints from the park."

"Will do."

"Thanks."

Bill exhaled. "Lot of trucks in Lee County."

"There are," I said. "Even a tire match wouldn't prove anything. Lots of people have Cooper Discoverer LT Roadblock whatever they were tires."

"You didn't have a motive for Scott, did you?"

"Not unless he knew about this other boyfriend she supposedly had."

"Maybe *he* drove a truck."

"That seems more likely. Still, I'd like to rule Scott out."

Cheryl knocked and peeked her head in. "The photos should be in your shared folder now."

"Thanks, Cheryl."

"And the mayor just walked in. I presume for you."

"Ask him to give me just a few minutes."

She nodded and withdrew. I walked around to my computer and tapped the necessary buttons to bring the photos up on the screen. Only one of the photos from Caitlin's recycle bin, the one with Scott crouching in front of his truck, showed the tires with any clarity. Even so, and even with zooming in, I couldn't confirm that the tread pattern did or didn't match the print that had been made in the muddy spot in the parking lot.

"Do me a favor, Bill."

"Name it."

"Cheryl looked through the garbage cans at the park for a gun. She's going to the Ericksons. But would you take a look at those cans again for any sign of a water bottle, steel wool—on the off chance the killer ditched the silencer there."

"Sure."

"Take Lake with you if you'd like."

"Will do."

"Unless you'd rather talk to the mayor?"

Bill held up his hands with a grin. "The pleasure's all yours."

I chugged the rest of my coffee, then went and welcomed Mayor O'Reilly back to my office. This time he sat in one of the chairs facing my desk. The screen behind him was now black.

"Any progress, Cash?"

"In a manner of speaking."

"That sounds like a no."

"I don't have a suspect in cuffs, if that's what you mean. But we're following up on several leads, trying to rule out some persons of interest."

"We're pushing thirty-six hours, Cash."

Half of which had been overnight Sunday and Monday, but I wasn't in the mood to argue with him.

He sighed. "I don't mean to step on your toes. I just fear the town's a little on edge."

"Be honest with you, Mayor, I'm hearing more concerns with road construction than a murder."

"Don't I know it," he said. He dropped his hands into his lap. "Cash, I keep telling people, we had to get this done, and before winter sets in."

"And before an election?" I asked with a grin.

He slyly rubbed his nose.

"Give them a couple days and they'll all settle down and get used to it," I said. "Then they'll get on my case."

"You mind telling me what you do have in terms of leads?" he asked.

I did the same dance as yesterday, telling him without going into exhausting detail. I again promised to keep him updated and he again offered any help I could use. Then I walked him out to the front lobby, where we both looked out at the construction on Main Street for a moment.

"How are things looking, election-wise?" I asked.

"Oh, all right."

"Just all right?"

"Finances are a little tight at the moment, but that's been the case before. Money always comes in."

"If people can find their way to the bank through all this," I said.

"All right, all right, I get it," he said, returning my smirk. "Confidentially?"

I nodded. "Of course."

"My polling suggests seventy-thirty."

"That's pretty comfortable."

"Closest election was the first one, fifty-eight to thirty-seven. Third term was almost eighty-five percent. So it's comfortable, but you never want to assume. And weird things have a way of happening before elections."

"Not just then," I said.

He gave me a wink. Then we shook hands, he left, and I went to get rid of some old coffee and brew myself another cup of new coffee.

Fifteen

TI'ANA'S younger sister informed me that the Parker family had just returned from a long weekend visiting relatives in Sioux City, explaining why no one had answered the door the day before. Ti'Ana was at work at Runza until three. Her mom, Estelle, came to the door and informed me, after I explained why I was there, that Ti'Ana knew of Caitlin's death from Ashlee but had been gone all weekend. I assured her I wasn't there because Ti'Ana was a suspect, but that I hoped to talk to her anyhow. I was told not so politely to come back after three.

Next I called Jackie Cooper and confirmed that Scott was again working, to no surprise. I was glad I hadn't made another trip to their house for nothing. Instead, on something of a whim, I drove east on Highway 28 almost to the eastern county line to the feed yard where Scott worked. I wanted to atone for being a little sloppy the night before and inspect his truck tires up close. I also wanted to catch him off guard, as something still bugged me a little about his demeanor. People grieved in different ways, but I couldn't shake the feeling I wasn't getting the whole truth from him.

Loehr's Cattle Company covers 160 acres north of Yankee Hill Road, with pens capable of holding and feeding a combined 7,500 cattle. As you might imagine, there was a fragrance in the air as I parked in front of a gray pole building with a brick façade around the right corner. Growing up in rural Nebraska, I had long-since gotten used to "country air," but as my grandpa used to say, you could get used to hanging too if you did it long enough. I hurried inside, having not seen Scott's navy-blue F-150 in the small gravel lot in front of the building and figuring employees parked elsewhere.

A middle-aged woman with a trucker's cap stenciled with LCC on the front, worn over wavy auburn hair, sat at a reception desk. She looked up from a keyboard and smiled briefly. "How can I help you . . . Sheriff?" she asked as her eyes homed in on my badge.

"I'm Sheriff Nelson," I said, figuring it was proper even if the badge identified me.

"Mandy."

I nodded. "Do you have a Scott Cooper working for you?"

"We do," she said. "Is there some trouble?"

"No trouble, but I would like to speak with him if he's available. I also don't want to take him away from work," I said as Mandy reached for a walkie-talkie on its base to her left. "But if he has a break coming up soon where I could have a few minutes, I would appreciate it."

Mandy pivoted and, instead of picking up the walkie-talkie, grabbed a clipboard off a hook on the wall. "Let's see . . ." she said. "Looks like he's on the noon lunch shift in . . . about fifteen minutes. The employee break room is through this door, down the hall and on your right—you can't miss it. There's also a meeting room across the hall if you want to speak with him in private."

"That would be great, thank you."

"I am going to let Mr. Loehr know that you're here," she said almost apologetically. "He likes to know who's on the property and why."

"No problem at all," I said. "I can wait for him in the break room?"

She nodded and reached for her phone, not the walkie-talkie, as I made my way to the employee break room. It had seating for a dozen at two tables, with a counter and sink, microwaves, and a refrigerator along one wall. Not that dissimilar from the break room at the sheriff's department, which reminded me, I hadn't availed myself of any of

Bonnie's buffalo ranch dip yet, and my stomach was just about done with the morning's pancakes and ready for more.

The break room was empty, so I sat down and pulled out my phone to see if I had any text updates from my deputies. I didn't, but Jessi had sent a short clip of her stomach bouncing and moving as the baby presumably kicked and thrashed in the womb. I sent her a snarky reply asking if she'd had a bad breakfast burrito, and she taught me that there is a tongue-out emoji.

Calvin Loehr, the second-generation CEO of Loehr's Cattle Company, arrived before any of his workers. He stood six-three, broad shouldered, looking very much like a cowboy of yesteryear with his wide-brimmed cowboy hat, crisp work shirt and jeans, and the obligatory boots. Black, polished, with silver tips. He had not been treading through the mud and manure this morning. We shook hands and introduced ourselves, even though we knew who the other was, and then he invited me across the hall to the conference room.

"Have a seat, Sheriff," he said, and I did, eyeing a sparse but functional conference room with views across the front lawn to the road. "Please don't get the wrong impression," he said in his drawl (the Loehr family had its roots somewhere in Texas, and thirty years of living in Nebraska hadn't changed anything). He raised both hands. "I'm not trying to obfuscate justice or throw up any roadblocks. But I also want to have my employees' backs."

"I understand that, Mr. Loehr."

"Ah, call me Cal," he said, waving a hand.

"Cash," I said.

He narrowed his eyes. "You're too young to be named after Johnny Cash, aren't you?"

"I am not," I said. "My dad grew up listening to the Man in Black, and his and Mom's first date was to see the Highwaymen when they came to Ames, Iowa."

"No kidding. Cash Nelson?"

"Middle name's Leroy, after Mom's dad," I said, knowing what he was thinking. Anyone who learned the reason for my name, combined with my surname, was bound to ask if I happened to be Cash Waylon Kris Nelson or Cash Jennings Haggard Nelson or something of the like.

Cal Loehr blew out a breath. "Anyhow, you mind if I ask what sort of trouble Scott's in?"

I briefly recapped the death of Caitlin Thomas, of which he'd heard, and the fact that Scott had been her boyfriend, which he hadn't known. I said that I'd spoken with Scott the night before, but had some follow-up questions, and assured him that Scott was not a suspect nor in any trouble. That was true, at least pending his answers.

"I appreciate your straightforwardness, Cash," he said when I was done. "Gonna give you a little in return."

I nodded.

"When Mr. Cooper comes in for lunch in a few minutes, I'll let him know you're wishing to speak to him, and I'll offer that our legal counsel can be present if he chooses. That fair?"

"It's a free country," I said.

He looked at me. "Yeah, sort of."

I sensed Cal and I were of the same cloth. We stood, shook hands again, and then I waited for Scott to come in. He did, about ten minutes later, with a small cooler bag and a bottle of Mountain Dew but without Cal or a lawyer. He wore dirty jeans and another sleeveless shirt, along with an American-flag bandana as a headband. He did not smell, particularly, of manure.

"Mr. Loehr said you had more questions for me," he said.

"I do."

"You mind if I eat while we talk?"

"Go for it," I said, and gave him a moment to pull a sandwich out of the cooler bag. He opened a small bag of chips, and then I said, "We think Caitlin's killer may have driven a pickup truck, based on tire prints found at the park."

He chewed on his sandwich but said nothing.

"Do you happen to know the brand and model of the tires on your truck?" I asked.

He gulped down the bite. "You think I killed her?"

"I think I'd like to rule you out as a suspect, Scott. But we also have reason to believe Caitlin may have been seeing someone else, and that would add a motive."

Scott set down his sandwich. "What do you mean? Like . . . she had another boyfriend?"

I nodded.

"Who?"

"We don't know."

"Then why do you think she did?"

"One of her friends said she was dating someone else, someone older. And after her date with you last night, she went home, changed into nicer clothes, and snuck out to the park, we think to meet him."

Scott shook his head a few times. "Then he'd be your killer."

"Maybe. But if you knew, it would also—"

"I didn't." He shook his head some more, then dropped his head into his hands, his elbows on the table. I waited for a minute, literally, until he lifted his head and looked right at me. "Caitlin . . . broke up with me Sunday night. She didn't say anything about a boyfriend."

"What did she say?"

Scott swallowed. "She said it wasn't worth us going any farther since she'd be leaving later this month."

"Farther how?"

"In a relationship. Continuing dating."

"Not farther physically?"

He frowned, then shook his head. "No, is that what you're thinking?"

"I'm just asking questions, Scott."

He bit his lip and looked away. "There was nothing physical," he said softly. He turned his head back. "Okay? We didn't even *kiss*. We were hardly a couple, just friends . . . without benefits."

"Was that okay with you?"

"I guess. I mean, I'm not gonna lie, she was hot, and . . . I can't believe we're having this conversation," he said. "If you're asking if I killed her because she wouldn't sleep with me, the answer's no. And she didn't break up with me because I was pressuring her, okay?"

"Okay," I said. "Okay."

"I liked Caitlin, okay? Probably more than she liked me. And I knew . . . I knew it wasn't going anywhere, but I wanted it to, someday. So when she said it was over . . . it hurt. I was mad, but not at her. Just mad that it hurt. You know what I mean?"

"Yeah, I do."

The girl before Jessi had broken my heart. Had this conversation been in a different setting for a different purpose, I might have told him I was glad she had. But although I believed Scott, I needed to ask a few more questions.

He finally picked up his sandwich again. "I don't know what kind of tires I've got," he said, holding the sandwich in front of him. "Whatever Kevin had on hand. We can go look at them if you want."

I nodded, then marveled at Scott's ability to eat while we walked through the "country air" to the employee parking lot where his F-150 was parked with a dozen other trucks and cars. I knelt down to look at the tires, which did not appear to match the Cooper Discoverer Rugged Trek LT tires Nessa had said made the print. I took a few photos of them anyhow, just to be sure.

"I have to ask, Scott, do you own a gun?"

He stuffed the rest of his sandwich in his mouth with a nod. Then he nodded again, this time at the back of his cab. "In there."

"May I?"

"I haven't shot it in months."

I opened his unlocked truck and folded forward the seat to climb into the back, where a .22 caliber Henry was mounted on a rack against the tinted rear window, right next to a moderately inappropriate, anti-

Democrat window cling. Caitlin had been killed by a pair of nine-millimeter bullets, not rounds from a .22.

"You can go to my house, search my room, search the garage, whatever," he said when I rejoined him by the rear bumper. "I didn't kill Caitlin. I came home after dropping her off at her car, made something to eat, and spent three hours in my room playing *Call of Duty* online. The guys I played with can verify it."

I nodded. Maybe the time would come to toss his bedroom for a nine-millimeter handgun hidden under the mattress. And I took the names of his online pals to verify. But the thing Scott had been hiding—that Caitlin had broken up with him—had been disclosed, and, while it would make for a stronger motive, my sense and the lack of evidence told me this trail had gone cold . . . at least for now.

I thanked Scott for his time, then went back to my truck, rubbed the pine scent air freshener hanging from the rearview mirror under my nose a few times, and headed back to town.

Sixteen

GRIEF played out in dark circles under Molly Erickson's eyes, in a face that looked longer and thinner than it had the previous morning, in a faraway look in her face even as she welcomed me to their front door a little after two that afternoon. I had driven the dusty dirt roads to see Jackie Cooper again, asking her to confirm what she had heard Sunday night. She'd told me she'd heard Scott come in and then do something in the kitchen. She could neither confirm nor deny that he'd been in his room playing video games for a while after that. I had Lake, who played the occasional video game himself, following up on the names Scott had given me, who could hopefully confirm that. I had also asked Jackie if they kept a gun in the house, and she had said no. I had Cheryl looking up gun registration records to confirm. I had been able to tell I was upsetting her, so I'd finished by assuring her that I did not suspect Scott, but was just making sure. Tying up those loose ends.

I had gone from Jackie's back into town, around the construction, to the Ericksons house. As she had the day before, Molly invited me into the living room, where we sat down.

"Pat went into the office to take care of a few things today," she said.

"How are you holding up?"

Molly let out a breath. "We're surviving moment by moment. She's in a better place now, with her parents again." She forced a smile. "That sustains me."

I believe in heaven, in a "better place" in the afterlife, but not that everyone defaults there when they die. If everyone goes to heaven, and no one goes to hell, it kind of makes life on earth meaningless; an innocent victim like Caitlin and her murderer both end up in heaven? I couldn't speak for Caitlin or her parents, nor did I think now was the time to get into it with Molly. So I just nodded.

"I wanted to stop by and give you an update," I said. "But unfortunately, I don't have much. We are working some leads, but we don't have anything concrete yet."

"Deputy Johnson was here this morning and said you were looking at photographs on her computer?"

"We think it's likely she and her killer knew each other, so we're trying to identify people she might have known."

"A boy?"

I nodded, not able to bring myself to tell her it was likely a man—a grown man. But I didn't know that yet, either. I had it secondhand from Ashlee Blaine, and until I could confirm what she'd said, there was no point further upsetting Molly.

"No idea who it was?"

"No," I said. "But we're digging. And I promise you, Molly, we're going to get to the bottom of this."

She bit her lip as she nodded, then dabbed her eyes with a tissue. I gave her a moment while kicking myself for making a promise I wasn't sure I could keep. I asked her about funeral plans, if there was anything my department could do to help, and then left, letting her know I'd be in touch.

Cheryl and Lake were both waiting to talk to me when I got back, practically jostling each other for position. So I knocked on Bill's open door and stuck my head in. "Anything at the park?" I asked.

"Some bottles in the trash, but none with any hints of steel wool."

"Thanks for checking."

"How'd it go with Scott?" he asked. I'd texted him before heading to Loehr's to let him know my plans.

"I don't think it's him. I sent Cheryl a couple pics of his tires—"

"Not a match," she said from behind me.

"And he's got a .22 in the back of his truck, not a nine mil."

"You mention the other boyfriend?"

"I did. He confessed that Caitlin broke up with him Sunday night."

"She what?" Lake asked from behind me.

I stepped into Bill's office so I could look at my other deputies too.

"That makes for a pretty good motive," Cheryl said.

"It does, but the evidence doesn't point there. Unless Lake couldn't confirm his alibi."

"I got ahold of two of his three playing companions. They said he was online from quarter after eleven until almost two, and on video too. Said he got up once for two minutes and then was back. One of them said he seemed a little off, a little gloomy."

"Because his girlfriend dumped him," Cheryl said.

"According to him, they weren't so much boyfriend-girlfriend as close friends," I said.

"Close friends don't get dumped," Lake said.

I shrugged. "He's got a solid alibi."

"We need to find the other boyfriend," Bill said.

I nodded and turned my attention to Lake and Cheryl. "Ladies first."

Cheryl gestured for me to follow her back to her desk, where she slid into her seat and opened a tab on her browser. It displayed a pair of black, high-heeled sandals, not that dissimilar from the ones Jessi had produced last night when I'd asked what she'd wear with a twist-neck blouse and leather skirt. "These were missing from Caitlin's closet," Cheryl said.

Bill—who had followed us—and Lake joined me in leaning in closer.

"Three-point-two-five-inch heel, adjustable buckle closure, non-slip outsole. Forty-nine ninety-five on Amazon when she bought them three weeks ago."

I was suddenly aware of another face beside ours, and turned to see Bonnie bent over to look at the screen. She raised her eyes to me and Bill, and by extension Lake. "Not your style, I don't think."

"Brrrnnng," Lake said.

"Funny," she said, walking off.

"Fifty bucks," I said.

"That's a lot for a pair of sandals," Bill said.

"You don't buy women's shoes a lot, do you?" Cheryl asked.

"This is a pretty good price, actually," Lake said.

We all turned his way.

"What? Just because I'm not seeing anyone now doesn't mean I never have."

I exhaled and stood up. "Fifty bucks for a pair of shoes. I have trouble believing the killer would have taken them for their dollar-value."

"It would also mean her killer was a woman," Cheryl said.

"Or a guy who knows about ladies' shoes," Bill said with an eye to Lake.

"Hey, I get good reviews from ex-girlfriends."

"How do you get reviews?" Cheryl asked.

"I ask them," he said with a shrug.

"Someday we're going to probe that," I said, "but this does mean there's a good chance the killer took her shoes, and if they weren't taken because the killer—male or female—wanted a pair of high heels, then that means they were taken for another reason."

"A trophy," Bill muttered. "Meaning we're dealing with a creep."

"Or they somehow had evidence on them that would tie back to the killer," I said.

"Or," Cheryl said, "she met up with her other boyfriend, left her shoes in his car to take a barefoot walk in the park, and he killed her and drove off with them. It doesn't really tell us much, but they were missing from her closet."

I sighed.

"There's more."

We looked at her.

"I cracked her e-mail password, which was also her social media password. I'm still pouring through Instagram posts and a Facebook account that looks dormant, but I did get into her e-mail."

"What'd you find?"

"Not much. She kept a pretty clean inbox, and from what I can tell, most of her e-mails are school-related, either at Lincoln Southwest before moving here, at Lee High, or at UNL. I didn't see anything with friends or to suspicious accounts, and I went back to last year."

"Kids don't e-mail much anymore, do they?" I asked.

"Boss, adults don't e-mail much anymore."

"She did have a long thread back and forth with Daisy Schubert, the assistant soccer coach at Nebraska. It was mostly technical stuff, dealing with her recruitment, training regimens, fall camp—nothing of interest. But there were several references to calls and texts too between them. Maybe more of the same, or maybe Daisy was something of a mentor. Might be worth checking out?"

I nodded.

"And I found a flash drive at the Ericksons' house that looks to have schoolwork on it, including a portfolio of artwork. I'll check it and social media accounts for any males over high school age or anything else of note."

"Good work, Cheryl." I looked to Lake. "Okay, what's your news?"

"My news?"

"That you were waiting to tell me when I got here."

"Oh, yeah. Uh, I talked to Cooper's buddies who played *Call of Duty* with him last night. His alibi checks."

"That's it?" Bill asked.

"I caught a guy doing thirty-five on Lincoln on my way to lunch." He shrugged.

"Help Cheryl go through the social media posts. Look for anybody who stands out—anyone who isn't a classmate or teammate or any affinity she has with someone who isn't on our radar."

"Will do, Boss."

"What's your next move?" Bill asked.

I looked at the clock. "Waiting for Ti'Ana Parker to get home."

Seventeen

THREE-THIRTY came and went, and Ti'Ana had not yet returned from her shift at Runza. Somewhat reluctantly, her mom texted her and got no response. Ti'Ana sometimes grabbed a bite to eat after work, so it was possible she was hanging out there and simply not answering her phone. Since it wasn't that far away, downtown construction notwithstanding, I asked Estelle to call me if she returned and drove to Lee's only fast-food restaurant.

Runza is a Nebraska institution, selling the trademark meat-filled bread pockets as identifiable with Nebraska as corn fields and Cornhuskers. They also have pretty good chicken tenders or sandwiches, and soft-serve ice cream or lemonade drinks that would hit the spot on a late summer day. Ti'Ana was not camped out in one of Runza's booths, nor at the patio tables, nor—according to her shift manager—still on the premises. In fact, she'd claimed she wasn't feeling well and, with business slow in the mid-afternoon, had been let off about an hour early. A coworker claimed to have seen her leave alone but had no idea where she was going.

I checked my phone—nothing from Estelle, so I resisted the aromas from the kitchen and drove back to the Parker home. Still no Ti'Ana, nor answers to texts or a call from her mom or a text from her sister. I could see the concern playing out on both of their faces and couldn't help but share it. One dead teenage girl and now one missing. It was too early to assume anything about Ti'Ana, but not too early for minds to wander and wonder.

Estelle, still clutching her phone, searched my eyes, which I tried to keep stoic.

"Is there anywhere else she might have gone, or would usually go?"

"Maybe a friend's house, but why is she not answering her phone?"

"Do you have her friends' numbers? Maybe we should give them a call."

"Kyra?" she asked, turning to Ti'Ana's sister.

"Some," she said, looking up from her phone.

"Will you call Dana and Justine? I'll call Ashlee."

"Ashlee Blaine?" I asked.

Estelle nodded, swiped and tapped, and then set the phone on the coffee table between us. Kyra stood and walked into the other room.

"Hello?"

"Ashlee, it's Estelle Parker."

"Hi."

"Is Ti'Ana by any chance with you?"

"No."

"Have you heard from her today?"

There was a pause. Then, "She texted me a few times this morning, before going to work."

"Did she say anything about where she might be? She didn't come home from work and isn't answering her calls."

The pause was longer this time.

"Ashlee, it's Sheriff Nelson. It's important that we find her," I said, trying to send Estelle a reassuring look.

Some kind of noise came through the phone, one I associated with Ashlee almost speaking but not doing so.

"Please, Ashlee," Estelle said.

"I don't know anything," she said finally, "but there's a place where she might be."

"Where?"

"It's easier if I show you."

"How about you show me?" I asked. "That way Estelle can wait here in case she returns?" I looked at Estelle for her agreement as much as Ashlee's. Estelle nodded. Ashlee paused again.

"Ashlee?" I said finally.

"Okay."

"I'm leaving now," I said. "I'll pick you up in a couple minutes?"

"Okay."

"Thank you, Ashlee," Estelle said. She ended the call and looked at me as I stood.

"Try not to worry," I said. "There are any number of explanations."

She nodded.

"I'll let you know as soon as I know something."

"And I will call you if I hear from her."

I waited just a moment as Kyra returned and said she had struck out, then drove across town to the Blaine house on Arbor Court. Ashlee answered the door wearing a V-neck pullover and shorts barely longer than underwear. She invited me inside and then said she had to get shoes. I nearly suggested pants, but decided to save my comments about teenage girls' apparel in case Jessi was right and a baby girl going on teenager was growing inside her. Ashlee's shoes were a pair of flip-flops, and she had also grabbed a purse which she slung over her shoulder.

"Either of your parents home?" I asked.

"No."

"Do you need to let them know where you're going?"

She looked at me like I was from Jupiter.

"You want to tell *me* where we're going?"

"It's easier to show you."

We walked out to my truck. I got the door for Ashlee, which earned me another look. Then, while she trussed her hair up on top of her head, I called Bill and let him know I was following a lead with Ashlee Blaine.

In the old days, Andy Griffith could have ridden around Mayberry with a teenage girl and nobody would have batted an eye. A quarter of a way through the twenty-first century, in the current climate, I figured an extra layer of accountability couldn't hurt.

Ashlee directed me to go north out of town, then occupied herself with her phone while I drove. She looked up as we crossed the West Fork of the Big Blue River. "Um, turn here," she said as we crossed Pioneers Road.

I raised my eyebrow and looked at her.

"Sorry," she said, scooting a little farther back in the seat to sit a little straighter. "You can take the next road, I think."

The next road was a dirt road, and I followed her earlier point to the west. After two miles, she directed me to turn south, and then almost immediately pointed to a rutted path that ran along the edge of a cornfield on the north and prairie with a few clumps of brush and wannabe trees on the south. Up ahead, a row of trees defined the edge of both.

"Whose land is this?" I asked.

Ashlee shrugged.

We bounced along for a quarter mile until we were almost to the tree line. Ashlee sat up a little straighter again and said, "You can park right up there." She pointed to a small area of dirt and short grass on the right, separated from the edge of the cornfield by a small copse of trees. Low-hanging branches and scrub obscured the gray Toyota Corolla already parked there until I started my turn.

"That's her car," Ashlee said.

I parked beside the Corolla and looked toward the tree line. "Is that Pioneers Creek?"

She nodded.

I had a lot of questions but left them unasked as we got out. I waited for Ashley to come around, and she led the way to a narrow but obvious path through the trees. The West Fork of the Big Blue River is only a few paces wide through most of the county, and Pioneers Creek is a three-mile-long tributary. Sometimes wider than the river itself, the creek is at no point so deep that a child couldn't wade across it without getting his or her shirt wet. The trees and brush around it obscure a shallow bank, except where the path Ashlee led me on opened up. There a sandbar about the size of my office protruded into a bend in the creek.

We stopped suddenly at the sandbar. Across five feet of river was another bank of sloped grass on a small island in the creek. At least when it rained. The other "fork" of the creek that created the island was so thin and shallow it was dry half the time. But the island was maybe thirty-five or forty feet long and about a dozen feet wide, with a few gnarly trees and a mess of scrub on its north end. A very small, dilapidated wooden structure resembling an outhouse had more or less collapsed at the edge of the scrub. But none of that was what stopped us. Rather, it was the body lying face up on the sandy bank of the island.

It was a girl, medium-brown skin and dark hair, wearing a black tank top and khaki pants, no shoes or socks. Ti'Ana Parker, I presumed. And, I feared, the second dead teenager of the week.

Eighteen

ASHLEE shouted Ti'Ana's name as she kicked off her flip-flops and splashed through dirty brown water a foot deep. I trudged in cargo tactical pants and boots, observing several empty beer cans in the grass beside Ti'Ana and several more upright cans at arm's reach beside her. They gave me hope, and then I saw her diaphragm rise and fall under her tank top as Ashlee shouted her name again.

Ti'Ana groaned, then opened her eyes. She blinked against the sunlight, then raised a hand to shade her eyes, which settled first on Ashlee, then on me. She groaned again.

"Are you okay?" Ashlee asked.

"I'm . . . fine. What is he doing here?"

"Your mom's worried. You didn't come home and you weren't answering your phone."

"I'm fine," she said again.

I looked at the beer cans. "Have you been drinking?" I asked.

Ti'Ana moaned and looked at Ashlee. "Wh-why . . . didge you bring . . . him?"

Ashlee bit her lip and turned to me.

Ti'Ana gave me a sour look, then rolled onto her side and slowly stood, stumbling once. When she did stand, she was uneasy on her feet and accepted an arm from Ashlee to help her balance. She was a few inches over five feet, maybe a hundred pounds if you counted the long dreadlocks that were half fastened on top of her head and half flowing over and around her shoulders. It wouldn't take a ton of alcohol to impact her limited body mass, especially if she had consumed it quickly.

"How much have you had to drink?" I asked, looking from her to the ground and back. I counted three empties in the grass.

"A couple," she said at last. "I'm not even sshure I'm d-dru . . . unk." She wobbled, and I thought she might puke. Instead, she planted her feet a little wider and deeper in the sand.

"The statute on underage drinking doesn't specify an amount," I said.

Ti'Ana tipped her head back and forth a few times, wiped her eyes, and then fell back onto her rear on the sand. For several minutes she interchanged sobs with mostly incoherent phrases while Ashlee sat beside her, rubbed her back, and sobbed too. I gathered from it that Caitlin's death was what had set Ti'Ana off and caused her to drive out to the creek and shotgun Coors Light. I gave them a few minutes and sent a quick text to Estelle, letting her know I had found Ti'Ana and she was okay. Relatively speaking, at least.

I rejoined the girls, and Ti'Ana looked up at me. She had gotten control of her crying and spoke clearly. "Are you going to tell my mom and dad?"

I nodded.

"Do you have to?" Ashlee asked.

"Yeah, I do."

"What if she promises to never do it again?"

"Are you going to arrest me too?" Ti'Ana asked.

"Do you want me to?"

"No," she said without any conviction.

I took a step forward and dropped to a crouch, so I was on her level. "How about this," I said. "If you answer a few questions for me, I'll take you home and tell your parents what happened. And given the circumstances, I think we can do without an arrest this time."

She blinked some tears.

"But only this time," I said. "Alcohol is nothing to mess around with."

She nodded, then swallowed. "What questions?"

"For starters, where'd you get the beer?"

"I don't know."

I sighed.

"No, I don't know."

"We don't," Ashlee said.

"We?"

She bit her lip again.

I stood. "I'm willing to be lenient, but it is a limited-time offer, ladies."

"Just tell him," Ti'Ana said.

"Some of us come out here sometimes to hang out and . . . sometimes drink. We've had different people buy us beer before, and we keep it in a cooler in the shed," she said, nodding over her shoulder at the dilapidated structure.

"Which different people?"

She bit her lip again.

"My cousin," Ti'Ana said. "He lives in Lincoln."

"Who else?"

They reluctantly gave me a couple names, and I entered them in my phone to track down later. Right now, I didn't see a tie to Caitlin's death. To that end, I asked, "Did Caitlin ever come drinking with you?"

"Once," Ti'Ana said.

"I think she had one beer and then didn't want anymore," Ashlee said. "She never came back out here."

I nodded. Then I asked Ti'Ana the questions I'd asked Ashlee and Riley the day before and got mostly the same answers. Caitlin seemed fine lately, all things considered, and hadn't been in any trouble she knew of. Ti'Ana had been gone since Friday afternoon and knew nothing about Caitlin's weekend plans. She had no idea who might want to harm her.

She also knew that Caitlin had been "dating" Scott Cooper, but didn't know about her plans to break up with him. Neither did Ashlee. Nor did Ti'Ana have any knowledge of another boyfriend, much less his identity.

I had Ashlee show me where the cooler was and found it contained a couple cases of Coors Light and Bud Light. I wondered about teens so desperate to drink that they'd chug warm beer, but that really wasn't the point. I carried the cooler back to where Ti'Ana sat, then loaded the remaining unopened cans into it. "You ladies ready?" I asked.

Ashlee helped Ti'Ana up and helped her back across the creek and along the path to where we had parked. I put the cooler in the back of my pickup, then turned to Ashlee. "Do you have your driver's license?" I asked.

She nodded.

"Will you drive Ti'Ana's car? Follow me back to her house, then I'll give you a lift home?"

"Are you going to tell my parents about the drinking too?"

"No," I said. "You are."

Her countenance fell, but she didn't object.

Ti'Ana retrieved her footwear, purse, and Runza work shirt from her car. Fairly confident she wasn't about to dispense her beer, I helped her into the passenger seat of my truck. Whether out of genuine remorse or in a plea for me to cut her more slack, she apologized three times on the drive back into town and to her house. Estelle was relieved to see her, but relief turned to controlled rage when I explained where I had found her and what I had found her doing. I explained my deal with Ti'Ana, then left her in the hands of her mom and drove Ashlee home. Her parents were still both gone, so I told her to have one of them call me after she had informed them about the drinking. If I didn't hear from them, I said, I would call them and let them know myself. She agreed reluctantly, but then said, "Are you going to find whoever did this to Caitlin?"

"I'm going to do my very best."

With that, I left her and returned to the office to inform my deputies that I had reached another dead end in terms of finding Caitlin but that we did have a new place in the county to check for kids engaged in underage drinking. Ever the optimist, Lake said, "At least she wasn't snorting cocaine."

Nineteen

EVERY Tuesday in the summer, Lee County residents descend on East Park on the southeast edge of town to watch softball. The joke is there's nothing else to do in Lee, so why not, but there's been a long-running affinity for slow-pitch "beer league" softball in town. Half a dozen teams sponsored by local businesses and organizations play each week, with family, friends, and people with "nothing else to do" packing the bleachers behind the home plate cage. Tuesdays at East Park are a social event. People come to chat and gossip while drinking beer and eating hot dogs, burgers, nachos, or popcorn from the concession stand behind first base. Families and couples catch up from row to row. Men congregate in circles to talk about their crops, their jobs, or whether *this* is finally the year for the Husker football team. Women do the same, only I assume their topics are different. Meanwhile, the kids run and play in the grassy field between the right-field fence and the county fairgrounds to the east, staging their own pick-up games or playing pickle or tossing a football around—all while running the concession stand low on candy bars, cotton candy, and popcorn. Tuesdays are a slice of Americana, with BNSF trains rumbling past the outfield fence and the dual Lee landmarks—the double ellipsoidal water tower beyond right-center field and the silos of the Lee Co-operative grain elevator left of the left field foul pole—gleaming a pale blue in the shadow of the setting sun until the field's floodlights take over. As popular as the game is, some nights the softball is an afterthought.

Even so, I seriously considered not going to the games. I questioned the optics of the sheriff sitting in the bleachers watching middle-aged men with beer bellies hit pop-ups to shallow right while there was an unsolved murder on his docket. Never mind the optics, I also felt like I should be doing something to solve said murder. Unfortunately, I was short on leads to follow. The key seemed to be identifying Caitlin's other boyfriend and assessing whether or not he had a motive and opportunity. Sadly, Caitlin seemed to have taken the secret of his identity to the grave.

Jessi persuaded me to go. She said I shouldn't let optics determine my behavior, and my presence in the back row just left of home plate was a fixture at these games. She said sometimes it was good to get away and clear the mind. She said Steve, her younger brother and star of the Lee Co-op team, would be sad if we didn't come to support him. (I wasn't so sure about that pitch.) And she persuaded me by looking rather cute in her full-length maternity sundress, navy blue to match the Farmer's Co-Op logo on her red baseball cap. I know there are parts of the country where a lady covering her mid-length blond hair with a hat emblazoned with the same logo as adorns the local grain elevator wouldn't be considered attractive, but I'm happy to report Lee County, Nebraska, isn't one of them.

Steve's game was at eight, but we went for the seven o'clock game as well, and got there early to grab supper from the concession stand. The evening air was warm but absent the recent humidity, just perfect for sitting back and watching ball. The usual gang filled in around us, and through most of the first game we talked about everything from the weather to the shame it was that money was ruining collegiate athletics to whether or not Jessi and I had names picked out for Junior. I fended off a few casual questions about the murder investigation and stayed out of a couple complaints about the noise and hassle of road construction. Only a few times did my attention really settle on the game, when Caleb Tucker launched a homer that had to come close to landing on the railroad siding and when a close play at third prompted the typical and mostly good-natured heckling of the umpire. Tonight it was Don Mecklenburg, a lifelong resident and retired master plumber. He takes the heckling in stride and gives as good as he gets.

In the last inning, a whistle from below got my attention. Jessi and I both turned around and looked down from the top of the bleachers—about a dozen feet up in the air—at Steve, standing behind them. He wore the red and white raglan top that all the Farmer's Co-Op players did, with a hat like Jessi's currently backward over curly brown hair. He held an aluminum bat over his shoulder, his glove hung over the knob. Five years younger than Jessi, Steve wears the permanent smirk of a twenty-something stuck between a boy and a man.

"How's Junior?" he shouted up.

Jessi glared at me.

"After years of looking after me, you're perfectly prepared to be a boy mom," he said to her.

"*She* is doing just fine," Jessi called back down with a hand on her belly. She wrinkled her nose. "Shouldn't you be warming up or something? Stretching so you don't pull something?"

"I'm too young to pull anything. Seriously though, baby's fine?"

"Baby's fine," she answered.

"Kicking good? I don't want him to be some unathletic, uncoordinated weenie."

"Kicking like a little soccer player," she said, knowing how Steve detested the "European" sport. "Won't be long until Uncle Steve is handing out juice boxes at halftime of *her* pee-wee games."

"Ugh. I better go warm up. See you guys after?"

"Sure thing," I said as Jessi wiggled her fingers in a wave as he turned. Her eyes warmed with the appreciation she had for Steve's concern, while her mouth held back a smirk. We'd talked several times about what a good uncle Steve would be, whether it was playing catch with a little boy or having fake tea parties with a little girl. We also dreaded the thought of giving him any real responsibility.

"Is it awful that I kind of want to see him pull a hamstring trying to leg out a triple?" Jessi asked with a crooked look on her face.

"No. If you'd said throw out his back, maybe."

She smiled.

"You want some popcorn or something?" I asked.

"No, thanks."

I had a few minutes before the next game, so I picked my way down through the bleachers and headed back to the concession stand. I got in line behind a woman with dark hair threaded in a ponytail through the back of a pale pink baseball cap. She wore a purple tank top and jean shorts, and could have been any number of women in town, and, yet, I got the feeling I recognized her. As we inched forward, she turned around and confirmed it. Kassondra Ives.

"Sheriff," she said with a trace of surprise. She pushed her glasses up.

"Miss Ives."

"Kassondra, remember?"

"Right. Cash."

She looked toward the head of the line, just a few people in front of us, then to the lack of people behind me. "Do you have a second?" she asked.

"Sure."

We stepped out of line and around to the side of the concession stand, where smoke from the currently unmanned grill and the frying oil combined to create an aroma that was somewhere between appetizing and nauseating. It granted us relative privacy, without it being obvious.

"What's on your mind, Kassondra?"

"I wanted to ask how things are going in the Caitlin Thomas investigation."

I debated between giving her the standard but courteous "the investigation is ongoing" brush-off that I gave most citizens, since it wasn't prudent to discuss police business with them, and the basic briefings I gave the mayor, since she was running for office. I was pretty sure presidential candidates were given some sort of intel on geopolitical affairs, but briefing the potential future leader of the free world about national security concerns was a long way from updating a long-shot mayoral candidate on a murder investigation. So I split the difference.

"Honestly, and confidentially," I added, and she nodded agreement, "leads are pretty thin at the moment. I've talked to several friends, a boyfriend, and no one knows of a motive anyone would have for killing her, no one knows why she was in the park."

"Forensics?"

"There was evidence on one of the bullets that would suggest the killer used a homemade suppressor."

"A suppressor. A silencer?"

I nodded.

"So it was premeditated?"

"We think so. Again, I'm telling you because of your position in the mayoral race, but please keep this confidential."

"Of course."

I said nothing more, because there really was nothing more. When Kassondra realized that, she adjusted her glasses again and said, "Have you considered bringing in outside help?"

"Outside help?"

"The state police, maybe even the FBI. I mean, if there was a premeditated murder—a professional killing—it might warrant their attention."

I thought that was a rather delicate way of saying "You're in over your head, Sheriff," and I appreciated the tact.

"We don't know it was a pro," I said. "Right now, I'm not assuming or discounting any possibilities, and that includes utilizing whatever resources are available. But there's nothing as of yet to suggest that any aspects of this crime extend beyond our jurisdiction, so I don't know that any outside authority would be available. They've got even more on their plates than we do."

She nodded, whether with conviction and concurrence or in acknowledgment that I had dismissed her idea. She thanked me for my time, we got back in line, and I returned to my seat with a box of popcorn just as the Farmers Co-Op team took the field.

"What was that about?" Jessi asked, sticking a hand into my box.

I looked at her. "I thought you didn't want anything."

She gave me that cute shrug that women—especially women bearing your child—can give you to get away with anything. Then I took a handful myself and, before depositing it in my mouth, said, "She was curious about the progress of the case."

"What'd you tell her?"

I crunched on my popcorn. "There isn't much to tell."

Jessi put her hand on my thigh, either as consolation or a preparatory move toward more popcorn. I moved the box to the bleacher on the other side and ground on a kernel still in my mouth. Something about my answer to Kassondra bugged me, but I couldn't place my mind on what. So I focused on softball and what passed for married-person flirting with my wife over the popcorn.

As the sun turned red and sunk beyond the trees of town and floodlights splashed the ballfield with a bright, white glow, Steve hit a pair of doubles (no hamstring pulls digging for third) and flied out. With his team down one run in the bottom of the last inning, he smashed a ball as far as I'd ever seen but foul, drawing oohs and aahs from the fans as it blended into the faded paint on the side of the grain elevator. He hammered the next pitch hard as well, but right at the shortstop, who was still shaking out his glove hand a minute later when the game ended.

"Stay for the nightcap?" I asked Jessi, extending the mostly empty popcorn box to her.

"No, I'm actually feeling tired."

I was softballed out and didn't put up a fight. We waited until Steve had said goodbyes to a few of his teammates and then walked with him toward the parking lot. His hat was tipped back on his head now, and all he could talk about was how hard he'd ripped those last two balls. Maybe that was a sign of immaturity, or maybe it was the beauty of how little the result of a beer league softball game mattered.

"In the handshake line," Steve said, "their shortstop—Bobby, Billy, whatever it was—showed me he had a bruise forming on his hand already. Through his glove."

"You must be really proud," Jessi said.

He tugged her hat askew, then draped his arm over her shoulder. "Hey, Cash, why don't you play on Tuesday nights?"

"I have trouble with the cur . . ."

A brown, square-body pickup truck had pulled out of the spot two over from where I'd parked my truck.

"Urve," I said softly, walking to where the truck had been parked.

"Cash?" Jessi called.

The ambient light from the field lights made a dark patch of the gravel parking lot stand out. I whipped out my cell phone and flicked on the flashlight to get a closer look at a wet stain, several inches in diameter. A faint rainbow of color spread across its greasy surface. Oil.

I stood quickly.

"What is it?" Jessi asked.

"Steve, can you take her home?"

"Yeah, sure. What's going on?"

"Maybe nothing," I said, "but I've got to follow that truck." I planted a quick kiss on Jessi's cheek, knocking her cap further askew with the brim of my own. "I'll be home soon," I said, then nodded goodbye to Steve as I fished out my keys. Careful not to run anyone over, I quickly backed out of the parking spot and spun gravel exiting the lot. I turned west on Denton Road, a few vehicles behind the pickup which was identifiable by the old-fashioned design of its taillights.

I remembered to buckle my seatbelt and then settled into my seat. Half the county drove a pickup truck, and I was sure that more than one of them had an oil leak. But maybe, just maybe, I finally had a lead.

Twenty

THE truck turned left on Junction Street, going past the grain elevator and, I suspected, bypassing downtown. One of the cars between us followed, and did so again when the truck turned right on Monroe, giving me a little cover. We all turned right on West Street, then left onto Main/Highway 28 as it headed out of town. I thought about calling Wally or Lake, my two deputies on duty at the time, to see if one of them could help in pursuit. But it would be hard for them to get ahead of us so that I could pass off the tail to them and, whereas my pickup was nondescript, they would have officially marked LCSD vehicles.

A couple miles west of town, the pickup signaled for a right turn. I did likewise. The vehicle between us kept sailing west. Without being conspicuous, I hoped, I closed the gap such that I could read the truck's license plate. In Nebraska, except in the most highly populated counties, the license plates identify the county with the first digit or two—in this case, 94, Lee County's identifier—and then have random digits thereafter. The truck belonged to a county resident, which was no surprise.

It kept a steady pace, right around the speed limit on the gravel county roads. I toyed with the idea of pulling the driver over. In theory, I had grounds, albeit shaky ones. But I decided not to tip my hand, and actually eased back a little. We drove for two miles, stopping at Old Cheney Road. I thought I saw a baseball cap on the driver but couldn't tell for sure. There were no other markings or identifiers on the GMC Sierra, nor could I see the tires well enough to tell their tread pattern.

We crossed Old Cheney and, a mile and a half north, the West Fork of the Big Blue River. Almost immediately after, the pickup's brake lights came on, then the right blinker. I slowed as well and watched as the pickup turned into a gravel driveway leading at an angle to the east, and stayed at a slow pace just long enough to read the address on the fire sign beside the driveway before accelerating and continuing north.

I kept going past Pioneers Road, just in case the pickup driver had been suspicious and was watching; I wanted him to think I had a destination north instead of turning back east. I did that at the next road, and then a mile east turned back south. It was hard to tell in the dark, but I was pretty sure I came past the rutted path to which Ashlee Blaine had directed me earlier—the one that led to the drinking sandbar in Pioneers Creek. I'd have to check the county map back at the office to be sure, but the property the pickup had turned into may have very well backed up against the other side of Pioneers Creek, not too far from the sandbar. I supposed that *could* have been coincidence.

I returned to town and made my way around downtown and back to East Park, where the final game of the night was in the middle innings. I found the spot where the pickup had been parked still unoccupied, and parked nearby. I took a flashlight and a pair of evidence bags and walked back to the oil spot. I collected a sample of the oil, then carefully searched the entire spot with my flashlight. One passerby asked if I had lost something, and I said no, hoping they wouldn't recognize me. Other than the oil slick, there was no foreign matter in the area, nor any sign of dirt that didn't belong, although it would be almost impossible to tell.

I went back to the truck and, before I forgot, wrote down the license plate and the fire sign address. I thought about swinging by the office to drop off the sample and set the night shift on the case. But I decided to save it until morning, when fresh eyes and minds could assess what, if anything, we had discovered.

I was sure Jessi would be waiting curiously for my report, but I was wrong. She was already fast asleep.

Twenty-One

JESSI was still out when I left the house at seven the next morning. I swung by City Park and found the stain of the oil slick in the parking lot. The spot had dried, but I chipped away a few cobbles of pavement in the hope that the lab could get a sample of the oil and compare it to the sample I'd collected the night before. A long shot, perhaps.

Lake was manning the office and was willing to run an errand. So I dispatched him to take the two samples to Lincoln. He left as Bill and Cheryl were arriving, and I briefed them on my findings at the softball games. Cheryl immediately got to work tracing the license plate and address, while Bill fetched us mugs of coffee.

"Plate's registered to a Tonia Savicki," Cheryl reported, tilting her screen as if we might not believe her. She looked at us as we drank coffee.

"Name's familiar," Bill said with a swallow.

"Doesn't ring a bell," I said. I leaned in toward the screen. "That's the address. What do we know about her?"

"At first blush, she's forty-one, redhead, green eyes, non-corrective."

"Not sure a physical description's going to help us," I said.

"Redheads," Bill said with a shake of his head, then a drink of coffee.

I left that unprobed.

"Looks like she's from the area, attended Lee High, graduated class of—"

"How long of red hair?"

They both looked at me.

"You got a picture or anything? The person I followed last night didn't have long hair."

"You saw that?" Bill asked as Cheryl clicked up the driver's license photo. Kind of curly reddish brown hair was at least past Tonia's shoulders. I studied the face for a second, not recognizing it even a little, then stood upright. "I suppose she could have had it in a ponytail. I just saw a silhouette of someone wearing a cap, I think."

"You think it wasn't her driving?" Bill asked.

"No idea. Just thinking." I looked over as Bonnie came in, carrying her purse and a plastic container.

"Peanut butter cookies," she said, holding the container aloft.

"You know a Tonia . . . Sawicki?" I asked.

"Savicki," Cheryl corrected.

Bonnie stopped. "Tonia Savicki? Yeah, why?"

"You know her?"

She came over to see Cheryl's screen. "She's dating my cousin Jerry. At least she was. I haven't talked to him in a while. Why?"

"Maybe nothing," I said. "You know anything about her?"

"I think she's into horses. I don't know her well."

The bell over the front door clanged, and Bonnie quickly set her purse in a desk drawer and waved the container of cookies as a reminder before setting them on her desk. Then she went to see who had come in. A moment later, she motioned to me. "Mayor O'Reilly's here to see you."

I looked at the clock. He was early.

"Mayor," I said, greeting him at the door to the lobby. I invited him back to my office, and we took our seats. "How are you this morning?" I asked.

"Hot," he said. "How's the case coming?"

I took a beat, not in the mood to be hurried. I sensed impatience in the mayor.

"Admittedly, we don't have a lot of leads."

"But you do have some?"

I stifled a sigh before giving him the runaround. I didn't mind keeping him in the loop, but reporting back to him as a superior was a different story. And that's what this was starting to feel like.

"Nothing in terms of motive from her life, her past, her friends and coworkers and the like?"

"The other boyfriend, if we had anybody who knew he was. If there's a connection, we'll find it."

He leaned back, disagreement in his posture. "Maybe . . . it's time to bring in some outside assistance."

"Outside? Like the feds?"

"They do have specialists. Maybe someone in Lincoln or Omaha who's dealt with this kind of thing before."

"Have you by chance spoken to Kassondra Ives recently?" I asked, deciding to push back a little. He hadn't been quite as delicate as she had the night before.

"Ives? No, not recently. Why?"

"She suggested the very same thing to me last night, at the softball games."

"You talked to her about the case?"

"She asked how things were going, and I gave her a high-level overview. I figured it was acceptable, given the fact she's running for mayor."

O'Reilly nodded for a moment. "No, I haven't spoken to her. But the county board has been talking. It's bad for public relations and town morale to have an unsolved murder. They want this tied up."

"No more than I do, I assure you."

"I believe you, Cash. And I have your back—I do. But I'm not your boss; they are."

I bit my tongue. Technically, in a sense, I answered to the Lee County Board of Commissioners. But ultimately, I was answerable to the citizens of the county via election every four years.

I took a breath. "I understand the urgency. We're doing everything we can."

"I'll let you get to it then," he said. We both stood and shook hands, and O'Reilly left the office.

I refilled my coffee and found Bill and Cheryl sitting around her desk. "You and Lake have any work left to do on Caitlin's portfolio or classmates' social media?" I knew she had found nothing the previous afternoon, but wasn't sure how many Facebook and X and Instagram and TikTok and whatever other accounts there were they still had to sort through.

"Her portfolio, no," Cheryl answered. "But I don't know how far Lake got on social media."

"I think that's grasping at straws anyhow," I said. "We'll let him pick that up when he gets back. Right now, I want anything and everything we can find on Tonia Savicki. Particularly, is there any connection at all to Caitlin, to Scott Cooper, to anyone we know has a connection to her."

"You got it, Sheriff," Bill said.

"What time's Wally in today?"

"Noon," Bonnie called from her desk. She has the ears of an owl.

"Thank you." I looked back at my deputies. "Somebody should ride patrol today. We've been slacking on that a little. I've also got a half dozen permits pending we really should get to this week. Anybody have druthers on one or the other?"

"I'll handle the permits this afternoon when Wally comes in," Bill said.

"Okay."

"You go on patrol," Cheryl said. "We'll compile everything there is on Tonia and report when you get back."

"That good with you?" I asked Bill. He nodded.

It may not seem like much, or important at a time like this, but having the sheriff's department conduct routine patrols was both a crime deterrent and a comfort to the community, and thus a vital part of what we did. And it wasn't like I'd just be cruising the backroads listening to Toby Keith and Lainey Wilson on the radio. I realized the mayor and the wannabe mayor had a point. It was time to enlist some outside help.

Twenty-Two

CAPTAIN John P. "Jack" Nelson had served as the commander of the New Orleans Police Department's Eighth District for five years, after four years as an assistant district commander with the department. The better part of a decade had almost made a northerner "one of us" to the people of the Crescent City, at least as of last telling. Eleven years after leaving Lee County, his name was still well regarded in the community. Truth be told, it certainly hadn't hurt my election campaign two years ago and was another reason I was determined to fulfill my oath to the people to the best of my abilities. On a warm but pleasant Wednesday morning, that meant calling my old man as I cruised the backroads of the county.

"Cash, how are you?" he boomed with a voice that seemed to cut through the miles as if he was sitting right beside me in my truck.

"I'm not taking you away from anything important, am I?"

"Naw. That's why I have a staff. Besides, it's the middle of the week and too hot for people to cause much trouble."

"I wish that was the case here."

"So I hear."

"Oh?"

"Jessi shot us a text Monday morning. Said there had been a murder in town, and you might could use some extra prayer this week."

"She wasn't wrong on that."

In typical Dad fashion, he asked, "How is she doing?"

"Pretty well. Gets tired quickly, but that's to be expected."

"You picked out names yet?"

"Keeping with the family motif, we're settling on Jagger, Hendrix, or Presley."

"That's what I get for asking," he said. "What's on your mind, son?"

Because Dad had always been a man who offered sage advice and counsel—and not just because he had a lot more experience at policework than I did—I walked him through the last fifty-two hours of my life. I had already cruised most of the streets in town and made a decent dent on the county's main thoroughfares while recounting conversations and evidence and also laying out the potential next steps Bill, Cheryl, and I had discussed—everything from talking to every classmate or teammate of Caitlin's to probing her life in Lincoln prior to moving to Lee. Maybe Caitlin had secretly turned to drugs to cope with her parents' death and her supplier went to school with her. Maybe she had made contact with the drunk driver who had killed her parents or a relative of his and their meeting had gone sideways.

"Sounds like you're reaching," Dad said.

I blew out a breath. "I know."

"Piece of advice?"

"It's why I called."

"Before you start latching onto wild theories—and I don't deny one of them *could* be correct . . . But before you do, run whatever leads you have to ground. Experience tells me you usually have the answer before you know the answer. You just have to figure it out."

"I keep coming back to the boyfriend no one can identify and the oddity of her being barefoot and a pair of shoes missing."

"I would agree, he seems like a good place to start if you can figure out who he is. You say the best friend told you about him?"

"Yeah."

"You the one who talked to her?"

"Yeah."

"You have a female deputy?"

"Yeah. Cheryl Johnson."

"Might be worth her having a conversation—woman to woman."

"You think Ashlee's not telling me something because I'm a man?"

"More like a conversation between two women might naturally go places a man talking to a teenage girl wouldn't and open her mind to things she doesn't recall while you're asking questions."

"Hmm."

"Just a thought."

"No, it's a good one."

"As for the shoes . . . could be a number of explanations. Bigger thing to me is the cell phone."

"I figured it had the killer's identity on it somehow."

"You pulled call and text records?"

"We did. There's a burner we can't identify that we're guessing might be his."

"Hmm. Pictures, maybe, that she didn't upload to social media."

"Maybe."

"Here I've got us grasping at straws," he said with a sigh.

My phone beeped, indicating another call. I glanced at the display. Bill.

"Dad, I'm getting another call. I've got to go."

"I'll chew on it and call you if I think of anything."

"Thanks."

"Keep me posted?"

"Will do. Bye, Dad."

I interrupted his goodbye by ending the call and swiping to accept Bill's. "What's up?" I asked.

"Lake's back, and he and Cheryl are back onto social media accounts, looking for anything."

"You and Cheryl find anything on Tonia?"

"Basic bio. I sent you an e-mail. There's nothing there that raises any flags, nor any ties to Caitlin we could find."

"I suppose a lot of vehicles in the county leak oil," I said. "Lake happen to say if the lab gave him any indication of what results they might pull?" I wasn't sure if they could get beyond identifying the brand and viscosity, say to determining it had run through the same engine. More grasping at straws.

"He didn't," Bill said. "I can ask."

"Nah, forget it. We can't sit around and wait anyhow."

"What's our next move?"

"What'd you find on Tonia's job?"

"Self-employed, as a farrier and a CPA specializing in tax prep."

"A farrier?"

"Yeah, a person who takes care of horses' hooves—trimming, shoeing."

"Yeah, I know. You just don't often see those two professions go together."

"Small town," he said.

"Yeah." I sighed. "Well, I'm at Old Cheney and D. Not quite lunchtime. I'll bum out to her place and see if she's around. See if I can get it straight from the well-shod horse's mouth."

Twenty-Three

IN the light of day, without worrying about being surreptitious, I paid closer attention as I drove across the West Fork of the Big Blue River on Road B. Tonia Savicki's property was second on the right, beyond a hobby farm run by a homeschooling family of nine or ten at last count. Depends who you asked, they were either a little odd and old-fashioned or salt of the earth, authentic people. At any rate, they were known around the county for selling chicken eggs, homegrown honey, vegetables people had never heard of like kohlrabi and celeriac, and the occasional quarter cow or pig. I guess it wasn't just a hobby.

On the other side of the road, with a driveway between the two on the east, was the old DeBoer farm. DeBoers ran thick in Lee County, and I couldn't remember which if any of them had ties to the property. In recent years, it had become famous for the largest drug bust in county history. Before my time as sheriff, the department had raided a meth lab under the barn, albeit without recovering the meth. I was a little hazy on all the details, only that the news had rocked the county. Meth labs were found in the seedier parts of Omaha and Lincoln, not rural Lee County. Now I guessed that was second place compared to the murder of a teenage girl.

Tonia's gravel driveway had an iron headgate overhead, its supports anchored in small clumps of evergreen bushes and, on the north side, several spruce trees. SAVICKI STABLES was scrawled in iron between the two arched bars of the headgate. Seeing it in the daylight reminded me of seeing it on other passes down this road, and I kicked myself for not recognizing the property the night before.

The driveway ran for a hundred yards over flat terrain before curving to a two-stall garage separated from a ranch house on the left. A horse barn with a gated corral was southeast, and beyond it a field of grass bound by a fading white picket fence that seemed to stretch all the way to the trees that lined the west bank of Pioneers Creek. I didn't see any horses. I did see a brown, square-body GMC pickup parked in front of the garage but aimed at the house where the driveway widened with just enough room to make a turn. I saw no signs of people and felt like I was in one of those Westerns where it was quiet—too quiet.

There was no answer when I rang the doorbell, nor when I opened the screen door and gave an old-fashioned fist-banging knock. I came down off the front stoop and, without being creepy, tried to look in the front window. Midday sunlight reflecting off it made that a no-go.

I heard the jingle of metal and turned around as the sound was accompanied by clopping. The sliding door of the horse barn had been left open, and from the darkness a woman emerged. She was leading a dappled gray horse and accompanied by a shaggy golden retriever. Seeing me, the dog bounded from behind her into a slow trot over toward me.

"He's friendly," the woman called, which was generally a given with retrievers. I focused not on the dog but her. Red hair spilled out from under a low-riding Stetson. She wore a brown leather vest open over a blue T-shirt, faded jeans with a few tears and no chaps, and the obligatory dusty boots. I confirmed from seeing her picture on Cheryl's screen and again on the bio Bill had sent to my phone that this was Tonia Savicki. That made sense, seeing as how this was her place.

The dog gave a soft bark—really more of a snort—as it approached and sniffed a few places, then circled back to Tonia. She and the gray stopped a dozen feet from me. "Can I help you, mister?"

"I'm Sheriff Nelson, with LCSD," I said.

She squinted at my shirt. "Sorry, I didn't see the badge. Sheriff, what I can do for you?"

"Is that your truck?" I asked, cutting a glance at the Sierra.

"It is."

"Seems to be in pretty good shape for being, what forty years old?"

"She leaks like the Longhorns run defense," Tonia said, tipping her head slightly to the side. "You mind if I tie Marble up?"

"No," I said, and she led the horse—which I noted was saddled—over to a hitching post next to the stoop I had assumed was for show. She turned around, scratched the dog behind the ears once, and then put her hands on her hips.

"Sheriff, why the interest in my truck?"

"Were you at East Park last night?"

"Yeah, I go a lot of Tuesdays. Why?"

"Would you mind telling me where you were this past Sunday night?"

She looked at me for a moment, crossing her arms. "Omaha."

"Till when?"

"Midnight. Maybe later. We were at a Brooks & Dunn concert, and it got out late, we stopped for something to eat on the way back. Might have been closer to twelve-thirty."

"We?" I asked.

"My boyfriend Jerry and some of our friends. Sheriff, what's going on? Why do I feel like a criminal all the sudden?"

The golden retriever would have stiffened and snarled if this was the movies. Instead, having sniffed a few places on the gravel driveway, it wandered over to the lawn and laid down.

"Did you take the truck to the concert?" I asked.

Tonia eyed me again for a moment before answering. "No. Jerry picked me up and dropped me off."

I nodded. "Did you hear about the murder of Caitlin Thomas?"

"Yeah, of course. Why?"

"We found a patch of oil in the parking lot near where her body was found, as well as some tire prints presumably from a pickup truck. Last night, I happened to see a pickup truck leaving East Park, leaving an oil stain behind. I followed that truck here."

She nodded. "That was you behind me?"

"It was."

"And you think because my truck leaks oil it's the truck that left an oil stain at your murder scene?"

"I think it's a possibility. I've sent samples of both oil leaks to the lab and they'll analyze them and determine if they are or aren't the same, and, just looking at your tires, it appears they might be a match to the tracks we found . . . Cooper Discoverer Rugged Trek LT tires."

"They are," she said. "But I didn't kill anybody."

"We put the time of death between eleven and midnight," I said. "If you don't mind, I'll take the name of your friends to verify you were at the concert, but that would put you ninety miles away at the time of death."

Tonia nodded. "Not to be a smart aleck, but I'm sure there are a lot of pickups in the county that leak oil, and these tires aren't common, but they aren't uncommon either."

My turn to nod. "Do you mind if I ask you a few more questions, just routine?"

"Would it stop you if I said no?" she said with a grin.

"You have no legal obligation to answer."

"What you got, Sheriff?"

"First, if you don't mind, the names of the people who went to the concert with you."

She gave me Jerry Klein, her boyfriend and Bonnie's cousin, and three other couples. She, Jerry, and another couple had ridden in Jerry's vehicle and the other couples in another vehicle. According to Tonia, they had followed each other to Omaha and back, stopping at the same place for dinner on the way there and for a midnight snack on the way back, and had never been apart longer than it took to go to the bathroom. There was no way she could have left the concert, driven back to Lee, killed Caitlin, and then driven back to Omaha, but I wanted to be thorough.

"Does anyone else drive your truck?"

She shook her head.

"No employees?"

"This is a one-woman operation."

"That's a lot of work for one woman, or one man."

"I like it that way."

I nodded. "Do you have any security cameras here?"

"No."

"So if someone had stolen your truck . . ."

"They'd have been somebody pretty sharp because they parked it right where I left it."

"In the garage?"

"Right here."

I nodded again. "Did you know Caitlin Thomas?"

"Not personally. I know Pat and Molly casually, and knew they had taken her in."

"Any idea where your paths may have crossed? You do any work for the Ericksons, have any association with the school or the girls soccer team, anything of that sort?" I asked, while she shook her head. I nodded. "Thank you for your time," I said, reaching into my shirt pocket. I came out with a business card. "If you should think of anything," I said, extending it to her. "Sorry for the scare."

"No worries," she said, sticking the card into a pocket in her vest.

I touched the brim of my cap, and she reciprocated with her Stetson.

Another lead run to ground and another dead end.

Twenty-Four

TECHNICALLY, the lead wasn't run to ground until we verified Tonia's alibi for Sunday night. But unless there had been an eight-person conspiracy to commit murder or Tonia was dumber than her horse to give such an easily debunked story, I was pretty confident that would happen.

I stopped at the end of the driveway, and my eyes settled on the broken-down barn across the street at the DeBoer property. Whatever color it had been originally, it was now worn and faded gray, with boards missing and the north end looking ready to collapse with one good gust or moderately heavy snowfall. The grass and weeds and bushes around it were head high at least. An old-fashioned concrete silo beside it was a degree or two crooked, crumbling in places, and surrounded by just as many weeds and scraggly bushes. A garage or shed behind the house had fallen in on itself, and the square, two-story house from early in the previous century or before was uncared for, its windows black or boarded, its porch sagging and overcome by weeds, the path to it from the driveway indiscernible. Only the driveway itself, which ran between the barn and the house and past the garage to the fields beyond, was even moderately kept, and that appeared from fresh use. The field in the distance was planted with soybeans, and a field south of the house with corn.

There was no sign of activity on the grounds, and, on a whim, I turned south on Road B and then into the driveway of the DeBoer property. I stopped between the house and barn and cut the engine. I got out, listened for a moment to the dinging of the warning for leaving my keys in the ignition, then swung my door shut. Five years ago, the sheriff's department had raided a meth lab on this property. Three days ago, a teenage girl had been murdered, quite possibly by someone driving the truck of the woman who lived across the street. That wasn't for certain, and although a few people had mentioned drugs, there was no evidence of drug use by Caitlin. And yet, I couldn't bring myself to shrug that off as a coincidence.

I walked to the front of my truck and examined the rutted driveway. Tractor tire prints were evident in the ruts, and grass and weeds between them were several inches high. In spots, gravel or dirt indicated the driveway had at one point been more than just ruts, especially as I looked over toward the remains of the garage.

Proceeding carefully through knee-high and higher grass, I approached the front porch. I stopped short of setting foot on it, since it was apparent no one else had beaten this path anytime recently. I made my way around to a backdoor adjacent to a root cellar entrance, neither of which showed any signs of activity. The cellar doors were padlocked, and the backdoor accessible through a screened-in porch that had disconnected from the house and didn't appear as if it would hold a human's weight anymore.

I eyed the garage for a minute, then approached the barn. The front door was open, and the grass and weeds flowed into the opening. I went and got my flashlight, then returned to peer into the darkness. Even though it was the middle of the day and a hot sun was beating down on me, I had to fight off a shiver as grass brushed against my face and cobwebs refracted as much light as they let through. I did not see any beady eyes looking back at me and walked to the threshold of the barn. The flashlight beam revealed that it was mostly empty aside from a lot of cobwebs. A few fallen pieces of lumber had dropped from the hay mow above, and a stack of decaying hay bales that had fallen in the corner had collapsed into a clump. No stanchions left in the concrete floor, no farming equipment, and no containers or filters or sheets of cloth—meth lab supplies.

I backed out and returned to my truck. On the way, I happened to cut my eyes across the road to Tonia's place. From where I stood, I could see the west half of her ranch house on one side of the clump of spruces on the north side of her headgate. As I walked back in front of and around my truck to the driver's side, the view changed slightly, blocking her house but opening the view of the garage and her GMC Sierra parked in front of it.

I stopped and stood, one hand on the door of my truck. I leaned there for several minutes, looking at Tonia's truck, looking over my shoulder at the front porch of the DeBoer house, and thinking.

"Hmm."

I got in my truck and pulled out my phone.

"Any luck?" Bill asked.

"Maybe. Wally in yet?"

"Just got here."

"I'm going to text him some names. Have him start calling them and verifying their whereabouts on Sunday night."

"Okay."

"Tonia Savicki claims she was at a concert with them in Omaha until after midnight."

"And you doubt her?"

"No, I believe her, but I want to make sure."

"Got it."

"And would you pull together a briefing on the DeBoer drug bust?"

The confusion came through the phone. "Sure. Why, you think there's a connection?"

"Tonia's house is across the street from the DeBoer property."

Bill repeated the address. "Of course. Why didn't I think of that?"

"Same reason I didn't."

"Who's the briefing for?"

"Me. I want to make sure I've got all the facts straight. You were here, you worked the raid. I've heard bits and pieces and rumors and retellings. I want to know it like I was there."

"I'll get right on it."

"I'm headed back soon, so I'll take care of those permits while you do that."

"That's not necessary, Sheriff."

"You can relieve me when you get that briefing together."

"All right."

"I'll send Wally those names right away, if you want to touch base with him."

"Will do."

I ended the call and pulled up the list I'd typed of names Tonia had given me. I was halfway through entering them into a text message when I happened to glance up into the rearview mirror. Tonia was walking from the barn to her truck. I was curious. She had just been leading a saddled horse *out* of the barn, as if to go for a ride. Maybe twenty minutes had passed, and now she was getting into her truck. I turned around in my seat and watched as she opened her door and signaled for the golden retriever, who jumped up into the truck a second later. Then she got in, closed the door, and appeared to reach up to the sun visor. A few seconds later, the truck started moving and headed down the driveway.

I turned back around. There was no way I could follow her without being spotted, and my earlier curiosity at where she was going so soon after saddling a horse was replaced with skepticism. Tonia could have reached up for the visor because she was about to start driving. But her truck had been parked north and the sun was high in the southern sky. People didn't usually flip the visor down in anticipation of high sun but because the sun was already in or about to be in their eyes. What if, however, she had been reaching up to get the keys? It may sound crazy to city folk, but lots of people living in rural areas don't lock their doors at night or lock their car when they park in town, and some even keep their keys in their vehicles. Did Tonia keep her keys above her visor, making her oil-leaking truck an easy target?

I watched as she turned north out of her driveway, then lowered my head and finished my text to Wally. I started my own truck and backed out of the DeBoer driveway, waited for a southbound vehicle, and headed back to town. I found myself humming as I was thinking, and realized it was "That Ain't No Way to Go" by Brooks & Dunn.

My phone interrupted me, and I glanced at the display to see it was Jessi as I raised it to my ear. "Hey, Babe."

"Cash," she said tensely, and immediately I knew something was wrong.

"What is it?"

"I think I'm going into labor."

Twenty-Five

LEE County has a small medical center on the west side of town, where in theory they could deliver a baby in an emergency. But then again, so could the county veterinarian. Jessi's doctor was in Lincoln, and, worse than that, on the east side of town. On a normal day, it would take about an hour to get there. Using the removable beacon on the roof of my truck, we did ninety-five on the interstate. A couple times, Jessi asked me to slow down, and I finally listened when I realized I was doing sixty on Superior Street in Lincoln. But her contractions were fairly steady and, while she wasn't sure, she thought her water had broken. I wasn't sure how a woman didn't know but wasn't going to ask. Nor was I going to take chances.

During the drive, I went through the math a dozen times, going over every statistic and percentage I knew about prenatal development and, while eight weeks was early, modern medicine and technology meant the survival rate was still high. Outwardly, I projected strength and calm—other than for my driving. Inwardly, the new father was a mess. When I wasn't doing math and dodging sane drivers, I was praying, even though I couldn't form a coherent thought.

It didn't take long for Jessi to get admitted, dressed in a gown, and hooked up to a monitor around her abdomen. Naturally, her OB/GYN was on vacation, but the on-call doctor was a middle-aged man with an easy-going but competent manner and disarming wit. He confirmed that both Jessi's and the baby's heartrates were good and asked a handful of questions relating to the frequency and duration of Jessi's contractions; other symptoms she was experiencing and if anything had relieved them, and her recent activity and diet. All the while, he reviewed her e-chart and gave soothing responses and comments. Not in the almost arrogant way some doctors had of making you feel like an idiot for even being there, but in a way that made me trust him. After listening to the baby's heartbeat again and pronouncing it as "ideal" he stood. "We'll leave you hooked up for a little while just to keep monitoring everything, and we can do an ultrasound too, for your peace of mind."

We nodded.

"But I don't see any signs that your baby's in any distress."

I allowed my heart to start beating again as he gave us a few minutes alone.

"So, how was *your* morning?" Jessi asked.

I gave her the brief rundown.

"So that's why you tore out of the game like a crazy man—ow!" She reached for her abdomen. "Contraction," she said with a wince, seeing my eyes widen. "Talk to me."

"Yes. I followed her based on the oil stain."

"I had an old Honda that leaked oil."

"I know it's common, but we were looking for a truck, and she drove a truck. I'm hoping the lab can match the oil, but she has the same kind of tires too."

"And you think there's a connection to the DeBoer family?"

"They lived right across the street."

"Don't the—ow—Norwoods live right next door?" she asked, referring to the homeschool family of close to a dozen.

"They do. You want me to call the doctor?"

"He'll be back." She rubbed her abdomen. "I'm starting to think you're right about him being a boy."

"Oh?"

"He's got an ornery streak," she said with a wince, followed by a relaxed sigh and a deep breath.

"It's over?"

She nodded.

A nurse brought Jessi some juice, and she and another nurse wheeled over the ultrasound machine and monitor. The sight of little Junior alive and definitely kicking brought more relief to both of us, and tears to Jessi's eyes. Then the doctor returned.

He sat down on the other side of Jessi's bed and folded his hands in his lap. "I *think* you're having Braxton Hicks contractions. Also known as false labor."

Jessi nodded.

"Quite common for women in their second or third trimester, and they don't mean anything in terms of imminent labor or that anything is wrong with the baby. They will come and go, and can become more frequent as your due date approaches."

"Doc, I'm sorry," I said, "but do I hear a 'but' coming."

He gave a slight nod. "Usually, Braxton Hicks contractions are a little shorter than what Jessi's experiencing. And they usually aren't as frequent or consistent as what you're having."

"I've read about Braxton Hicks," Jessi said, "but that's what made me think it wasn't them. And these are really painful."

The doctor nodded. "It is possible that you're starting labor, and the only way to know for sure is to check if you've dilated any. That doesn't happen with Braxton Hicks, so that will confirm for us."

"Water doesn't break, I assume, with Braxton Hicks," I said.

"No."

Jessi described what she thought might have been her water breaking, and they talked "discharge" for a minute, and what would be normal and what wouldn't. Then the doc prepared to go under the hood.

"You're welcome to stay, or step outside," he said to me.

I looked to Jessi. I'd heard fathers say that real men stayed in the delivery room through everything, that they watched their children emerge from the birth canal, that they were ready to cut the umbilical cord. It was described in a way that made me think they popped open a hunting knife like they were about to skin a deer. Other fathers, masculine and tough fathers, swore that the delivery room was no place for a man or, at the very least, if it was, he stayed well north of the equator. I had expected a couple more months to figure out which sort of a man I was. Now, I let Jessi make the decision, and she said, "It's okay."

Like any man, I covered my vulnerability. "I should make a couple quick calls." I leaned in to kiss her forehead while still squeezing her hand. "I'll be right outside."

She smiled, and I nodded at the doctor and got the heck out of Dodge.

I found a small lobby seating area and called Bill, updating him on what the doctor had said. He put me on with Wally, who had so far spoken to Jerry Klein and two others—one from each car that had gone to Omaha for the concert. They all confirmed Tonia's alibi. I then asked the two of them to try to cross reference the concert goers and their family with anyone who had lived or worked at the DeBoer property to see if there was a connection. If I had, presumably, seen Tonia reach for her keys from the driveway, so might anyone else who lived at the DeBoer house. And if one of those people knew she would be gone for hours . . .

It was a long shot, admittedly. Someone could have seen her park at the grocery store or the co-op and gained the same knowledge. But we were down to long shots, so it was worth a try.

I ended the call and shifted into expectant father mode, pacing up and down the hall, stuck between worrying about Jessi and Junior and trying to solve a murder without enough evidence. As if on cue, my phone buzzed.

"Sheriff Nelson."

"Sheriff, it's Nessa Sterling from the State Patrol Crime Laboratory."

"Nessa, good afternoon."

"It is," she said. "Do you have a minute?"

I looked back at the door to Jessi's room. "Yeah."

"I was able to match the samples of oil you sent in."

"You were? That's great."

"Yes. Both oil samples definitely ran through the same engine, likely an older engine based on the level of contaminants and wear metals."

"I'm looking at a truck from 1986."

Nessa whistled.

"Yeah."

"Anyhow, if you get to that point, it will hold up in court to tie the two samples together."

"That's good to know. Say, while I've got you on the line, I've got another question."

"Okay."

"You said one of the two dirt samples I sent had traces of manure in it."

"Yes, that's right."

"Can you identify the animal?"

"You mean, it was a cow not a pig, or can I match it to a particular sample and confirm the same animal made both . . . deposits?"

I grinned at her terminology. "The former. I suspect it's horse manure."

"I can confirm."

"I'd appreciate it," I said, even though I realized as I said it that the oil samples were enough to link Tonia's truck to the City Park parking lot.

"I'll let you know shortly," Nessa said.

I thanked her and ended the call just as the doctor emerged from Jessi's room. He caught my eye and motioned for me to join them.

Twenty-Six

JESSI and I were home by quarter after four. She hadn't dilated any, indicating the labor she was experiencing was false labor, or Braxton Hicks contractions. With further confirmation that her and the baby's heartbeats were good, her blood pressure was good, and there were no signs of distress or trouble, the doctor had sent her home with recommendations for rest and plenty of hydration, and a few steps to alleviate the contractions if they continued or returned.

She didn't have a single one on the drive home. Jessi's not a psychosomatic, but I couldn't help wondering if the diagnosis had also been something of a cure. The doctor hadn't said anything about stress causing Braxton Hicks, nor was Jessi's life particularly stressful. But when had stress ever had a *positive* health impact?

"You can go back to work," she said when I had helped her settle comfortably on the couch and taken a seat in the chair next to it. "You do have a murder to solve."

"I've got competent deputies working on it. Besides, I think I should stay with you, at least for a while."

"That's sweet, Cash, but I don't think I'm going to suddenly start actual labor now."

"You were prescribed rest. Somebody's got to make dinner."

"I can call for pizza as well as you."

"Uh-huh," I said.

She settled into the pillows behind her. "Were you worried?"

I looked at her. "Yeah."

"Me too. And I feel silly, like a first timer who freaked out."

"You *are* a first timer, and you said it yourself, the contractions didn't seem like Braxton Hicks. Better safe than sorry."

"Still, the last thing you need now is a distraction," she said with a slight wince and an adjustment of her posture, causing the blanket she was under to slide off her feet. She sat up to fix it, but I quickly jumped up and pulled the blanket back down. How she could sit under a blanket when it was eighty-five degrees outside, I had no idea. Then again, I also had no idea how she suddenly had a taste for Bugles with her yogurt either.

"You are not a distraction," I said, kissing her forehead again. I stopped to make eye contact, then backed up to my chair.

"Mmm, tell that to Pat and Molly."

"I have no idea how they can function right now," I said. "To lose a child, even if it's not your natural child . . . and after losing Molly's sister and brother-in-law . . ."

"I know."

"I always used to think of those sorts of things, but it was like the thought landed a glancing blow. Now, with fatherhood potentially imminent . . . it hits like a shovel to the face."

"That's a lovely image," she said with another wince.

"You know what I mean."

"I do. And it scares me, to bring a life into this hostile world. Sometimes I still wonder if we did the right thing. I mean, there's so much that could go wrong. And I know you can't think about that, but as a parent, how do you not?"

I nodded.

She smiled. "Maybe that's why the Norwoods have so many, so they stay too busy to worry about it."

"I thought Keith always said it was because we couldn't stave off the Commies with only two and three kids per family."

"Speaking of family, I texted your folks the other day, to let them know what you were facing."

"I know. I talked to Dad this morning."

"You did?"

"Needed some captainly advice."

"We should invite them for Thanksgiving. Return the favor for last year."

"Might be a crazy time with an eight-week-old on our hands."

"They'll want to see her."

"We're back to it being a her?" I asked. Neither of us had looked at the sonogram image closely enough to confirm our gender preference.

"She calmed down," Jessi said.

I nodded. "I'm going to get something to drink. You want something besides that water?" I asked with another nod at the glass on the coffee table.

"No."

"Doc mentioned herbal tea or warm milk might help."

"If I was having contractions, and I'm not."

While in the kitchen, I began contemplating what I could make for supper. I had just taken some ground beef out to thaw a little so that I could make a homemade version of Hamburger Helper when Jessi announced that Marjorie Murtaugh had texted and said she and Bill would bring supper at five-thirty. I stuck the package of ground beef back in the freezer. "Do all women have a ninety-minute casserole at the ready for such situations, like those soup-in-jar Christmas gifts the homestyle ladies give?"

"Homestyle ladies?"

"You know what I mean," I said as I sat back down.

"I have no earthly idea what you mean. And no. We just know how to get our rear in gear when it's called for."

I sat back and wondered if making meals for sick or grieving families, or for young mothers-to-be who had a false alarm, was a rural, Midwestern thing or if they did it in L.A. and Seattle and Miami and New York too.

Twenty-Seven

MARJORIE Murtaugh brought a chicken and rice dish, along with homemade applesauce she had canned last fall, peas, and brownies for dessert. She apologized that the peas were from the store, but they were all she had on hand.

Bill brought a file on the DeBoer family, but set it aside while we all sat at the dining room table and dined together. Jessi had insisted when she saw how much food Marjorie brought, and it had been a while since the four of us had gathered. I was Bill's boss, but in many ways, I looked up to him as a model of how a man should carry himself, and Jessi and I both admired Bill and Marjorie's marriage of nearly thirty years. An hour flew by, followed by brief clean-up as I assured Marjorie I would take care of the rest later. Then she settled Jessi back on the couch and sat down to chat with her while Bill and I adjourned to our back deck with the DeBoer file.

"Wally and I spent the afternoon looking for any ties to anyone in there and the folks Tonia mentioned had gone to the concert with her."

"Anything?" I asked, opening the file and skimming through thirty pages of notes, dossiers and rap sheets, evidence lists, and photographs.

"Nothing," Bill said. "Want me to summarize that for you?"

"Yeah. I'll read it in full later."

"We suspected for several years that meth was flowing into the county, we thought originally from Lincoln or Omaha or maybe even Denver. Finally, we got a tip that led us to the DeBoer place."

"What kind of tip?"

"We arrested a kid—I say kid, he was twenty or twenty-one—for vandalism at the cemetery, and he was high on meth and had some on him. He wouldn't roll on his dealer, but claimed it was being manufactured locally. We didn't put much into the ambiguous claims of a kid high on meth, but, a month later, Waste Collections contacted us and said they suspected the DeBoer place because of some of the stuff they were collecting—particularly chemical containers. We investigated, found some other signs, and called in the state boys. We raided the place and found they had a huge lab set up on the ground floor of the barn and in an old root cellar beneath it."

"But no drugs, right?"

Bill shook his head. "We arrested the mastermind behind it all and a flunky on some lesser charges, confiscated all their equipment and production, but never found any more than trace elements of meth. Unless they just left everything out in plain sight, they had recently finished a run, meaning either they delivered it right away or it's still hidden somewhere. Five years later, not a trace of it."

"That's odd."

"Uh-huh."

"Who was the mastermind?"

"Guy named Justin Tyrell."

"Justin. For some reason, I was thinking Jason. Not a DeBoer?"

"A cousin to the family, I think. Originally from Kansas City."

"What about the flunky?"

"I don't recall the name, but it's in there. Darryl, Dylan, something like that. He had some kind of connections, I think through an ex-wife, to the property behind the DeBoer place, over on A."

"What about the crankhead?"

"Aaron Butterfield, of the Butterfield clan up in York."

"The car dealership people?"

He nodded. "He spent a couple years in prison. The flunky pled down to a smaller charge. Tyrell served a nickel at NSP."

"But he's out now?"

"Yeah."

"Whereabouts?"

"No idea. Nor the flunky."

"We should track that down."

"I'm pulling the graveyard shift tonight. I'll look into it."

"Thanks, Bill."

He nodded dutifully.

"What about the DeBoer place now?"

"At the time, it was owned by a Helen DeBoer. Bank foreclosed on her three years ago and she moved to a retirement home in Beatrice. Died last year."

"She connected to the meth?"

"Not that we could ever tell.

"Who owns the place now?"

"It's in the file. Place was sold at auction by the bank."

"You been out that way recently?"

Bill shook his head.

"It's abandoned except someone's using the fields."

"I can look into it."

"If you get time," I said. I sighed, tapping the folder on the arm of my chair. "Bill, I can't believe there's a stash of meth that's been missing for five years, meth manufactured across the street from the woman whose truck leaked oil in the parking lot next to where Caitlin was found murdered—I can't believe that's a coincidence."

"Me neither. Then again, and I know cops are supposed to hate coincidences, but twenty-five years' experience talking here . . . some things are just coincidental."

"Hmm."

Bill clapped his hands. "Well, I should be getting Marjorie home and then getting back to relieve Cheryl. She's been at it all day."

We headed back inside, where Jessi and I both thanked Bill and Marjorie profusely. They left, and I, still holding the folder, sat down in the chair adjacent to Jessi.

"What do godparents do again?" she asked.

"Mostly buy gifts for birthdays now, I think."

"Hmm."

"I don't know, look after the kid if you die."

"They'd make good ones."

"For us or Junior?"

"Touché."

"How are you feeling?"

She touched her stomach. "Full. I'm thinking I'm going to take a hot bath and then get to bed early. I have been worn out the last few days."

"You need help?"

"That's sweet," she said with a smile, "but pretty sure I can draw a bath and finagle my way in and out of the tub."

"Okay," I said, tapping the folder again. "Then I'm going to go see another woman."

Twenty-Eight

GOLDEN hour, as the period before sunset is called, worked well for Tonia Savicki's property, from the light glinting off the iron of her headgate to the long shadows cast by the spruce trees beside it to the tones it created in the grass surrounding her driveway to the warmth it gave the stained siding of her house, garage, and horse barn. Her 1986 GMC Sierra, parked in the same spot as it had been on my earlier visit, looked like it belonged in a retro commercial. I could almost hear Bob Seeger singing in the background. Only this was a GMC not a Chevy.

Tonia answered the ring on her doorbell this time and invited me into a house that matched what I would have expected—a cross between an old farmhouse and a Montana hunting lodge. The décor was rustic more than feminine, but I didn't give it more than a glance. Tonia was dressed the same as earlier, only without the hat and with her hair in a ponytail. Her golden retriever sniffed me again and then retreated to a doggy bed in the corner.

"Can I get you something to drink, Sheriff?"

"No thanks."

She offered me a seat in her living room. "How can I help you?"

"First of all, we did conduct a routine check with some of the people who attended the concert with you, and everything you said checks out. I'm not here because you're a suspect."

"That's good to know."

"But I did want to ask you a few more questions."

"Okay."

"How long have you owned your truck?"

She blew out a breath. "Um, forever." She closed one eye. "Has to be close to fifteen years."

It was seventeen, per Cheryl's search of DMV records, but I'd asked not to verify but as a lead-in.

"Do you always park it in the same spot?"

"I do." She paused. "Why, right, when I have a two-stall garage?"

I shrugged. "People use garages for a lot of things. I was asking as it pertains to a routine, as in could someone know it would be outside, accessible?"

"It would be accessible in the garage, too. I don't have an opener—they're manual lift—and I don't lock anything around here."

"Including your truck?"

"Including my truck."

"I stopped at the DeBoer place when I left earlier, and I saw you leave. You keep the keys above the visor?"

"I do."

"Always?"

"Pretty near." She shrugged. "Easier if you always know where they are."

It was the same for me, only they were in my pocket, but to each his or her own.

"You think someone stole my truck Sunday night?"

"I do. The oil spot we found near the murder scene matches the oil I found where you'd parked at East Park. The lab says it came from the same vehicle. We also found a trace element of horse manure near the murder scene," I said, having had that confirmed by Nessa on the drive back from Lincoln earlier.

"And there's plenty of that around here."

I nodded.

"Who would steal my truck?" She shook her head. "There's nobody at the DeBoer place. Hasn't been for years."

"Do you know who uses the fields?"

She shook her head.

"What about when you're in town? Grocery store, hardware store, gas station—do you keep the keys above the visor then?"

"In Lee County, yeah. You think someone saw me at the grocery store and filed away the fact that if they ever needed to commit a murder, my truck would be an easy target?"

"I'm considering all options."

"And how did they know it would be free on Sunday night?"

"We ran the names of everyone you were attending the concert with, and their families, looking for any connection to Caitlin or to the DeBoer family, thinking word might have gotten out about the concert and provided a window of opportunity." I shook my head. "No connection."

"Why the DeBoer family? You think they had something to do with the murder?"

"Truth be told, I don't know what's become of the DeBoer family anymore. You said it, the place has been abandoned for years. But if you've parked the truck where you've parked it for years, kept the keys where you've kept them, anyone who lived or worked there even years ago would have known about it."

"No disrespect, Sheriff, but that seems thin."

I nodded.

"Like I told you earlier, if somebody stole the truck, they parked it in the same place and left it like they found it. I just cleaned it Saturday afternoon and didn't notice anything there that shouldn't have been after Sunday night."

"Would you be all right if I sent one of my deputies out tomorrow to dust it for prints, see if they can find any forensic evidence?"

"No, that's fine."

"You've used it since, I saw your dog hop in earlier, so any evidence they may have left behind is probably contaminated, but it's worth a try."

"I should be here all day."

"I'll have someone call in the morning."

She nodded.

"Five years ago, when they were running the meth lab, did you have any interaction with anyone there?"

"Not really. They kept to themselves, and I didn't reach out."

"The name Justin Tyrell mean anything to you?"

"He was the guy, wasn't he, the one they arrested?"

I nodded.

Tonia shrugged. "All I know is his name. Don't think I'd recognize him if I saw him walking down Main Street."

I thanked Tonia again for her time and drove back to the office to see Wally, who I'd texted before leaving home to see if he could run a deep dive on Justin Tyrell. He had just punched out, so I talked to Bill who said that Wally had sent me everything in an e-mail. I could access that as well at home as at the office, and call Wally just as easily from my couch if I had any questions. Plus I wasn't too keen on leaving Jessi home alone after the events of the afternoon.

She was sitting up in bed reading when I returned home. She wore flannel pajamas, and I shook my head. "How are you going to manage come winter?"

"Last week I almost crawled into the refrigerator. My temperature vacillates."

"Which means boy and which means girl of hot and cold, per the old wives?"

"Um, I don't know."

"Any more contractions?"

"Maybe a couple small ones."

"You feel okay?"

"Just tired."

"You turning in soon?"

"I think so."

"I'm going to do a little more work while I watch the Royals."

Jessi winced. "Getaway day. They lost 5-2."

"Then I guess I'm stuck with *Woman's Day*."

"Ha, ha."

I gave her a goodnight kiss, changed into sweatpants and a T-shirt, and fired up my laptop. Justin Tyrell was a career loser. A couple stints in juvie in Kansas City, probation in Lincoln a decade ago, and then a domestic assault case that had been dismissed a year before he had showed up in Lee County. Wally had indeed dived deep, but I saw nothing to connect either event in Lincoln to Caitlin Thomas or her family. Then again, it was a city of over a quarter million, so his being from there and her being from there was likely a coincidence.

Tyrell's mother's sister had married a DeBoer, which linked to the family tree but didn't explain how or why he had come to Lee County. That DeBoer was a nephew of Helen DeBoer, and I tried to figure out who my mom's sister's husband's aunt was and concluded I had absolutely no knowledge of such a person. In fact, I didn't know any of my aunts' or uncles' spouses' aunts or uncles. Who did? Yet somehow, Tyrell had found his way to Helen's farm and cooked up meth in her barn.

The details of Tyrell's conviction, sentence, and release were included, as was his current address, at an apartment on Monroe Avenue in Lee. Tyrell was at least a person of interest in a murder case, and I would have been well within reason to pay him a visit. But I wanted to make sure of my hand before I laid it on the table.

There was no record of employment post-release in April. As a convicted felon, Tyrell couldn't legally own a gun, but neither had he legally been allowed to cook meth. We hadn't pulled any financial records and couldn't without a warrant or exigent circumstances, and we had neither as of yet.

I also read through Tyrell's psych eval during his trial and prior to his release from the Nebraska State Penitentiary. According to a pair of professional psychologists, Tyrell was a product of his upbringing and could almost blame it for his fall into crime. He displayed what one of them considered a borderline personality disorder, at times showing he was capable of being a functional adult, holding down a job, being thoughtful and mature. On the other hand, he was the guy who had punched out his girlfriend, been heavily fined for a fight in which he had broken up the bar as well as several fellow combatants, and disturbed the peace on numerous occasions. Yet neither described him as psychotic. He didn't lose his temper or blow his stack from a lack of self-control. Far scarier, he acted with calculated and premeditated anger.

I shut my laptop and went outside onto the deck. Tyrell looked good for any crime, given his past. And he had a definite link to the DeBoer farm. He could have seen where Tonia parked her truck and kept her keys. But remembering that five-plus years later? Knowing the truck would be available the night he needed it? And we still had nothing to tie him to Caitlin. Even knowing it was Tonia's truck that had been at the City Park parking lot and even if we could prove Tyrell knew about the keys above the visor, we needed the connection to Caitlin and the motive. And a murder weapon. And we still had nothing on any of those fronts.

I wandered through the backyard, enjoying a beautiful summer night. I thought through all that happened that day, thought about the risk of pregnancy and the greater risk of bringing a child into a world full of Justin Tyrells. Look where it had gotten Caitlin Thomas's parents.

Then again, that's one of the reasons I had become a cop—to make the world a little safer for people and their kids. I had failed Caitlin's parents and aunt and uncle, but I was determined not to fail them in bringing her killer to justice, whether that was Justin Tyrell or someone else.

Twenty-Nine

HAZE hung over the cornfields as I headed out early Thursday morning. It reminded me of Monday morning, when we had found Caitlin's body next to a cornfield, which reminded me that it was three days and counting and we still didn't have a solid suspect or motive, just some vague circumstantial connections. I hadn't slept well, in part because of that and in part because my mind was running with random thoughts and possible straws to grasp next. The problem with the former was, I never knew when my random thoughts were just that and when they were my subconscious desperately trying to get my attention. But for some reason, I couldn't stop thinking about when Jessi had sat up on the couch and the blanket had been pulled over her toes. Was it because it reminded me that Caitlin had been found barefoot in the park and a pair of shoes had been missing from her closet? That oddity still bugged me, like one of those loose ends that always bothered TV cops and mystery novel detectives, but it had been pushed to the back of my mind because of oil leaks and meth labs.

As for the straws to grasp, I had several ideas today. The first was Henry Schroeder, the farmer who had bought the DeBoer property at auction three years ago. Bill had texted me early in the morning, having dug up his name and address—among a few other things—on his graveyard shift. Schroeder lived in the next county over and raised both beef and dairy cattle on his 160 acres. With a thermos of coffee, I headed out shortly after sunrise, knowing it was best to catch a farmer or rancher early.

Schroeder's missus (she actually introduced herself to me as "his missus") told me he was already in the field when I knocked on their front door, then directed me where to find him. I drove my truck down a bumpy, rutted lane that led between fenced-in fields of hay to the "back forty" where he was round-baling a crop of hay. I parked at the end of the field and waited until he made the loop back to me. He cut the power takeoff and the baler ground to a halt as he sat idling in the tractor, a Case IH job with tires taller than me and an enclosed cab that I was sure had everything from air-conditioning to satellite radio. The former would definitely be appreciated today.

I started across the harvested field. When I was halfway there, the door on the cab swung open and a man emerged, in his sixties or seventies, judging by the gray hair and slight bend in his posture. Belying his age, he took a few steps down and then hopped to the ground. He wore overalls over a T-shirt and a faded seed-company trucker's cap, a stereotype of the Midwest that had been earned.

"You the law?"

"Sheriff Nelson from Lee County."

"Henry Schroeder," he said as he reached me and extended a long, weathered arm and hand. "My missus called me and said the law was after me." He winked.

"Not at all. Just have a few questions."

"Shoot."

"I understand you're the owner of the former DeBoer property on Road A in Lee County?"

"I am. Bought it for a song at auction, oh . . . three years ago."

"How do you use the property?"

"I don't."

"You don't?"

"I rent it out to a guy over in Lee County. Harry McConkey."

I knew the name.

"He farms the land. Fertile soil on the banks of the creek."

"So you bought it to rent it?"

"I've got several such properties in the area. Diversifying, I think the educated folks call it."

Some people bought duplexes and rented them. In the Midwest, farmers bought fields and rented them.

"Do you ever go on the property?"

"Not since I bought it. I understand the bank foreclosed after some sort of drug bust happened there." Schroeder shook his head. "Buildings were already in disrepair, and I didn't buy it for the house or barn. In fact, when I signed the papers with McConkey, I warned him they probably would fall over if he idled his tractor by them too long."

"He the only one you've leased to?"

"Yup. Three years running now."

"Have you had any complaints about trespassers? You have any cameras there or anything?"

Schroeder shook his head. "Nope. Nope." More shaking. "Why, something going on?"

"We're looking for a connection between the property and former owners and a crime that was committed in Lee, and I'm just chasing down every loose end."

He nodded. "Well, I wish I could help you. Check with Harry. He's been on the land. I drove past it a month ago or so and saw he had crops coming up."

"I'll do that." I extended my hand. "Thanks for your time."

Schroeder returned to baling, and I returned to Lee County. Harry McConkey was an old dairy farmer who lived a few miles north of the DeBoer property. He was single and known to be a little salty, but I doubted he was involved. Still, worth a few questions. Maybe he had seen something. But he didn't answer when I knocked on his door, nor did I see any signs of him in his barn or shed.

I returned to the office, where everyone but Bill was already in. I learned I wasn't the only one who couldn't sleep with an unsolved murder hanging over our heads. Or with the banging of construction, Lake added.

"They weren't working overnight, were they?" Cheryl asked.

"No, but it's like when you're in a plane or on a boat during the day and you get in bed and it still feels like it's rocking and swaying," he said, demonstrating with his hands as if he was trying to keep his balance on an Alaskan fishing trawler. "I swear I hear jackhammers in my sleep."

"It was pretty loud here yesterday afternoon," Cheryl said. "By the way, how's Jessi?"

"Fine," I said.

"Braxton Hicks?"

I nodded.

"Who's he?" Lake asked.

"They're naming the baby Braxton Hicks," Wally said with a straight face.

"Not a bad idea," I said, pointing at him.

"Who's Braxton Hicks?"

I explained as briefly as I could to my sharp but in some ways naïve deputy, and then we got to work. Using a pair of white boards, we listed everyone who had become a person of interest and divvied up their bios, looking for any connection to Caitlin, Justin Tyrell, or one another. We found connections, but never more than two. Nobody tied to Caitlin was tied to Tyrell or vice versa, nor was anyone tied to Caitlin tied to someone tied to Tyrell, and so forth.

"Maybe Tyrell's the other boyfriend," Wally said.

"Crossed my mind," I said. "But there's no proof."

"How old is he?"

"Uh . . . thirty-one," Lake said, referencing a file on his desk.

"That's old," Cheryl said.

"Hence the 'older' comment," Wally said.

"And the secrecy," Lake added.

"How would Caitlin have ever met Tyrell?" Cheryl asked.

"They lived in the same town for a while." Wally said. "Both were in Lincoln previously."

"When she was, like, twelve. He's been in prison for five years."

He shrugged.

"Okay, but what would she see in a repeat criminal, a drug dealer, after her parents died at the hands of a drunk driver?"

"Drugs and alcohol are two different things," Lake said.

"And attraction doesn't always make sense," Wally added.

"It's a theory," I said, "but we've got nothing to establish it as more than that."

"What if we show his mugshot to Caitlin's friends and teammates?" Lake asked. "Maybe they've seen her with him or seen him around, but didn't know the connection."

"That's a good idea. And we should also push into the drug angle. You start asking teenage girls if their dead friend was doing drugs, you're probably not going to get a straight answer, but we need to probe it."

"Who do you want us to talk to?" Cheryl asked.

"You track down Ashlee Blaine and Ti'Ana Parker. I think I've worn out my welcome with them. Lake and I will talk to Rylie Kučera and see if she can guide us to any other teammates."

"Got it."

"And me, Cash?" Wally asked.

"Would you run over to Tonia Savicki's and see if there are any prints or DNA in her truck? Probably nothing viable this long after, but worth a try."

"Will do."

The bell over the door clanged, and I sighed. "That who I think it is?"

"Mayor to see you," Bonnie announced a moment later.

"Okay. You two head out. Lake, we'll go when I finish with the mayor. In the meantime, see if you can find anything on Harry McConkey that would tie him to any of this."

"Got it."

I took a deep breath, then stood to greet the mayor.

Thirty

MAYOR O'Reilly was somewhat pacified by the scant details of our investigation over the last twenty-four hours. He didn't say much when I mentioned the Justin Tyrell theory, other than to ask if we had any actual evidence of his involvement. I said we didn't, which was the low point of the conversation. But he said the leads we were chasing had some promise. He left after fifteen minutes and I found myself dreading each of our talks more and more, and realized I needed not to let my barometer of success be the mayor's approval or lack thereof.

For the second time, Rylie Kučera wasn't home when I visited. Neither was her mother, this time.

"People are always home when the TV detectives show up," Lake said.

"Else they sit across the street with the windows down and banter until they come home on cue," I said, taking off my LCSD cap and wiping my sleeve across my forehead. "Let's run over to the school, see if Rylie happens to be training."

"In this heat?"

"She was Monday."

Lake shrugged, and we got back in my truck. I had recapped my talk with the mayor on the way to the Kučera house, so now I asked what Lake had found about Harry McConkey.

"Nothing." He shrugged. "I mean, nothing that ties to Caitlin or Tyrell. He's never married, farmed his whole life, has a brother over in

Sutton that he takes care of financially. He's in a nursing home. No trouble with the law ever, nothing of note."

"I suppose he could need money for his brother, but I find it hard to believe he's anything other than the guy who rents the DeBoer fields from Schroeder."

Lake shrugged.

There were two females on the football field at the school again. This time, both were girls, both in soccer/training gear. Rylie Kučera and a taller girl with short, blondish-brown hair. They were doing one-on-one dribbling drills when we walked onto the field, both sweating profusely in the morning sun. They stopped as we approached.

"Sheriff Nelson," Rylie said, her wrists on her hips as she panted for breath. The girl beside her used the strap of her tank top to wipe perspiration from her face.

"Rylie. This is Deputy Lake Ryan."

He nodded.

"Michaela Friedlander," the other girl said, offering a sweaty hand. We both shook it.

"I have a few more questions about Caitlin," I said.

"Do you mind if we walk over to the bench?" Rylie asked, nodding at where a couple towels and water bottles sat on the sidelines.

"Not at all."

We gave the girls a minute to slug water and towel off a little. Then I said, "Rylie, you said the other day that Caitlin had a boyfriend, Scott Cooper."

She nodded.

"Were you aware that she planned to break up with him?"

Rylie frowned. "No."

I cut my eyes quickly to Michaela.

"I didn't even know she was dating him," she said.

"Did either of you know anything about another boyfriend?"

"Another boyfriend?" Rylie asked. "No. I barely knew about Scott."

Michaela just shook her head.

"Do you think Scott had something to do with it?" Rylie asked. "He's a little odd, but he wouldn't kill her."

"You know him?"

"From school last year. He was kind of a clumsy farm boy, you know the stereotype," she said, then wiped her towel over her face again. "But he seemed nice."

"I knew who he was," Michaela said, "but didn't know him."

I nodded at Lake, who lifted up his tablet with a picture of Justin Tyrell on it. "Either of you ever seen him?" I asked.

They both looked at the tablet.

"No," Rylie said as Michaela shook her head. "He the other boyfriend?"

"We don't know."

"You're sure?" Lake asked. "Could have been with Caitlin, could have been a face in a crowd . . ."

"Lot of faces in the crowd, but he doesn't look familiar."

"No," Michaela said. "I haven't seen him."

I took a breath as Lake lowered the tablet. "This next question's a little more delicate," I said.

They both looked at me.

"Is there any chance Caitlin was into any illicit substances?"

"Drugs?" Michaela asked.

I nodded.

"No," Rylie said.

"No way," Michaela echoed.

"I mean, it's not like we talked about it," Rylie said, "but she wasn't the type."

"Even after what she went through with her parents?" Lake asked.

"No. That gutted her, obviously, but . . . I just can't see it."

"Her scholarship at NU meant everything to her," Michaela said. "No chance she'd jeopardize that, even with her grief."

I nodded. "Another question, and on my word as Sheriff, this one comes with full immunity . . . Have either of you ever been out to the sandbar on Pioneers Creek?"

Rylie's face showed no recognition.

Michaela shook her head. "I've heard some kids go drinking out there, but I never went. My dad would kill me. I mean, literally, you'd have a homicide on your hands if he caught me drinking."

"What about Caitlin?" Lake asked.

"Not that I know of."

"I don't even know what you're talking about," Rylie said, and I believed her.

"You should talk to her coach at Nebraska," she said. "Daisy, I think. They seemed to have a bond, from comments that Caitlin made. Almost like she was a mother figure or something after everything that happened. Like Michaela said, I can't believe Caitlin was into anything like that with everything that she had on the line, but if she was struggling and tempted . . ."

"She'd have gone to Daisy first before throwing her future away," Michaela said.

"Yeah."

"I'll reach out to her," I said, having already planned at least a phone call to the University of Nebraska athletic department.

"Have you talked to Jenna?" Michaela asked.

"Jenna?"

"Jenna Updike. She was the star of the team before Caitlin."

"As in Caitlin took her spot?" Lake asked.

"No, she graduated spring before last. She goes to Kearney, but still comes back, helps as an assistant coach or trainer when she can since we have a spring season and college plays in the fall. She's kind of like the team's big sister."

"Sometimes the coaches have trouble relating to the girls," Rylie offered. "She bridges the gap."

"She and Caitlin kind of clicked, I think, being on the same level talent-wise. Or closer to it. Caitlin ran circles around the rest of us."

"I should have thought to mention her the other day," Rylie said. "I wasn't thinking."

"It's fine," I said. "Is there anything else either of you can think of you haven't mentioned, anything about her behavior or friends?"

They both shook their heads, so we thanked them for their time and headed back to the truck. On the way, Lake looked up Jenna Updike's address on the tablet. "Lives in the Towns End Apartments on 3rd and Jackson."

"South of the construction," I said.

He nodded.

"Let's run to Harry's place first, then we'll swing back around from the west."

"Deal."

Thirty-One

LAKE and I struck out twice. Harry still wasn't home, and neither was Jenna. We drove back to the office, and I dispatched Lake to find out if she had a job and try to find her there. Meanwhile, with no word yet from Cheryl or Wally, I drove to the Erickson house again. I showed Tyrell's photo to Molly, who didn't recognize him.

"Do you think he's the one who killed her?"

"We don't know yet."

"Who is he?"

"He's a resident of Lee County, a former criminal."

"Why would he have killed Caitlin?"

"We don't have a motive yet."

Molly frowned.

I explained about finding the oil spot and the trace of horse manure in the parking lot at City Park, tying the oil and manure to a truck owned by a person who had a solid alibi, suspecting the truck may have been stolen, and Tyrell's one-time proximity to Tonia's property. I did so without mentioning names, or why Tyrell had been where he'd been. Then I asked Molly to look at his picture again and try to envision him at one of Caitlin's soccer games, with any of her friends, or out in public in passing.

Molly continued to shake her head. "I've never seen him."

I nodded. Licked my lips. "Molly, I know I asked you about any oddities in Caitlin's behavior, but I want to ask a few more."

She frowned slightly but nodded.

"Did you notice any changes recently in her eating or sleeping habits?"

"No. No, I don't think so."

"Was she hotter or colder than normal?"

"No."

"Had she been sick, or complained of any symptoms of sickness, headaches, any physical issues like chest pain, racing heartbeat, that sort of thing?"

"No. What are you getting at, Sheriff?"

"There's no easy way to say this, Molly, but Tyrell was in prison for five years for manufacturing methamphetamine. One possible connection to Caitlin would have been if she was using any kind of drugs."

Molly looked down.

I didn't push but waited for close to a minute.

She lifted her head. "Sheriff, Caitlin was the sweetest girl. She really was. And I can't believe she would do drugs. I know that sounds like every naïve parent or friend who says that about someone, but she wouldn't."

I waited, sensing there was something she wasn't saying.

Molly swallowed. "The accident changed her, obviously, to the point where I can't say there's no way, because people do desperate things when they're stricken with grief. But I still find it hard to believe, and I didn't see any of the things you've mentioned."

I went through a few more symptoms of use—depression, anxiety, paranoia, sadness, hopelessness. Caitlin checked the boxes for all of them, but no worse recently. Actually, Molly said, the fact that the calendar had turned to August and the date of her enrollment at UNL was approaching had seemed to buoy her.

We talked for another fifteen minutes, confirming a few of the things Rylie and Michaela had said, and also talking about funeral preparations.

The funeral was set for Saturday, and some extended family members were arriving tomorrow. Molly and Pat's friends, neighbors, and members of the community had been overwhelming with support, and they were doing as well as could be considering what had happened. I assured her the department was doing all it could, and left her with a promise that we would get to the bottom of what happened.

It was still a little early for lunch, and my phone had buzzed a few times while I'd been speaking with Molly. It was Wally, saying he and Cheryl both had news. I drove back to the station where the two of them and Lake were waiting.

"Ladies first," I said when they were all seated, this time in my office.

"I talked to Ashlee again. She didn't recognize Tyrell and swore she knew nothing more than she had told you before."

"You believe her?"

"I do."

"Did you ask her about Caitlin using drugs?"

"I worked my way around to it. She balked at the idea. Said she didn't know anyone who did drugs. Said the occasional drinking was one thing, but none of her friends were dumb enough to start using, and certainly not Caitlin."

"Even though she was going through a tragedy?"

"Even so."

I nodded.

"Same story from Ti'Ana, albeit without so much of a strong rebuke about drugs in general. But she did assure me there was no way Caitlin would use."

"Nothing on Tyrell?"

"When I showed her the picture, she thought he was that actor from *NCIS*."

"Which actor?"

"The same one who was on *That '70s Show*."

I shook my head.

"Wilmer Valderrama," Lake said.

"How do you even know about that show?" Cheryl asked.

"I'm not that young. And there are reruns."

"Did you find Jenna?" I asked.

He grinned. "She's a waitress at The Edge, just starting her shift."

Located right across the street, The Edge of Town Bar & Grill is a cross between a small-town bar and a family-friendly honky-tonk. The owners are a husband and wife team who double as bartenders, triple as wait staff, and quadruple as informal host and hostess. The building is old, brick, having been remodeled a couple times without losing its old charm. Most importantly, the simple fare is as tasty as it comes.

"You talk to her?" I asked.

He nodded.

"How'd you get there from here?" Cheryl asked.

"Wasn't easy."

"What'd she have to say?" I asked.

"Like the girls said, she was something of a mentor to the girls soccer team, and the softball team, and the basketball team. Kind of an all-sports star in high school."

"Jenna Updike?" Wally asked.

"Yeah."

"I know her name. She was a good athlete."

"I didn't take you for a fan of girls high school sports."

"Sports are sports."

"She know Caitlin?" I asked.

"Not terribly well, but admitted they had talked a few times, mostly about training, physical fitness, the psychological aspect of sports. She didn't know anything about another boyfriend, did know that Caitlin had a casual relationship with a guy. She actually thought she was pretty happy, all things considered, making progress in part because of the boyfriend. Caitlin was bridging to being an adult and he was an adult—and I don't mean that crudely. He wasn't childish, she said."

I nodded.

"Jenna didn't recognize Tyrell, said she would be stunned if Caitlin had used drugs, and had no clue who might want to hurt her or why."

I sighed. "What are the odds of a seventeen-year-old girl using drugs and not only does nobody in her life have a clue, but they all vehemently deny it?"

"I'm sure it happens," Wally said, "but probably not great."

"And what are the odds Caitlin was connected to Tyrell if drugs *weren't* the connection?"

"Between slim and none," Cheryl said.

"Which either means Tyrell had a different motive for killing her, or he's not connected and Tonia's truck being stolen is just a coincidence." I looked to Wally. "You find anything?"

"Bunch of partials and smudges. All hers. Hair that matches hers or the dog's in color. Nothing else."

"If Tyrell did steal it, good chance he wore gloves and was careful."

"Yeah."

"Here," Lake said, holding up his phone. "That's Wilmer Valderrama."

I raised my eyebrows.

"There's a resemblance," he said with a shrug. "Which is odd, since Tyrell's not Hispanic."

I sat forward and tapped the table with my knuckles. "There has to be a connection somewhere in all of this. Lake, dive through social media again, this time looking for Tyrell, any drug references, whether it was Caitlin, one of her friends, anybody. See who's friends with who. Maybe there's a connection there."

He nodded.

"Wally, I want you to find Harry McConkey, run that lead to ground. Then see what you can find about Tyrell since he's been released. We know where he lives but where does he work, where does he eat, where does he shop, where does he hang out? He has to have a footprint, let's find it."

He nodded.

"Without alerting him that you're looking."

"I'll be discreet."

"Cheryl, see what you can find about Caitlin's life in Lincoln. Did she have a boyfriend there, any secrets in her or her family's past, any criminal connections somehow to her family?"

"Will do."

I sighed. "I'm going to grab some lunch and then head for Lincoln to talk to Daisy."

"The soccer coach?" Wally asked.

"Yeah." I tapped my knuckles on the desk again before standing. "Caitlin's funeral's Saturday. I want to be able to look Pat and Molly in the eye and tell them we got the guy."

Thirty-Two

OVER sandwiches and lemonade, I briefed Jessi on the morning's progress. As I recapped it, it didn't feel much like progress. More like spinning our wheels. It seemed there just *had* to be a connection between the DeBoer property being used by Justin Tyrell as a meth lab right across the road from Tonia Savicki and her truck that we had forensically tied to the parking lot less than a hundred feet from where Caitlin had been murdered. And yet, Molly Erickson and all of Caitlin's friends and teammates denied that she had been using or even would use drugs. Nor did any of them recognize Tyrell, who was a good candidate for the secret older boyfriend no one could identify. Henry Schroeder, the current owner of the DeBoer property, wasn't using it, and the current lessee, Harry McConkey, didn't seem like a promising lead.

Jessi mulled for a few bites, then said, "Maybe it is all coincidence."

"Maybe."

"More likely a connection you can't find."

I looked at her.

"That's what you think, isn't it?"

I ground on my whole wheat bread, roast beef, and Swiss cheese. "Yeah."

We ate in silence for a minute.

"I don't remember too much about Tyrell or the meth lab," she said after a drink of lemonade. "I remember it was in the news, of course, and that the whole town was shocked that there would be a meth lab in Lee

County. I still am, in fact. I mean, I know drugs are everywhere and every politician talks about Fentanyl coming across the border, but I just can't believe a girl was murdered here because of drugs."

She took a bite, then tipped her head to the side.

"What is it?" I asked.

Jessi swallowed. "I was just thinking, Kassondra Ives said something about it in her initial press conference. Do you remember that?"

"No. How do you?"

"It was in the paper."

"You remember specifically what she said?" I asked, my subconscious telling me that any connection to Kassondra Ives—Rylie Kučera's aunt—was worth at least paying attention to.

Jessi set down her sandwich. "She blamed O'Reilly for letting drugs into Lee County and I think mentioned the DeBoer meth lab. Yeah, I remember now, she was talking about how she wasn't here at the time, and it came off as kind of petty I thought, but she said drugs were a problem everywhere and we couldn't afford to think we were immune. And she said she offered a new, fresh perspective as someone new to the county."

"What perspective?"

"That I don't remember." She shrugged. "Probably just a lot of empty rhetoric. She's a politician."

"Ouch."

She shrugged again.

"Mayor O'Reilly talks the talk occasionally, but I think he's generally real."

"Oh, I do too. I didn't mean all politicians; I mean, she strikes me as the stereotypical, smooth-talking politician."

I stuck my tongue in my cheek, thinking back on my conversations with Kassondra over the last few days. They hadn't been political conversations in any way, and yet I had seen her projecting control, trying to massage the conversation.

"You don't think so?" Jessi asked.

"I don't know her well enough to say."

Jessie narrowed her eyes. "You think she has a chance?"

"No."

"Not even . . ."

"What?"

"I maybe shouldn't say."

"You started to. Say it."

"Even if there's an unsolved murder, and I'm not saying there still will be, but . . ."

"That might hinder *my* chances at reelection."

"It reflects on the mayor too. More than you think, maybe."

I stuck my tongue back in my cheek, thinking again. Maybe Jessi had a point. O'Reilly had been especially concerned about our progress. But to go from that to the unsaid assertion, that Kassondra was benefitting from a murder and thus somehow involved—that was a bridge too far without evidence.

Jessi seemed to sense it too. "And throw in the construction which has the whole town mad."

"That may factor in," I said. "But no. I don't think she has a chance. Not in rural, conservative, blue-collar Lee County."

"Misogynistic Lee County."

"Did she say that in her press conference too?"

"No, but she's hinted at it. Lot of older people, lot of white people, lot of people with no college education . . ."

I nodded. "No chance."

We finished our sandwiches with talk about how Jessi was feeling and her plans for the afternoon. She had taken the doctor's advice to take it easy, but was getting restless and said she was going to spend some time in the garden after her women's prayer meeting at two. I worried just a little bit about her having more false labor and fainting, and me coming home to find her face-down among her beans and cucumbers.

But she had a good head on her shoulders, and I knew she'd be careful. So a little before one, I gave her a kiss on the cheek and hopped in the truck for a second drive to the capital in as many days.

Interstates are known for being long and straight, but I-80 in east-central Nebraska is exceptionally so, running over seventy miles with hardly any variation. It's virtually flat too, making for a lot of long views of corn and soybeans and hay. Some find it boring—flyover country. I think row after row after row after row of corn, dark green with golden tassels poking the sky on a hot summer day, has a pastoral charm. So does that same corn when it's dried and beige and the sky is streaked with October clouds.

There's a connection between people and land, and it's not just in Nebraska. But there's something about the people of this state that embrace the struggle, the grit and determination that the unforgiving prairie requires. They work hard, just like the corn that has to fight through often hard, dry soil. They stand tall, just like the corn when the wind and rain come howling. They are dependent on the harvest to sustain them another year, and thus live within their means and aren't given to extravagance. At the same time, they enjoy the simple things because they know how fickle and fleeting life—or the harvest—can be. Those are stereotypes and generalizations, to be sure, but ones that exist for a reason. And while so many outsiders tend to scoff or sneer at such glowing depictions of Nebraskans or Midwesterners in general, those of us who live here know it truly is the good life.

I thought about that as I drove, in particular as it related to Kassondra Ives. I didn't know her past, other than she wasn't from Lee County originally. I didn't even know if she was a native Nebraskan. Not that either was a requirement to be mayor, but it did raise some questions as to who she really was and why she was campaigning for the job. I hadn't thought about it before because I hadn't cared because I had no consideration of voting for her. But now, I realized, maybe it would be prudent to at least ask a few questions.

Then again, I couldn't bring myself to truly believe Kassondra was involved somehow in Caitlin's death. Nor that she was so uncaring about the community she was seeking to lead that she would try to manipulate a tragedy for her benefit. I'm not naïve about human nature, nor the nature of politics, but I chose to believe better until proven otherwise.

Thirty-Three

DAISY Schubert met me in the lobby of Hibner Soccer Stadium in north Lincoln. It had taken a few calls to reach her late that morning, but when I had explained who I was and why I was calling, she had found time for me and suggested the meeting location. The soccer stadium was only used on gamedays and was not directly adjacent to the UNL campus. While she hadn't said it in so many words, I got the feeling a conversation with the sheriff about a murdered recruit wasn't something she wanted in public. I could understand that—even if school hadn't started and Caitlin's would-have-been teammates hadn't arrived on campus.

Daisy was tall, close to six feet, with brown hair trimmed short yet in a feminine style. She wore a scarlet and gray polo with an N on the breast and khaki shorts, revealing an athletic figure that suggested she had played before transitioning to coaching. We introduced ourselves as we shook hands, and she suggested we walk and talk. I agreed, and we exited glass doors and walked through a gate to the soccer field. A red grandstand and press box on the right looked across the field at a video scoreboard on the left. To the south, the Bob Devaney Sports Center, Memorial Stadium, and the downtown skyline—including the iconic capitol building—were all visible. Not a bad place for a game, but that wasn't my focus.

"I can't believe Caitlin's dead," Daisy said, stuffing her hands in the pockets of her shorts.

"When was the last time you communicated with her?"

"Last week sometime," she said. She closed one eye. "Wednesday or Thursday? We talked for maybe fifteen minutes about the start of camp, various logistics of her arrival."

"Anything personal?"

"Not this time."

"Other times?"

"Sure. I first recruited Caitlin her junior year, when she was at Southwest here in Lincoln. She committed that spring, and we kept in pretty consistent conversation. Some of that was soccer related. We'd talk about training, technique—she played for Sporting Nebraska, Under 19 youth soccer—in the summer, until this year, and we talked about her games. But we also talked about life. As a coach, I always try to build relationships with players. That's what it's really about, not just scoring goals and winning games. I felt like I got to know her pretty well."

"Did she confide in you?"

"Some. We didn't talk about her dating life or her relationship with her parents as much as school, her intended major, her future, silly stuff from pop culture which may not seem like much, but it builds a relationship. Then, of course, when her parents died, that changed. That absolutely devastated her, as you'd expect. We had a couple really long conversations then, and I was impressed by her resolve. She was hurting, and a lot of people might have gone to really dark places. She didn't. I think soccer and the future it offered were a part of that."

"Had anything changed recently?"

We were almost to the end of the field, which transitioned to a grass-covered berm. Daisy stopped, crossing her arms over her chest and turning toward me. "Not really. I mean, she had made gradual improvement since the accident. Besides the grief and uncertainty, she didn't like being in a small town, didn't like leaving behind everything and everyone she knew here. But she made some friends, she was part of the soccer team there. You don't 'get over' grief, but you do start to live with it, and I think that was her."

"What about the last few weeks or last month?"

"There was building excitement for the season, for coming back to Lincoln."

"Any complaints about not feeling well, physically or mentally, or any signs of it you observed?"

"No, she was in good shape physically, and mentally and emotionally—other than the obvious, she was doing well as far as I could tell."

"She never mentioned boyfriends?"

Daisy shook her head.

I showed her the picture of Justin Tyrell on my phone. "Do you recognize him?"

"No," she said, shaking her head again. "No, I don't think so. Who is he?"

"Convicted felon who's a person of interest."

"How?"

"That depends. Did Caitlin ever say anything that made you think there was a chance she was using or might use drugs?"

"No. Absolutely not. That would have jeopardized her soccer career, and nothing was more important to her than that. And I saw absolutely no signs of it whenever I was around her or talked to her, texted her, anything."

I nodded.

"Sheriff, that scholarship was her way out. And I don't mean that dismissively of Lee, but . . ."

"Small towns aren't for everybody."

"Especially considering what a small town meant to Caitlin. It wasn't just a small town, it was a shakeup of everything she knew and it symbolized the death of her parents. This was a chance at a fresh start."

"Not that I don't believe you, Daisy, but *if* she had been using . . . would you have noticed?"

"I'd like to think so. I've got a complicated family, with addicts and alcoholics, and it's hard to hide if you know where to look."

I nodded.

"Is he a dealer?" she asked, nodding at my phone.

"Of sorts. We have very circumstantial evidence that *could* tie him to the scene."

"Have you questioned him?"

"No. I stress the *very* in very circumstantial."

Daisy wiped her hand over her forehead. "So you don't have any idea who did this to her?"

"Unfortunately, nothing conclusive."

"I just can't fathom anyone wanting to hurt Caitlin."

"I've been hearing that a lot."

"Have they set a time and date for the funeral?"

"Saturday, eleven o'clock in Lee."

She nodded.

"Is there anything you can think of from knowing her that would point you to a person, a motive?"

"No, nothing."

"I've been hearing that a lot too." I took a deep breath. "Thank you for seeing me."

"I wish there was more I could do to help."

We turned and headed back to the far corner of the field. I found myself thinking about how Caitlin should be running on this field this fall, playing soccer for the University of Nebraska. I wasn't ready to say it was my fault she wasn't, that I had failed to keep Lee safe, although maybe it was the truth. But I felt like it was my fault that every interview was leading to the same place—nowhere.

"Is Ron O'Reilly still the mayor of Lee?" Daisy asked as we walked back.

"You know Ron?"

"When I was in college, I was part of a . . . summit, I guess you'd call it, for troubled youth. There were business people, some politicians, other athletes and coaches, all trying to figure out ways to mentor and guide and help kids through athletics or apprenticeships or tutoring or just hanging out—to help them see that they could do something positive with their life. Anyhow, to make a long story short, Mayor O'Reilly and I ended up at a dinner table together and had a nice conversation. He said he had a granddaughter who was going through some things and could use a positive role model like me." She shrugged. "I got good grades and played soccer in college, which I didn't think much of at the time, but his comment kind of got me thinking too, that maybe I could make a difference. It's part of the reason I ended up going into coaching." She shrugged again. "He's stuck in my head because of that."

"Yeah . . ." I said after a pause. "Yeah, he's running for a fifth term this fall."

"Tell him I said hello, will you?"

"Of course."

We shook hands again, I thanked her again, and we went our separate ways.

Thirty-Four

LINCOLN'S downtown Haymarket District has a novelty shop that sells a special kind of "homemade" candy that Jessi absolutely adores. So I detoured south past Memorial Stadium to get her a box. Finding parking was another detour, thanks to several nearby buildings being renovated or torn down, and dumpsters and fencing blocking rows of spots. But I found Jessi's candy and was just headed back to my car when Wally called.

"How'd it go with the soccer coach?" he asked.

"About the same as with everyone else."

"Hmm. Well, I struck out with McConkey."

"Struck out as in didn't find him or—"

"He's been in the hospital in York since Friday with pneumonia."

"In the summer?"

"He's old."

"Okay, scratch him off the list," I said as I turned the corner.

"Already did. And I did some digging on Tyrell. There's no record of him having a job since being released from NSP. He had a 2014 Honda Civic licensed to him when he went away, and that license was renewed in May."

"In which county?"

"Lee. Nine-four, three-three-seven-two. I buzzed by his apartment, didn't see it there, but there is a garage. I've got nothing in terms of where he hangs out. Cheryl and I have confidentially talked to a couple dozen people, none of whom have seen him at their place of business or where they hang out or even around town."

"So he's a ghost."

"Close to it."

I reached my truck. "You got any good news?" I asked as I opened the door, then climbed in.

"Nope."

"At least you're honest, Wally."

He said nothing.

I closed my door. "Cheryl come up with anything on Caitlin's pre-Lee life?"

"I'll let her talk to you. One sec."

I started the truck to get air moving; I didn't want to bring Jessi chocolate syrup.

"Hey, Cash."

"What's the good word?"

"Caitlin's life in Lincoln seems pretty clean. Good grades, no trouble at school, no trouble outside of school that made any public record. Her parents were successful and well respected. If there's a black sheep in the family, he's well hidden. I'm seeing nothing so far as a motive."

I thought back to my conversation with Daisy, of telling her I'd been hearing a lot of no motive. And yet Caitlin was dead.

"How's Lake doing on social media?"

"I can let you talk—"

"Don't bother. If he hasn't shouted 'Eureka!' I take it he has nothing."

"I think that's fair, although I don't know that he knows what 'Eureka' means."

I heard garbled conversation in the background, and then a laugh from Cheryl. "He said he's insulted. *Eureka* is a sci-fi TV show from twenty years ago." She laughed again. "Starring . . . the Maytag Man?"

"I'm going to let you get back to work," I said.

"You coming back in?"

"Leaving Lincoln now."

I tucked my phone in my pocket and concentrated on getting out of the Haymarket and back onto I-80, then pondered my next steps. I doubted we could procure a warrant to probe much deeper into Tyrell's life. He had served his full term and not been paroled, so there was no one watching over him who might know the details of it. I could tip our hand and pay him a visit, or at the very least have a couple deputies keep an eye on him. But I had a feeling that if Tyrell was our guy—and my gut told me he was—we were only going to get one chance to do this right.

Traffic was busy on the two lanes heading west from the capital, more so than it had been the day before. Then again, I hadn't been paying much attention to traffic with Jessi's health on my mind. I had noticed, but not really paid attention to, road construction on the westbound lanes that slowed traffic even more west of the exit to Seward. Soon it ground to a halt as two lanes of would-be racecar drivers were forced to merge into one. I vaguely remembered doing so the day before, with hardly any hassle.

I turned on the radio to try to take my mind off everything, most notably the annoying line of orange barrels to my left. Maybe it was the lack of progress in the investigation, maybe it was the delay finding a parking spot in the Haymarket, or maybe it was construction traffic, but I found myself a little out of sorts. I probably should have prayed about it, but instead I cranked country music. I'll deny it to my dying day, but the intro to Shania Twain's "Man! I Feel Like A Woman!" eased the tension, as did finally successfully merging into one lane.

Even so, traffic continued to crawl, past barrel after barrel after barrel, then finally under an overpass that was partially covered by huge tarps. Dust puffed through slits and out from the top and bottom of the tarps, and the whine of concrete saws forced me to bump up the volume on the "Queen of Country Pop" until I was past the overpass. Traffic continued to crawl, and, as Shania Twain gave way to Darius Rucker, I found the frustration creeping back in. I took several deep breaths and tried to soothe myself with the beauty of unending cornfields that disappeared into the haze on the horizon. Only this time, cornfields reminded me of finding Caitlin's body next to one, which reminded me that we still hadn't made any progress, which reminded me that I had more or less wasted a trip to Lincoln which had led to me sitting in this infernal traffic jam.

Keith Urban singing "Where the Blacktop Ends" replaced Darius Rucker, and suddenly I sat up straight. Little alarm bells were going off in my head. Road construction barrels. Corn. Renovations in the Haymarket. No one having a motive to hurt Caitlin. Jessi's bare feet poking out from under the blanket on the couch last night. It was like having all my deputies talking to me at once, and I could hear snippets from each of them but not enough to make sense of what they were saying.

I punched off the radio in the middle of the chorus.

More alarm bells. The dust from behind the tarps. Snippets of conversation with Jessi last night. Mature corn, green now but soon to start drying out. Orange merge signs.

Traffic started moving around a pair of police cars with lights flashing behind a minor crash scene on the left side of the road. I almost wished it hadn't so I could sit there and think, but, in seconds, traffic was back up to seventy-five miles per hour.

The bells were ringing a cacophony in my head. Cornfields. Road construction. Downtown renovations. The blanket pulling off Jessi's feet on the couch. What had she said as it happened? We had been talking about her false alarm, about the Braxton Hicks contractions, and she had shifted and winced, causing the blanket to move, as she said . . . "the last thing you need now is a distraction."

A distraction . . .

Cornfields.

Road construction.

Downtown renovations.

A distraction . . .

And just like that, I realized I may have discovered the motive for Caitlin's death.

Thirty-Five

JESSI'S pretty blue eyes stared blankly at me over the dinner table. It took her thirty seconds to form words.

"You think Caitlin was killed as a distraction?"

"I think it's possible," I answered before biting into my fajita.

"Because her body wasn't hidden in the corn?"

"That's part of it, a part that never made any sense. Why would a killer who had—presumably—lured her to the park, double tapped her in the chest, policed his brass afterward, and not left so much as a hair or speck of DNA on her body or in the truck he stole—why would he leave the body laying out in the middle of a park where it would obviously be discovered within hours instead of dragging it a dozen rows into the immediately adjacent cornfield where it might not be found until a combine ran it over in the fall?"

Jessi winced.

"It suddenly hit me, what if the killer *wanted* the body found?"

"To cause a distraction?"

"And I remembered what you said the other night, sitting on the couch, about the last thing I needed was a distraction. And I remembered all the people complaining about the noise and the inaccessibility caused by the Main Street road construction. And I remembered, after buying you those chocolates—"

"Which I appreciate, by the way."

I nodded. "I remembered how so many buildings downtown are inaccessible, at least by the usual route, or at least by car, and I thought, what if this is all the perfect storm, to keep me and my deputies and the mayor and the whole town detoured and distracted?"

She picked up her fajita, almost took a bite, and then stopped. "Distracted from what, Cash? You're talking about murdering a teenage girl as a coverup. Even if we assume some dastardly criminal who has no regard for human life, that's still a big risk to take for a distraction."

"I know."

"Especially if you're talking about luring her, posing as a boyfriend and winning her trust . . ." She shook her head.

"I admit it's a little far afield, but Caitlin also makes the perfect victim. She's vulnerable emotionally, one could argue unstable, susceptible to manipulation. And she's from out of town, so while it's not like the people of Lee don't care, it's not the same as killing one of their own."

"That's cold, Cash."

"It's not me saying that, it's the killer's mindset."

Jessi bobbed her head in concession.

I took a bite.

"Still," she said, putting her fajita down without yet having bitten into it. "Distracted from what? What would be worth all this?"

"I don't know. But I have a theory."

"What's that?"

"Three million dollars of crystal meth."

Now Jessi's pretty blue eyes bugged out.

"When the cops raided Tyrell and his meth lab at the DeBoer place, they never found the meth. Maybe he sold it all just before they hit, or maybe he hid it somewhere else."

"And five years later after getting out of prison, he wants his money," she said.

I nodded.

"So he kills Caitlin at the same time the city has torn up half of Main Street, which keeps you busy chasing a killer and keeps the town in an uproar—"

"And largely away from downtown."

She frowned. "You think the drugs are hidden downtown?"

"Maybe."

"Where?"

"I don't know. Or maybe they're elsewhere."

Jessi shook her head, lifted her fajita, but then set it down again and sat back. "What'd Bill think?"

"I haven't talked to Bill yet."

"What did your other deputies think?"

"At first, that I'd spent too much time in the sun."

"And then?"

"That it was as good of a possibility as anything else. We have no known motive from anyone, no clue as to who killed Caitlin. And the suspect—Tyrell, who we can only link because his meth lab was across the street from Tonia Savicki's place and the truck we've linked to the City Park parking lot—has no apparent ties to Caitlin."

"But you think he's the other boyfriend?"

"I think he baited her, yes. But there's no reason why and no motive to kill her . . ."

"Unless she made an easy distraction."

I nodded.

Jessi finally took a bite of her fajita. "So how do you proceed?"

"I've got Cheryl and Lake doing a thorough deep dive on every building downtown—who owns it, who owned it five years ago, what is its status during construction, any ties back to Tyrell or his family or the DeBoer place. And Wally is pulling all the public records on the construction—the who, why, when—to see if we can trace a possible connection there."

"You think the killer arranged for road construction?"

"No, not exactly. Especially if it's Tyrell, because this project has been in the works for years, back to when he was in prison. But I also think this web might be larger than him, and someone connected to him or under his influence may have been able to impact the timing or scope, determined what got excavated when or to what extent." I sighed. "I'm grasping at straws."

"You mean your deputies are grasping at straws while you're having chicken fajitas with your wife?"

"Well, I did talk to the mayor for half an hour as well to get as much of that info from him."

"Did you tell him your theory?"

"No. I said I was running down a wild theory that somehow Caitlin's murder had a connection to the construction, mentioning the bit of cement on one of the bullets."

"He bought that?"

I made a face.

"Sorry, but O'Reilly doesn't strike me as the kind to tilt at windmills." She smirked. "That's a literature reference, if you didn't recognize it."

"I read literature."

"Zane Grey is not literature, Cash."

I looked at her.

She leaned on the table, teasing with her eyes. "Tell me, who tilted at windmills?"

"Don Quick Oats and his sidekick Pancho Villa, written by Miguel Cerveza," I said with faux intelligence.

Jessi shook her head but couldn't hold back a smile.

I finished my fajita and made another with the chicken, onion, red pepper, and rice mix Jessi had made.

"Are you going back in tonight?" she asked.

"No. Sadly, most of the info we need hasn't been digitized yet."

"You're serious?"

"It's a small town, a rural county. A lot of property records are still on paper, and construction permits and details haven't been scanned or uploaded. Or so Lake tells me. Then again, he also thinks a person could hypnotize themselves permanently, so . . ."

"So what are you doing tonight?"

"Well, I was thinking of taking my wife on a long drive in the country to get some ice cream and then mulling on this theory. I feel like I'm still missing a piece."

"A long drive where?"

"Clay Center."

She raised her eyebrows. "Any particular reason?"

"Caitlin went there with Scott Cooper the night she was killed."

"And you think there's a clue there?"

"I think that *maybe* an impartial observer saw something, heard something."

"You are down to long shots."

"It's mostly about the mulling and the ice cream," I said. "And the company."

"Nice save, Don Quick Oats."

Thirty-Six

FRIDAYS Cheryl "blessed" us with muffins. We had no idea why, but for years, she brought them without fail on Friday. Blueberry, orange-cranberry, apple cinnamon, pumpkin, chocolate, bran—you name it. Big muffins, with crumbles on top or caramel drizzle or cream cheese frosting (which Lake argued made them cupcakes) and all baked by her. None of us had the heart to tell her that something was amiss with her baking, and her muffins were drier than drought in the heartland. So we ate them, often on the go, so we could dispose of everything but the muffin top without it breaking her heart. It may have made us bad people, but we didn't care.

Some Fridays, Bonnie "forgot" about the muffins and brought in her own treats, anything from coffee cake to strudel to kolaches to muffins once. That hadn't gone well. The rest of us managed to show restraint with her baked goods so as not to offend Cheryl. But it was a delicate balance. I took advantage of a private office to choke down a dry banana nut muffin and savor two small pieces of apple cinnamon strudel while poring over information.

After a good night's sleep, my theory that Caitlin had been killed as a distraction still seemed viable to me. But I realized there was the same problem with it as with any other theories—no evidence. To that end, I had Bill and Cheryl each separately reviewing the digital property records we *did* have, which Wally and Lake had pulled and categorized last night, along with the info Mayor O'Reilly had provided to me the previous afternoon. Meanwhile, Lake had been at City Hall at 8:01 a.m. with donuts (I thought about having him dispense of Cheryl's muffins there) to bribe the staff to put a rush on pulling and collating everything else we needed. The hope was that one of us would see *something* in all that data that would provide a link to Justin Tyrell that would give us a chance at a warrant that would lead to evidence of Caitlin's murder.

My phone blipped with a text from Jessi, telling me she was having lunch with a friend and wouldn't be there if I came home for lunch. I was typing a reply when another message came, saying how much she had enjoyed a simple getaway last night and appreciated me making time for her even amidst the investigation. I edited my reply to acknowledge the second text, then spent a moment thinking about ice cream in Clay Center. No one at the old-fashioned drive-in had even seen Caitlin Sunday night, much less overheard anything. One had remembered Scott and his truck, and thought there may have been a blond girl in the front seat. From an investigative standpoint, the night had been fruitless. But after four long days, having some quality time with Jessi—not with premature labor on our minds—had been refreshing.

I put down my phone and got up to get more coffee. Bill had the same idea.

"Find anything?" I asked.

"Maybe. You seen all these dump trucks with the suit of armor on the cab?"

"I hadn't paid much attention to them, but now that you mention it, yeah." I poured my coffee, then nodded at Bill's mug. He set it down, and I poured.

"I must have seen a dozen of them coming and going from the construction site," he said. "Thanks," he added, taking his mug as I put the pot back on the burner. "Thing is, I've never seen those trucks around before."

"Can't say as that I have either."

"Turns out Knight Trucking is from Wilber."

"Wilber?"

"Uh-huh," he said and took a swig.

Wilber was southeast of Lee, a good twenty-five or thirty miles as the crow flew and even further as the truck hauled.

"I suppose there *could* be reasons why they were picked instead of a company closer."

"Could be," Bill said. "But there's more."

"Boys only meeting?" Cheryl asked walking over.

"I was just telling Sheriff about Knight Trucking, the company that's hauling all the debris and dirt out of here."

"Oh?" she said, reaching for the pot.

"From Wilber, and owned by—"

"Wilber?"

He nodded.

"That's thirty miles away," she said, talking as she poured coffee. "Why not go to York, or even Lincoln? That has to be closer via the interstate."

"That's what I was getting to," Bill said. "Knight Trucking is owned by Carson Knight, who graduated from Lincoln East a decade ago."

"And now he's running a trucking company?" I asked.

"Was Billingsly Trucking when he joined on nine years ago. Worked his way up the ladder and bought the company from Paul Billingsly when Paul retired three years ago. Renamed and rebranded it as his own."

"Where's this going, Bill?"

"I just confirmed that Knight was a classmate with Justin Tyrell at Lincoln East. Same graduating class."

Cheryl stopped in the middle of stirring sugar into her coffee. "I thought Tyrell was from Kansas City?"

"He was. Moved here before his senior year. Well, moved to Lincoln, where his mom and boyfriend lived."

"East has to have a pretty high class size," I said.

"Five hundred sixty-one seniors in their graduating class."

"That's a lot of people."

"Could be just a coincidence, admittedly," he said. "But worth noting."

I nodded, said, "Good work," and dismissed the informal meeting as we each went back to work. Lake arrived a few minutes later with stacks of copies and USB drives with more information. He and Bonnie made copies of the copies while Cheryl uploaded the contents of the drive to our server, and soon we all had desks covered with folders and papers and our computer monitors full of digital records. I had already begged off with the mayor for the morning, having spoken to him and updated him last night, and now I locked myself in my office with a topped off mug of coffee. I turned off the TV that often ran at low volume or muted in the background and instead tuned in the local country radio station for some white noise compared to the grumble of construction equipment outside, and then tried to sort through all the data.

I focused first on the town council's scope of work. I'm far from an engineer, in skill or mindset, but from what I read, the mayor's assertion to me that the construction was needed seemed a bit hyperbolic. Yes, there were legitimate issues that needed to be addressed with cracks, potholes, and sinkage of both the road and sidewalks; utility and sewer upgrades that were past due; and landscaping renovations that would be both aesthetic and functional. None of them, however, were deemed urgent by either the town council or the outside consultants they had hired. And while there was something to the idea of fixing it all at once instead of in pieces, there hadn't been a consensus that such a move was prudent.

That was a long way from an argument that the Main Street construction had been implemented or scheduled with an ulterior motive in mind. But it opened the door to at least some speculation, especially with Bill's discovery that Knight Trucking was owned by a former classmate of Justin Tyrell's. Then I found a list of selected bidders for the project, and Knight Trucking was conspicuously absent.

I scanned the list three times, still not seeing it. I needed to stretch my legs and walked to Bill's office, where I asked if I was looking at the list right. He looked at the piece of paper, then at me, then back at the paper. Then he handed it back and began digging through papers on his desk. He pulled one out and handed it to me.

"What's this?"

"List of contracts signed."

"Should match, correct?"

"Should," Bill said as I began scanning them side by side. Both were alphabetical and matched until the tenth row down, when Knight Trucking on Bill's list was opposed by a utility company on my list. The utility company was next on his, so I began comparing alternate lines until I had another mismatch. S&L Landscaping on Bill's list was opposite Spencer & Sons Trucking on my list, one row below S&L Landscaping. I scanned the rest of Bill's list and didn't see Spencer & Sons Trucking.

"There," I said, handing him back my paper. "Spencer & Sons. Their bid was selected but there's no contract with them, but there is with Knight."

"That's odd."

"When was the contract signed? Do you have it?"

"Uh . . . yes, that was digital." He clicked a few times and pulled up a copy of the contract the town had signed with Knight Trucking. "May 14."

"Can you find the amount?"

Bill scrolled until he found it, and we compared the contracted amount with Spencer & Sons' bid. The latter was almost fifteen percent lower.

I stepped back and leaned against the doorpost. "So Spencer & Sons' bid came in lowest, was selected by the town, but then at the last minute, the contract is signed with Knight Trucking, who just happens to be owned by a classmate of Tyrell's."

"Could be legit reasons for the change," Bill said.

"Could be."

"I'll run it down."

I nodded and returned to my office. I had barely taken my seat when Cheryl rapped on the door frame. I looked up and saw she was flushed. "What is it?" I asked.

"Did I just hear you talking about Spencer & Sons?"

"Yeah, why?"

"From Milford?"

"I don't know."

"Yes, from Milford," I heard Bill's muffled voice say. Soon he stood beside Cheryl in my doorway.

"Why?" I asked.

"Owned by Ryan Spencer?"

I shrugged.

"The same Ryan Spencer that owns half of Seward County?"

"The real estate king," Bill said

She nodded.

"I've heard of him," I said. "What's the deal?"

"Spencer has two sons and one daughter, who married an insurance bigwig from Omaha."

"Why do you know the Spencer family tree?"

"Well, he's not Warren Buffet, but he's pretty active financially, everything from buying and selling all manner of property in the Midwest to rather large political contributions."

I nodded. "Both sides, right?"

"Yes. No one can figure out his political leanings because he's backed right-leaning candidates and left-leaning candidates."

"Okay."

"Most recently, he's been propping up one particular candidate, both privately and through his various companies funding nearly half her campaign."

"Who?" I asked, sensing the answer even though it made no sense.

"His granddaughter via the insurance bigwig from Omaha. Kassondra Ives."

Thirty-Seven

LUNCHTIME came and went, as did rumbling Knight Trucking dump trucks outside my window. Wally came in, and all five of us searched for a connection between Kassondra Ives and Justin Tyrell, one that didn't require us to play six degrees of separation. We also looked at every building affected by the downtown construction—who owned it, who had owned it previously, what it was used for, whether or not there was still money owed to the bank or a lien on the property, and so on. It was dry, boring work, and the lines on paper started to blur. No amount of coffee could stimulate or keep the headache away.

Then I found something.

The sheriff's department sits on the northeast corner of 4th and Main. East of the department is the parking lot, and east of that are two old brick buildings dating back almost a hundred years. Buddy's, owned by Butch Hanrahan, is on the corner of 5th and Main. Directly west of it—sharing a wall with it, in fact—is a building split in two, forming two, long stores. One is Marlee's, a health food retailer that I'd been to once on an errand for Jessi. It smelled like fermentation and sandals. The other had changed hands numerous times over the years and was currently vacant. Most recently, it had been headquarters of Kassondra Ives for Mayor.

I dug deeper. Five years ago, when Tyrell's operation had taken place at the DeBoer property, a pet store had occupied the space next to Marlee's. Three years ago, it had closed, and a ladies' boutique had moved in and lasted less than a year. Lee County 4-H had leased it for a year, then New Light Church had leased it a couple nights a week for a Bible study, and then Kassondra had moved in late last year when she had declared her candidacy. Seeing that jogged my memory, but back then she had been so far off my radar that I'd hardly paid her notice. Late June, she had relocated to larger offices in a multi-purpose building on the edge of town, and the space had remained vacant ever since.

I sat back in my chair, fingers interlaced behind my head. Kassondra's name kept coming up, but not in any way that made sense. Her niece, Rylie Kučera, had been a soccer teammate of Caitlin's, but with no apparent connection to her death. Kassondra had showed interest in solving the murder and suggested bringing in outside help, which didn't make sense if she were somehow involved—why would she want me and my department to have additional assistance? One of Kassondra's primary donors owned the company that had originally been contracted to work construction on Main Street, but then had somehow been replaced by a company with potential ties to Justin Tyrell. And Kassondra had vacated her downtown office, a downtown that was so beset with construction noise and mess—noise and mess I theorized was a distraction, along with Caitlin's murder, from something else, presumably tied to Tyrell's missing meth.

I felt the walls closing in, and got up to see how the others were doing. They had no breakthroughs, and I announced that I was going to go for a drive, patrol a little, see if a change of scenery caused something to click. I encouraged them to take a break too. Cheryl suggested I take a muffin for the road, and I figured it was an easy way to appease her. I grabbed one and a to-go cup of coffee and headed out to my truck.

It was yet another hot, hazy day—one of the dog days of summer—and in the middle of the afternoon, the black asphalt was cooking. Almost sticky. I shifted the muffin and to-go cup into one hand and reached for the handle of my truck—chrome and hot in the midday sun too—and then stopped.

The parking lot.

Sixteen months ago, the Victorian house next to the department had been razed and the parking lot built over the ruins. I turned and looked at the lot, trying to picture that house. It had been old, falling into disrepair and neglect, an eyesore downtown, and the town council had bought out the owner and demolished it. The debate over what to do with the property had been a little contentious, but the need for more parking had won out, and department employees and visitors now parked in the lot, freeing up spaces on the street.

Picturing the old house, my eyes settled on the two-story brick structure beside it, housing Marlee's on the east and the vacant former political office/4-H headquarters/pet store on the west.

A dump truck grumbled by on the torn up Main Street, causing the ground beneath me to vibrate.

And suddenly I had a new theory.

I turned and hurried back inside, drawing looks from my deputies as I burst into the bullpen. Bill had been sitting out there with them and wrinkled his face. "What's up, Sheriff?"

"Who owned the old house next door?"

"The one that's now a parking lot?" Wally asked.

"Yeah."

"Frank Mueller," Bill said.

"Always?"

"Well, back a ways, anyhow."

"Five years ago?"

He frowned. "No. I think he might have sold it, now that I think about it, a few years before it got torn down. Yeah, when he and Connie moved to Grand Island."

"Find out who owned it five years ago, when we raided the meth lab."

"Why?" Lake asked.

"Just a theory."

"I'm on it," Cheryl said, spinning toward her computer.

"Actually, I've got another task for you."

"What's that?"

"You ever shop at Marlee's?"

"Once or twice."

"I want you to run over there and ask how construction's been impacting business?"

"Okay."

"Particularly ask about walls shaking, stuff falling off shelves and breaking, power flickering," I said, remembering Butch's complaints a few mornings ago.

"Okay," she said with a frown.

"Also, do we know who lives upstairs?"

"Pretty sure it's Marlee, the owner."

"Okay, verify that. If not, let's find that person and ask them the same questions."

"Okay," she said again, standing. "I'm on my way."

I nodded my thanks, then invited the three other deputies to join me in my office. We all had seats.

"I want you all to speak freely, with no repercussions from anyone in this room, and what we say here stays here."

They nodded solemnly.

"I don't see any evidence conclusively linking Kassondra Ives to Caitlin's murder, but her name does keep coming up. I want to tread very carefully considering the fact she's running for public office, and considering it's well known I'm friendly with the current mayor and he's friendly with this office. But I also don't want to look the other way because things could get messy. If Ives was just another citizen, would she warrant further investigation?"

They were silent for a moment. Bill just beat Wally in finally speaking.

"I would place her as a person of interest," he said. "But before we would label her a suspect or potential suspect or make any move to that end, we need to find a link—need to find it internally."

"I was going to say pretty much the same thing," Wally said.

I looked to Lake.

"We go where the evidence leads, right, Boss?"

I nodded. "Okay. Wally, check into Carson Knight's possible connections to Tyrell. Did they know each other in high school, hang out in high school, have any connections since, or did they just happen to be at the same school at the same time? Bill, look into Ryan Spencer's campaign contributions a little more carefully. I know he's all over the map, but see if you can find any consistency in those he supports, especially if there's anything that could be related to drugs, drug prevention, drug abuse, drugs and the border, you name it. Lake, find out who owned the Mueller place five years ago when Tyrell's meth operations were going on at the DeBoer place. I'm going to reach out to Spencer & Sons Trucking and get the scoop from them on why they're not on this project. Was it their choice, did something fall through post-bid, what happened?"

"You going to tell us what you're thinking?" Wally asked. "What bee suddenly got in your bonnet?"

"Let's see what Cheryl finds next door and what we dig up here. Then I'll know if I'm barking up the wrong tree or not."

Thirty-Eight

CIRCUMSTANTIAL evidence was mounting against the Democratic challenger for mayor.

On the whiteboard in my office, lest anyone should walk in, we had established a timeline.

In mid-November the prior year, Kassondra Ives had launched her mayoral campaign.

Later in November, she had received a contribution of $10,000 from Ryan Spencer.

In February, Spencer & Sons Trucking had been selected as the lowest bidder for the Main Street construction project.

On May 2nd, Spencer & Sons had backed out of the project. Per my conversation with the COO of Spencer & Sons, the decision had been internal, based on some personnel cutbacks and overscheduling. That could have been a legitimate reason or could have been a hard-to-dispute load of hogwash.

On May 14th, Knight Trucking had been selected and had signed a contract with the town—which Spencer & Sons had never done.

A month and a half later, on June 26th, Kassondra had vacated her office downtown, leaving it unoccupied ever since. Her campaign, which hadn't gotten much traction throughout the winter, had taken off a little after spring elections, which hadn't involved her but had stirred up Democrat voters throughout the area who hoped to challenge Republican incumbents in the fall.

One week after that, on July 2nd, she had received another $5,000 from Ryan Spencer.

Following the money didn't necessarily lead anywhere. Kassondra didn't have the power to determine which company was hired, say in exchange for a campaign donation. Nor was there any conceivable reason for Spencer to make another donation after his company backed out of the project, if some sort of quid pro quo had been in the works.

Bill's research into Ryan Spencer hadn't turned up anything conclusive. He was a political moderate who stayed away from the really controversial subjects—abortion, immigration, matters of sex and gender—but backed candidates from both sides of the aisle who espoused projects or causes that were beneficial to the people of Nebraska or to business ventures of his. Or, in the case of Kassondra Ives, candidates who were family.

Wally's quest to find a connection between Carson Knight and Justin Tyrell had gone nowhere. They had both graduated from Lincoln East the same year, but through a dozen phone calls to teachers and a few friends of Knight's at the time as well as by tracking prison visitor logs and Knight's business records, he had established no post-high school interaction. The fact that the man whose company had benefited from Spencer & Sons' withdrawal from the project had gone to high school with the man who had five years ago been arrested for operating a meth lab in Lee County seemed to be just a coincidence. Nor had I established any connection between Knight Trucking and Spencer & Sons Trucking or their owners to suggest they were somehow working in cahoots with one another.

Cheryl had talked to Marlee Van Zandt, the owner of Marlee's, who complained of similar noise and disruption as had Butch Hanrahan and said she would have come to us about them had she not known how busy we were with Caitlin's murder. She reported tons of noise, lots of windows shaking and items rattling on or falling off of shelves, and several power spikes and flickers. Marlee lived upstairs and confirmed some of the same had befallen her apartment there, but never at night—only during construction. I'd asked Cheryl then to canvass all the business owners across the street, between 4th and 5th, to see if they had experienced the same. Noise, yes. The occasional window rattling, yes. No breakage or excessive vibrations, no power spikes.

Lake had confirmed that Frank and Connie Mueller had sold the Victorian house that had stood between the sheriff's house and the two-story brick building since 1890 eight years ago. The buyer at the time had been Happy Homes Limited, a company that upon further examination was nothing more than a shell, a front for a man named Philip Willis. Willis, via HHL, owned dozens of properties in south central Nebraska, some of which he rented directly to tenants, others he leased to others who rented them out. The house in downtown Lee had been the former, rented to four different people in the five and a half years before it had been torn down. For the first two years, it had been rented by a family of six, a family I remembered upon hearing the name. Then an old lady had lived there by herself for two years, followed by another family for six months after her death, followed by a single man for the last year before he'd been evicted by Willis and the house had been sold to the Town of Lee.

The single man had a criminal record, misdemeanors—including marijuana possession—decades ago. But the person of interest, upon further digging, was the old lady who had lived there by herself for two years. Delores Schiff, a widow of several decades, originally from Hastings. Lake, to his credit, had gone way down the rabbit hole and found not one but two connections.

"Delores had a daughter named Eileen," Lake reported to all of us, "who married a man named Donald Jones. Eileen and Donald's daughter, Theresa Jones, spent five years married to Brent Tyrell, Justin Tyrell's father."

I raised my eyebrows. Bill whistled. Cheryl and Wally exchanged glances.

Lake continued. "Theresa is not Justin's mother, but came on the scene after he moved to Lincoln with his mom and her boyfriend before his senior year. Now, I haven't established a link between Justin and his father's ex-second wife, nor can I connect Theresa to her grandmother, Delores. Theresa now lives in Waco, Texas, and what—if any—time she's spent in Lee County or in Hastings is a mystery. But the fact that there *is* a connection has to mean something, doesn't it?"

"My head's spinning with all the branches in the family tree," Bill said, "but I would have to think so."

"It gets better," Lake said. "I ran a few basic bios. Donald Jones—that would be Tyrell's dad's second wife's father for those of you keeping score—is a graduate from the University of Missouri's Trulaske College of Business. Guess who his roommate freshman and sophomore year at Mizzou was."

"Who?" I asked.

"Guess."

"Brad Pitt," Cheryl said.

"No," Lake said, looking at the rest of us.

I bored my eyes into him.

"Calvin Ives, Kassondra's father."

Bill and I both whistled this time.

"You're serious?" Wally asked.

"I double-checked," Lake said with a nod. "It's the right Calvin Ives and the right Donald Jones."

I sat forward. "So let me just make sure we've got this right. Justin Tyrell, busted for operating a meth lab on the property of his mom's brother-in-law's aunt Helen, has a stepmom, for lack of a better term, whose grandma lived in the house next door at the same time Tyrell was cooking meth at Helen's place and whose father was a college pal of Kassondra Ives' father?"

Bill shook his head as if clearing out cobwebs.

Cheryl was a step behind me doing the math in her head, but nodded in corroboration. So did Lake.

"I can't connect all the dots—it's a long way from having those relations to having relationships with all those people—but I can't believe this is all a coincidence."

"But it doesn't mean anything," Wally said.

We all looked at him.

"So what if they all are connected to each other and to a house that's now in ruins. What does any of that have to do with Caitlin's murder?"

I stood. Walked to the window and looked at the mess of torn-up Main Street. Turned back around to face my deputies. "When the cops raided Tyrell's meth lab, they never found the product. I think he hid it somewhere, just before he got nabbed and sent upriver. Five years later, he gets out, and wants to find his meth and make his millions selling it. There's only one problem. He'd hidden it in a building—at the time rented by a distant relative—that is no longer standing. A building that is now lying in ruins, perhaps with millions of dollars of meth hidden in the walls or under the floorboards or in the cellar, under our parking lot."

I had started pacing. Four sets of eyes went with me, and four faces showed gradual stages of understanding and accepting my theory.

"Tyrell's not going to give up on all that potential money, but neither can he dig up a parking lot. His only way would be to tunnel in from the side, from the basement of an adjacent building. He could never manage it from the sheriff's department, but the brick building next door would be perfect. He just had to clear it out, or at least half of it, so he would have access to the basement. When the backhoes started digging up Main Street and the dump trucks started rumbling through town, he had the cover, and the added vibration from his tunnelling would upset Marlee and Butch, but would easily be blamed on the road construction."

"You think he arranged for the town to do road construction?" Wally asked.

"That's quite a stretch, Sheriff," Bill said.

I shook my head. "The construction was a stroke of luck. He just had to wait till it started, and then to make sure this department didn't listen too closely to all the complaints about the construction or pay attention to what was going on next door, he killed Caitlin to keep us chasing a murder investigation."

"That's a big distraction," Bill said.

"I don't know, Cash," Cheryl said. "Killing a girl just to keep us busy? Wouldn't the construction have been enough cover?"

"For the shaking, the rattling, maybe. But somehow he had to get drilling or digging equipment into the basement. Somehow he had to get over three million dollars of meth out of there if he could recover it. Somehow he had to come and go as a convicted felon to a supposedly vacant building without attracting any attention."

"I don't know," Wally said.

"How does Kassondra tie into this?" Bill asked.

"Maybe not at all. Or maybe as an accomplice. Her whole campaign could be another distraction, to occupy the space next door so no other tenant could get in the way, then vacate it when it was about time for Tyrell to get to work. Her campaign hasn't been growing, yet she needs a bigger space, one that accommodates more staff?"

"I admit she keeps appearing in all this," Bill said, "but . . . I don't know, this is . . ."

"A wild theory?"

"Kind of, yeah."

"I'm with Bill," Wally said, "this seems a little far-fetched. But, not so far-fetched that we shouldn't at least follow it."

"Should be easy enough," Lake said. "Go look at the basement next door and see if there's a drilling operation going on."

"Not sure we've got enough for probable cause," Wally said.

"Or a warrant," Bill added.

"I've actually got another idea," I said. "One that might expose Tyrell and his potential accomplice, if we lay the trap just right."

Thirty-Nine

BOTH Mayor O'Reilly and Kassondra Ives had been hesitant when I proposed a five o'clock meeting in my office. The mayor was eager for another update, but hadn't been wild about the timing, nor about me inviting his political opponent. But I sold him on the fact that she had a right to know as events could impact not only the campaign but also her potential future job. I sold it as very hypothetical. Kassondra, for her part, was perfectly willing to come and grateful to be included, but had seemed a little suspicious at me suddenly inviting her to the briefings. I sold her on the right to know as potential future mayor too.

Before calling either of them, I had called Tonia Savicki and my wife, both in respect to evening plans. Both had willingly gone along with my suggestion. A couple more phone calls had ironed out the plans just in time.

I'd asked Bill to sit in the meeting with me and sent Wally on patrol and Cheryl home for the night, with Lake settling in for the first shift of the night. Bonnie, before leaving for the day, admitted Kassondra at five till five, and Mayor O'Reilly at five on the button. After some forced cordiality and a mutual declining of offered drinks, we were all seated, me behind the desk, Kassondra across from it on my left, O'Reilly across from it on my right, and Bill against the right wall under the window looking out at the bullpen.

"Thank you both for coming," I said.

"You said on the phone you had a breakthrough," O'Reilly said. "But not an arrest?"

"Not yet."

"You have a suspect?" Kassondra said.

"In a manner of speaking."

They both frowned.

"We're pretty sure the killer used Tonia Savicki's truck to commit the murder," I said. "Tonia has a solid alibi for last Sunday night, but forensics tie her truck to the parking lot near where Caitlin was found."

"So the killer stole the truck," Kassondra said.

"That's our assumption."

"And you know who it is?"

"I know *of whom* it might be."

They frowned again.

"Tonia's property is right across the road form the DeBoer farm where five years ago LCSD raided a meth lab. The mastermind and an accomplice were arrested and did time, and both are out of prison by now. The accomplice, Dylan Foster, is living in Butte, Montana. The mastermind, Justin Tyrell, lives in Lee."

Kassondra's eyebrows shot up.

"There were likely others involved in the operation, any of whom could have looked from the property down Tonia's driveway and seen that she kept the keys above her visor, making her truck an easy target five years later."

"How do you know she kept her keys above the visor?" O'Reilly asked. "Or is that speculation?"

"I saw her leave when I was looking around the DeBoer place after questioning her."

"Still, a stretch to assume she did that five years ago. Or even had the same truck."

"The latter we confirmed with the DMV," Bill piped up.

"And habits don't often change," I said.

The mayor mulled for a moment.

"What's the connection to Caitlin?" Kassondra asked.

"That we don't know," I said truthfully. "Could have been any number of things."

"So Tyrell's your main suspect?" O'Reilly said. "Have you questioned him?"

"He's *a* suspect," I said. "But we have nothing to link him to Caitlin."

"But he is a person of interest," Kassondra said. "Have you questioned him?"

"No. I have another plan."

"What's that?" O'Reilly asked.

"I have a meeting tomorrow morning with Judge Felix. I'm going to present the evidence we have and see if he will issue a warrant to let me search Savicki's truck for fingerprints or DNA. If Tyrell, or one of his associates who are in the system, took the truck, we can link them to the crime scene. From there, we can get a warrant to search homes, cars, bank accounts—everything."

"Why do you need a warrant?" Kassondra asked. "Will Savicki not let you search the truck?"

"No. She's one of these . . . I don't mean to be political, especially in this room," I said with a thin smile, "ultra-libertarians, prefers to be left alone by the law or the government, doesn't want intrusion into her personal affairs or property, that sort of thing."

"Have you tried reasoning with her?" O'Reilly asked.

"Several times."

He sighed and shifted in his chair. "What if the killer wore gloves? You said the crime scene was pretty sterile."

"It was, and that's distinctly possible. But I can't believe anyone could have stolen a truck, driven to the park, committed a murder, then returned in the truck and dropped it off without leaving *some* kind of DNA behind."

"It's worth a try, at least, I suppose," Kassondra said. "You said you're meeting with the judge in the morning?"

I nodded.

"You're not worried Savicki will destroy any evidence before that—accidentally, I mean?"

"If you've been to her place or seen her truck even from the outside, you'll know she's not the kind to keep things real tidy. And . . . it's been five days already," I said, looking at Bill. "Sadly, we thought this was a dead end until today when we put it all together." I exhaled. "Anyhow, I wanted you both to know, I do anticipate narrowing in on a suspect tomorrow."

"And you can't see the judge until then?"

"He had some engagements this evening," I said. I shrugged. "I could call another judge, but I know Felix and if I look him in the eye, show him what we have, I'm confident I can get the warrant. I'm not sure with another judge I don't know as well."

"Well, that makes sense," O'Reilly said. "Felix's a good judge."

"That depends," Kassondra said.

I put up a hand. "No politics today, please."

She nodded.

"Is there anything else?" The mayor asked. "Mrs. O'Reilly has supper on."

"No. Like I said, I think we're on the cusp of solving this, and I wanted to catch you both up to speed." I stood and so did they.

"Thank you, Cash," Kassondra said with an extended hand.

"My pleasure." I shook her hand, then O'Reilly's.

"Keep us posted?" he said.

"Will do."

Bill ushered them both out, then returned to my office and closed the door. He sat down in the seat O'Reilly had occupied a few minutes prior. "You think it worked?"

"We'll see."

"They both seemed to accept your reason for the meeting."

"Seemed to."

He took a breath.

"You've got doubts?" I asked.

"Honestly?"

"I'd have it no other way."

"Yes," he said. "But also belief."

"That worked for the demon-possessed boy's father in the Bible," I said.

"I reckon so." He tapped the arms of his chair with his palms. "You sure you don't want a second man there?"

"I'm sure, Bill. One of us should have dinner with our wives tonight."

Forty

CHIRPING crickets kept me company as I alternated between sitting on a hay bale and pacing on the dirt floor of Tonia Savicki's horse barn. The door at the far end of the barn was open, and my eyes had adjusted to the very dim ambient light. The sliding barn door that opened to her driveway was cracked a couple inches, which allowed me to peek out at her house, the garage if I craned my neck and looked sharply right, and down her driveway toward the road if I craned my neck and looked sharply left. Most importantly, I could clearly see her 1986 GMC Sierra, parked in the same spot as always. A quarter moon had risen high enough in the sky that it cast a sheen of light over the metal and glass, but it wasn't bright enough to give me away through the crack in the door.

I had been in the barn since six o'clock, fueled by a Stanley thermos of coffee and a couple of meat and cheese sandwiches Jessi had whipped up on short notice. The glow-in-the-dark hands on my watch indicated it was almost midnight. Too early to call off my stakeout but getting late enough that I was starting to wonder if the seed I'd planted hadn't been watered.

Having time alone to think could be a blessing and a curse. In this case, it had been both. I'd carefully reviewed every piece of evidence or tidbit of information we had gleaned in the last five days, confirming the hunch I was playing now. Then I'd reviewed it again and realized how many theories and hunches had led to this point, which made me start to doubt it. Doubts and belief, like Bill had said.

The last bit of coffee in my lid was cold, so I dumped it and screwed the lid back on. I stood to pace some more and stopped almost immediately. I wasn't sure if I'd heard something so much as sensed it, but I crept to the slightly cracked barn door and peeked through it. At first, all was still. But then I noticed a shadow moving through the mouth of the driveway, a figure dressed in black who paused in the blackness next to a bush. For two minutes, there was no movement, and I wondered if wishful looking had deceived me.

Then the figure inched forward to the rear bumper of Savicki's truck, pausing in a crouch there. Another minute passed, the figure's head turning left and right. All the lights in the house were off, including the porchlight. The yard light on a pole to the south of the horse barn was also out, a last-minute decision I'd weighed carefully, as I didn't want to make the trap too enticing.

The figure slipped around the far side of the truck and opened the driver's side door, causing the dome light to flick on. Through the passenger window, I couldn't see well enough to make out the figure's face. I waited patiently as the figure sat in the driver's seat and eased the door shut, dimming the light. I took that as my cue.

With my Glock 22 service weapon in my left hand, I eased the sliding door open. Tonia and I had greased the wheels and track that evening, making sure it didn't squeak. I slipped through the opening, then brandished my weapon and hurriedly crept to the side of the truck. I yanked open the passenger door, at the same time pointing my weapon at the figure inside.

"Police, don't move."

Justin Tyrell looked at me from under a hood that was halfway over his head.

"Very slowly, slide across the seat, and keep your hands up." I had spent enough time at the range shooting lefthanded that I was comfortable without switching the gun to my dominant hand.

Tyrell raised his hands, but instead of sliding, raked down the sun visor. No keys fell into his lap. He looked at me, and I patted my pocket with my right hand, then motioned for him to come out. "Slide over."

Tyrell instead shoved open the driver's-side door and leapt out to make a run for it. I had anticipated such a move and stepped to my left. Unfortunately, I couldn't shoot a fleeing suspect in the butt. But I could draw from my pocket a very smooth, one-inch diameter stone I'd found in the driveway earlier for just such an occasion. Reliving my days as a high-school third baseman, I set my feet and rifled the stone right at the center of Tyrell's skull. My aim and my ability to lead the target were perfect, and it hit him right behind the ear. With a cry as much of shock as pain, he staggered, reached for his head, then stumbled and fell into the driveway.

I was around the truck and on him in a flash. He tried to wrestle me off, but I had the upper positioning and planted him forcefully in the gravel with my right hand while sticking my gun in the nape of his neck with the left. Feeling the cold steel against his skin, he froze. I used my right hand to reach for my cuffs, clap them around his right wrist, and then grab his left wrist and secure it behind his back to the right. Having been kneeling on his lower back and buttocks, I now stood and stepped back.

"Justin Tyrell, you are under arrest for the murder of Caitlin Thomas."

He swore a blue streak at me, continuing as I read him his Miranda rights. Amidst all the swearing, he interjected something about a lawsuit and police brutality. When I lifted him up by the collar of his sweatshirt, I saw a gash behind the ear where the stone had hit him, but it didn't look terribly deep nor was it bleeding profusely, as even minor head wounds tend to do. Then my attention was diverted as he tried to wrestle free and perhaps head-butt me. I spun him around and slammed his chest into the tailgate and portions lower than his chest into the bumper. He cried out again.

"You can keep resisting," I said, "or you can come peacefully."

More swearing.

I turned him around, his back to the tailgate.

"I didn't murder nobody."

"Technically, that's a confession that you *did* murder *somebody*, but I doubt bad grammar will hold up in court."

He swore again.

I frisked him, surprisingly finding no weapon. No identification either, just two handkerchiefs and a cheap cell phone.

I held up the handkerchiefs. "What are these for?"

He said nothing.

"You have a cold? Or did you come here to wipe your prints off the truck you stole?"

"I ain't saying nothing, pig."

I grinned and took a few steps back to check out the cell phone. Very simple, clearly a burner, with only two numbers in it. Neither were familiar, likely burners too, but we'd run them to be sure. The call history showed one of them had placed a call to Tyrell's phone at 5:34 p.m. My meeting with Mayor O'Reilly and Kassondra Ives had ended around 5:25.

I held up the phone to Tyrell. "Whose number is this?"

He spat with poor aim, missing my face wide left.

"You know that Nebraska has the death penalty, right, Tyrell? Murdering a teenage girl in cold blood, as a convicted felon . . . you make a compelling case for lethal injection."

"You can't scare me, pig."

"Oh, it's not me scaring you. It's the fatal dose of fentanyl they're going to pump into your veins that should scare you. Maybe you'd prefer an overdose of crystal meth instead?"

"Man, shut up."

"You rat out your partner, I'll talk to the attorney general and see about taking the death penalty off the table. Life at NSP's better than a straight ticket to the afterlife with your record, don't you think?"

Tyrell sneered as he shook his head. He swore again, then said, "You never even sniffed my partner five years ago, and you ain't gon' sniff her now. And I ain't getting no lethal injection for killing some girl, neither."

He used a different word for "girl," and I wanted to find another rock to give him a matching scar behind his right ear. Instead, I pocketed the phone and told him to wait where he was, hoping he would make a run and I could take him down again. He stayed in place, and I closed both doors of Tonia's truck. Then, with another glance to make sure he wasn't in fact bleeding excessively from the gash—he wasn't—I marched him toward the garage, where my truck had been parked since a little before six that night. I opened the garage door, loaded and buckled Tyrell into the passenger seat with his arms still behind him, and then got in on my side. Before driving off, I sent Tonia a text, letting her know the coast was clear and she and Jerry could return from their long double-date at a friend's house outside Fairmont.

Appropriately, "I Got Stripes" by Johnny Cash was playing on the radio as we drove back to town.

Forty-One

NOT even crickets sounded as I walked from the driveway to the front door of my house a little before one a.m. There was only the sound of my footsteps in the otherwise deathly silence of a windless summer night. Deathly was an appropriate descriptor, seeing as it was five days almost to the hour since Caitlin had been murdered. And now her killer was behind bars.

I was pretty sure.

I had driven Tyrell back to the department and processed him, and Lake had cleaned and bandaged his wounds. In addition to the gash behind his ear, there were also a few scrapes on his face that had drawn blood. We had endured our fair share of cursing throughout, but Tyrell had never asked for a lawyer, and I was more than happy to wait on that until morning. Or longer.

Then I had recounted his arrest for Lake and supplied him with the burn phone. Neither number stored in Tyrell's phone was in the system anywhere, meaning they were both likely burners . . . and not Caitlin's. There were periodic calls to the number that had called at 5:34 Friday evening, but none that struck either of us as being particularly timely. The other number had been called and had called Tyrell frequently, including Sunday afternoon around four o'clock, but not since. I had asked Lake to do his tech thing with the phone to see if there was anything else he could find on it, then left him in charge of the prisoner while I went home to shower and catch a few winks before in fact meeting Judge Felix for breakfast Saturday morning to talk warrants.

I hoped searching Tyrell's apartment and his vehicle—which had been parked in the DeBoer driveway—would give us a conclusive tie to Kassondra, or at least enough to procure a warrant to see if she possessed the burner phone that had called Tyrell shortly after the meeting in which I had revealed the last chance to wipe down prints and DNA was overnight Friday. It still bugged me that we didn't have the smoking gun, so to speak, the concrete, irrefutable, unchallengeable-by-a-defense-attorney proof that she was involved. For that matter, we didn't have rock-solid proof that Tyrell had pulled the trigger. Thus the need for warrants, and also the trace of doubt as I stepped onto the front porch. As I'd recapped things for Lake, I couldn't help feel this niggling sense that something was off. Maybe it was nothing more than Tyrell's repeated insistence that he hadn't killed anyone while being defiant about everything else. Or maybe there was some piece of evidence I had overlooked or some leap in logic in all my hunches.

That was another reason I wanted to get a little sleep and hopefully recharge a brain that had been grinding all day.

I stopped myself just before closing the door, seeing a lump on the end of the couch. Jessi, asleep under a blanket. She had known my plans and, like any cop's wife I imagine, been worried, even though I had reassured her I'd be fine. Like any cop's wife—or any man's wife—I was sure she had wanted to believe me but was also smart enough to know I couldn't really back up that assurance. This wasn't the first time she had camped out on the couch to await my return, nor, I was sure, the last.

I eased the door shut behind me and flicked the deadbolt, then crept over to the couch. She looked so cute there, curled up on a couple throw pillows, her hair draped around her chin, a blanket almost tucked around her shoulders, her bare feet poking out the other end of the blanket.

The first thought that popped into my head seeing her there was a line from the bridge of Sara Evans' song "Suds in the Bucket." The second was the juxtaposition of my wife, so peaceful, and Caitlin Thomas gray and lifeless in the park. The third was actually a series of thoughts that came cascading from my brain into my chest and caused my heart to pound. I realized I'd had it all wrong, that the evidence actually pointed in a different direction.

Or, at least, *could* point in a different direction. This was another hunch, one a little crazier than all the rest.

But this time, I had a feeling I'd finally stumbled onto the truth.

It was time to wake up a judge.

Forty-Two

"MAYOR, did I wake you?" I asked at quarter to seven Saturday morning. It was a polite formality—I hadn't slept in twenty-four hours and didn't really care if the mayor was a little groggy. Besides, I had big news.

"No, but I am surprised by the early call. Was your stakeout successful?"

"It was," I said. "I have Caitlin's killer."

"You what? You've got him?"

"And I have more than that."

O'Reilly's confusion played out in silence. "Come again?" he finally said.

"He didn't act alone, and I've arranged to meet his accomplice in an hour."

"You're meeting the accomplice?"

"Yeah, but they don't know it's a trap."

"I'm afraid I'm not following, Cash."

"That's all right, I'm not leading real great working on no sleep. I'm calling because I'd like you to be there."

"Me?"

"There are some political ramifications, and I think you should be there to witness it."

Another confused pause. "I'm still in the dark here, Cash."

"I know, and it'll be much easier to show you than explain it."

"All right. Where are you meeting this accomplice?"

"Tell you what, if you can be at the sheriff's department at seven-thirty, I'll meet you there, and we'll go together."

"All right. You've got a deal."

"Good. See you then."

He clicked off before I could, and I took a swig of coffee. I was so many cups in that I was afraid that once the floodgates opened they wouldn't shut, but that was a problem for later. With another half-gulp, I dialed a second number, waiting through three rings.

"Kassondra Ives."

"Kassondra, it's Sheriff Nelson. I'm sorry if I woke you."

"At . . . quarter to seven on a Saturday, not a chance," she said with a trace of sarcasm.

"I'll make it worth your while," I said. "Can you meet me at your old campaign headquarters in an hour?"

"Do what?"

"Four-twelve Main Street," I said.

"I know the address. Why am I meeting you there at quarter to eight on a Saturday?"

"Because I know who killed Caitlin."

"You do?"

"I do."

"That's great. But why can't you tell me on the phone and after some breakfast?"

"It is a little complicated, and much easier to lay out in person."

She sighed. "Seven forty-five?"

"Please."

"Okay," she said through another sigh. "I'll be there."

"Thank you, Kassondra."

She ended the call, and I set my phone down on my desk. Another blast of coffee, then I massaged my temples and my neck. I hadn't been sure I'd be able to persuade Kassondra to come but had a hunch she wouldn't be able to stay away.

I stood and walked into the bullpen, where Wally sat at his computer, having replaced an exhausted Lake at six a.m. "You checked on our prisoner lately?" I asked.

"Out cold about fifteen minutes ago."

I nodded.

"You still want to try questioning him again this morning?"

"You wake up with your head a few feet from a stainless-steel toilet, it can change your perception of things."

"Yeah, maybe make him *want* the death penalty instead of a life of that."

"Then I'll flip the deal."

He winked and pointed at me, and I went to brew some fresh coffee, figuring an olive branch offered through jail bars couldn't hurt. Unless, of course, Tyrell flung the coffee back at me.

Forty-Three

MAYOR O'Reilly accepted his coffee much more graciously than Tyrell had when O'Reilly and I met on the front step of the sheriff's department office at seven-thirty on the button. For the first time I could remember, it wasn't hot and sunny, but cool and gray as a result of a front that had swept through overnight. It hadn't brought rain, but the air was damp and chilly for an August morning. It felt like funeral weather, which reminded me that Pat and Molly Erickson and their friends and loved ones would be gathering soon. I desperately wanted to be able to give them closure of a sort.

"You're shrouded in mystery this morning, Cash," the mayor said, taking his to-go cup of coffee. "Thank you."

I nodded. "I'm tired. Blame it on this."

"You said you've got the killer? In jail?"

I nodded and took a sip.

"He talking?"

"In four-letter words. No, he's defiant."

The mayor harrumphed. Then straightened his posture. "Where are we going?" he asked, gesturing with his thumb down the block. "I'm parked on 4th."

"We can walk," I said. "Come on."

I led a frowning mayor down the sidewalk, which on this side of the street was still intact except for where the access from Main Street to our parking lot had been removed via backhoe, the concrete still in a pile of chunks by the curb. We journeyed around it, then returned to the sidewalk until we came to the entrance to the first of two storefronts in the two-story brick building across the lot from the sheriff's department. I stopped in front of a single concrete step leading up to a glass door beneath the numbers 412 on the doorpost. A shop window next to it showed the faded inscription where "KASSONDRA IVES FOR MAYOR" and "CAMPAIGN HEADQUARTERS" had been stenciled at the top.

"What are we doing here?" O'Reilly asked.

"You'll see," I said as I reached for the door. "Do you know what this building used to be?"

"Yeah, my opponent's headquarters. It's unlocked?"

I nodded. "Before that. Way before that."

"Been a number of things, as I recall."

"In 1932, when it was built, it was a department store with a 'bargain basement.'"

"That's fascinating, Cash," he said as we stood on a dusty wood floor of a front room that spanned the width of this half of the building, less than twenty feet, and went back about thirty before a drywalled wall blocked half the room while the other half went back another dozen feet before hitting a wall. Left and right, the walls were both brick, running up past the drop ceiling to the second floor. He looked around at the empty space. "What are we doing here?"

"I told you, meeting the killer's accomplice. She should be here soon."

"*She*?"

I nodded. "You ever been in this building?" I asked, wandering back toward where the main room narrowed.

"Can't say as that I have. It was my opponent's headquarters," he said again.

Three doors opened to the right once the room narrowed, one to an eight-by-ten office, another to a mechanical closet, and a third to a bathroom. A doorway in the back wall, also drywalled, was dark, lit only by the red glow of an EXIT sign beyond it. An alley and small parking lot serviced both this building and Butch's bar next door, and had also become something of a staging ground for some of the construction equipment.

"Cash, you want to tell me what's going on?"

I turned back as I took a drink of my coffee. "In a minute."

We both waited without patience for several minutes until Kassondra walked past the shop window and approached the front door. She wore joggers and a knit pullover, a contrast to the mayor's slacks and button-up dress shirt. That spoke to several differences in the candidates, none of which mattered at the moment.

"Kassondra, thank you for coming," I said as she entered, her pace slowing when she saw the mayor.

"You?" he asked, then looked at me.

"I should have figured I wouldn't get a scoop," she said as the door closed behind her. "Mayor."

"Miss Ives. Cash, what is going on?"

"I promised you both an explanation, so please bear with me. This could take a minute."

"Just get it on with it," O'Reilly growled.

I nodded.

"One of the first questions my deputies and I asked when we found Caitlin's body was why had the killer left it laying in the park instead of dragging it a short distance to the cornfield where it likely wouldn't have been discovered for . . . weeks if not months."

"Maybe he or she was in a hurry," Kassondra said.

"We considered a range of possibilities," I said with a shrug, "but it still never quite made sense. Yesterday—well, no, two days ago now—as I was driving back from Lincoln, staring at field after field of corn and backed up in road construction, I had an epiphany. Caitlin's murder was not the primary crime, but a cover for something else."

"Not the primary crime?" O'Reilly asked. "How can the murder of a seventeen-year-old girl not be the primary crime?"

"A cover for what?" Kassondra asked.

"With all the noise and shaking and hassle of construction on Main Street—and that's not a political statement, just a fact," I said, holding up a hand at the mayor, "and with the entire town buzzing about a murder, and me and my deputies working almost exclusively on trying to solve said murder, absolutely no one was paying attention to this building," I said, pointing at the floor.

"My old headquarters? Why would they be?"

"Land's sakes, Cash, come to the point, will you?"

I held up my hand again. Then said, "Follow me."

I set my mostly empty coffee cup down on the floor before leading them back through the narrow part of the room and through the doorway shrouded in darkness. Six feet beyond it, a steel fire door opened to the alley. Instead, I turned left and reached for the knob on a wood door. "Kassondra, I assume you knew this place had a basement, dating back to its days as department store?"

"Yeah. We kept some supplies down there. It was old, drafty, dirty."

I nodded, feeling for a light switch on the left wall. "Follow me," I said, starting down a set of wooden stairs that clanked under our feet. The wall on the left was stud and drywall, unfinished, and the wall on the right century-old stonework. The same was true dead ahead at the bottom, and I turned left through a doorway cut into the studs and drywall. I found another switch on the left, which turned on a trio of lightbulbs in an unfinished basement the same size as the first floor. Behind me, Kassondra gasped.

The far third of the basement was piled to the ceiling with stone and mortar crumbles, scraps of wood and drywall, and miscellaneous building debris. Along the left wall, dirt was piled in several mounds that nearly reached the ceiling and fell off in pebbles and crumbles almost to our feet. There was just enough room for a battery powered generator, a pair of construction lights that were currently off, a collection of hand tools, and a free-standing, industrial-strength drill with at least a six-inch boring bit. It was currently backed away from a tunnel partially drilled and partially hand-carved into the dirt where the western basement wall had been.

"What . . . in . . . the . . ." Kassondra asked.

O'Reilly stepped forward, scanned the room, and turned back to look at me. "What is this, Cash?"

"This," I said, "is Justin Tyrell's effort to retrieve three million dollars' worth of meth from the remains of his stepmom's grandmother's house."

Forty-Four

THEY both looked at me with incredulity as I walked over beside the drill, crouched slightly, and shined my flashlight down the tunnel. It bored in a mostly straight line for thirty feet, I knew from having crawled through it around three a.m., before getting stuck in a mess of old lumber, drywall, and plaster. Several additional holes, about a foot in diameter, extended in radials from its end. One of them had been widened additionally and angled downward, appearing to be the new direction of the "main" tunnel.

I explained all this to Mayor O'Reilly and Kassondra, then played my flashlight against the wall where a folding table held some smaller hand tools, as well as a pair of hardhats with headlamps attached to them, like a coalminer's helmet of yesteryear. Interestingly enough, they bore the familiar stamp of Knight Trucking, which overnight research had confirmed did more than haul dirt and rock. They also provided a host of construction services.

"Feel free to take a look yourself," I said. "Although it is a little tight."

"You're telling me that the meth . . . from the raid five years ago is in there?" O'Reilly asked.

"Delores Schiff rented this place from Philip Willis, a.k.a. Happy Homes Limited, five years ago. Her granddaughter, Theresa Jones, was married to Justin Tyrell's father at the time."

"And you think Tyrell moved his product from out in the country to his stepmom's grandma's house right next to the sheriff's department?"

"Brazen, wasn't it? Sixteen months ago, the old place was sold to the town and razed for the purpose of expanding our nice, new parking lot. Since asphalt doesn't need all that much foundation, it was easier to just bury the house in its own hole, fill it in, and pave over it. All while Tyrell sat helplessly in the state pen."

"Do you have proof of this?" Kassondra asked.

"This isn't proof enough for you?" I asked, aiming the light at the tunnel.

"It's proof that *someone* had reason to go tunneling, but do you know it was Tyrell? And do you know it was to retrieve three million dollars' worth of meth?"

"Admittedly that was a hunch," I said. "Until early this morning when Judge Felix issued me a warrant to come search this place. I found the tunnel, found the stub of a branch at the end, and found what looks like the remains of a modern stud-and-sheetrock wall in the basement. It's hard to tell, given the way two stories of a house were packed into a basement and buried, but I also found stuffed in that wall a torn piece of foil and a powdery substance inside. Methamphetamine. Ice, crank, cotton candy."

She shook her head.

"How do you know it was Tyrell?" O'Reilly asked. "How do you know it was *that* meth?"

"Hunches and guesses," I said. "We linked the truck belonging to Tonia Savicki to the parking lot where Caitlin was found, and Savicki's place is right across the road from the DeBoer place where Tyrell cooked up his meth. Still, that would all be coincidence," I said, "if it wasn't for Tyrell showing up last night to try to erase any evidence he'd left behind in Savicki's truck. And here's the thing," I said, looking between them. "You two were the only two who knew about my plans to get a warrant to search Savicki's truck in the morning, which means only one of you two could have alerted Tyrell to the urgent need to wipe it down last night."

"Not necessarily," Kassondra said with a shrug. "He could have decided to on his own."

"I suppose, five days after the crime he could have suddenly thought he left behind a print or a sample of DNA in some manner and decided on his own to go back and try to erase it." I reached into my pocket. "But let's run a little test," I said, thumbing on the burner phone I'd found on Tyrell. "Ten minutes after the two of you left my office, a burn phone made a call to Tyrell." I pressed the call button on his phone and waited, looking at Kassondra.

A few seconds later, a muted, vibrating buzz sounded. I took a step toward her, and we both turned to look at Mayor O'Reilly, whose face had blanched.

I held up the burner in my left hand. "You gonna get that, Mayor?"

Forty-Five

O'REILLY fumbled in his pocket as I hovered my hand over my holster. But all he came out with was the vibrating cell phone, which he muted. His blank face quickly formed resolve.

"Cash, we can work something out."

I shook my head.

"I had no idea he was going to kill the girl. That was never part of the deal."

"What was the deal?"

"T-t-ten percent."

"That's a nice campaign donation," Kassondra said.

"A retirement supplement, in f-f-fact. Th-there's not m-much money in being a civil servant." He swallowed hard. "But it's yours, Cash. Over three hundred thousand, and I'll back out of the race and fade into retirement."

"You're forgetting something," I said.

He frowned.

"Tyrell's accomplice."

"There's someone else involved?" Kassondra asked, even as the mayor's face whitened again.

"There is, and I don't think it'd be right of you to make a deal and give away your cut of Tyrell's money without consulting the accomplice first. Unless she's getting her own cut."

"She?" Kassondra asked.

"No . . ." O'Reilly muttered, dropping his coffee cup. "You surely don't . . ."

"There were two numbers in Tyrell's phone," I said. "Yours, which is how I know you tipped him off and implicated yourself, and another that he texted and called frequently, including the day of Caitlin's murder, but not since. He told me when I collared him that we hadn't sniffed his partner five years ago and we weren't going to sniff *her* now. Kassondra, I'll be honest, for a little while, I thought you might have been working with Tyrell."

"Me?"

"This *was* your campaign HQ, your grandfather owns the company that was going to get a contract for the road construction until Knight Trucking—owned by a classmate of Tyrell's—got it at the last minute, and your father was a roommate with Theresa Jones' husband."

She shook her head. "That has . . . to be a coincidence. I had no idea, about any of it."

I nodded. "I realized that. I remembered a few things that hadn't added up, and started doing the math again, and I realized there was someone else who tied into this. I played another hunch and texted that other number on Tyrell's phone, asking her to meet me here at eight o'clock." I looked at my watch. "Three minutes."

"No," O'Reilly muttered, and started reaching for his pocket again.

"Don't do it, Mayor. You try to warn her, it will still implicate her."

"It doesn't matter," a female voice called from the base of the stairs. "I'm already here."

She stepped forward, and I took note of blond hair in a loose braid under a backward baseball cap, a flannel shirt open over a gray tee, and blue jeans. She had an attractive face, even with her jaw set in a hard glare. But I wasn't focused on her face or her clothes. My eyes were drawn to the suppressor-equipped pistol in her right hand and the hot pink work boots on her feet.

"Glad you could make it, Shelby."

Forty-Six

"YOU shouldn't be," she said, training her eyes—and her pistol—on me. "I had a feeling this might be a trap, so I came prepared."

"Shelby, why?" the mayor asked.

She shrugged. "I figured I couldn't lose. Either Justin had found the drugs, in which case he and I would be rich, or it was a trap, and the law would be here, in which case it probably meant that Justin was in jail, and I alone could be rich."

"Do we really need the gun?" Kassondra asked.

"Yes, Little Miss Pacifist, we do. In fact, Sheriff, how about using your *left* hand to slowly remove your gun from the holster and put it on the ground."

I extended my right palm and slowly did as she asked.

"Now kick it over here."

I did.

"In case you think one of your deputies is going to sneak up behind me, I bolted both doors when I came in, so it's just the four of us."

"Shelby, please don't do anything rash," O'Reilly said.

"It's a little late for that," Kassondra mumbled.

"No, he's right," I said. "You're in trouble, obviously, but if you two will come clean and implicate Tyrell for Caitlin's murder, I'll do everything I can to get you each a lesser sentence. Mayor, you know my word is good on that."

"I'll tell you all I know, take the full share of blame for my part, just please leave her out of this."

"I can't leave her out of it entirely," I said. "She's got me at gunpoint."

"Tyrell reached out to me through a back channel while he was still in prison. He knew my campaign chest was low, knew a few investments had gone south, and offered me over a quarter of a million dollars if I would do everything I could to expedite the Main Street construction project and evict the current owner of this building. I had no control over that, but I did what I could to push the construction up."

"Who was this back-channel contact?"

"I have no idea. We never met."

"I can't believe it," Kassondra said. "You sold out through some unknown messenger to a convicted felon? You know what that meth will do to our community if it's sold?"

"I figured it would be sold somewhere else, out of state probably."

"So it's okay to ruin other peoples' lives to pad your retirement account?"

"You'll get no argument from me," O'Reilly said. "I confess. I've got every message that was sent between us, and they implicate Tyrell. And I'll testify, he supplied me this phone," he said, holding it up, "and we spoke several times leading up to the start of construction. He said he'd found another way to get Kassondra to leave the building."

"How?" I asked.

"I don't know, he didn't say."

"I got a mysterious offer on the current building," she said, "out of the blue, more space and less rent. It was a no-brainer. He must have pulled a string somehow."

The mayor nodded. "Tyrell called me early Monday morning, said he'd arranged a distraction for the cops and I'd better not back out now because he and my granddaughter were both conspirators and he'd make sure we go down. I'll swear to it in court, he killed Caitlin Thomas. Just please leave my Shelby out of it."

"There's only one problem with that plan, Grandpa."

We all looked at her.

"Tyrell didn't kill Caitlin. I did."

"No!"

"It was his idea, and he seduced her and lured her to the park, but I was the one who pulled the trigger. Bang, bang," she said, flicking the gun the way a kid might fake a shooting with a thumb and forefinger. She smiled. "I don't think he had to work too hard to charm her, but it felt good anyhow, to see the girl who thought she could take my man go lifeless."

"Shelby."

"And then you helped yourself to her heels too," I said.

She looked at me with disbelief at first, then smiled. "They were just too adorable to let go to waste, and I figured no one would ever know. How did you?" she asked with a frown.

"The boots," I said. "All women have a thing for shoes, but those take it to a new level. Caitlin was barefoot, a pair of new shoes were missing from her closet, I knew a female was involved with Tyrell five years ago, and, now, you're on the construction crew and one of the bullets had cement dust on it. Daisy Schubert knew the mayor had a troubled granddaughter, one who had gone away several years ago, and then I did a little research and saw a birth record listing a Shelby Wallace as the mother of a boy born in Denver five years ago . . . the pieces all fit together."

"I thought you gave the baby up for adoption," O'Reilly said.

"I did, Grandpa." She turned to me. "Cement dust on the bullet and missing shoes?"

I nodded.

"This Hardy Boys-style recap is great," Kassondra said, "but can we start talking about a deal to end this peacefully?"

"There is no deal," Shelby said. "You and the sheriff are going to retrieve the meth from in there, and then I'm going to shoot you both and bury you. By the time anyone finds you, I'll be in another state and still no one will know I was involved."

"Except dear old Grandpa," I said.

"He won't rat me out, will you, Gramps? You never had the strong hand everyone seems to think you do, Mayor O'Reilly."

"How do you plan to get three mil of meth out of here?" I asked.

"I've got a pair of duffel bags upstairs."

"And if my deputies are waiting outside?"

Shelby reached into her back pocket and pulled out a cell phone. "They're not. Camera we mounted over the door, looking at the alley." She looked at the screen. "Nothing there but a mini excavator. I'm going to walk out of here with three million dollars' worth of product and never be seen again."

"What about your man, Tyrell? You going to let him rot in prison?"

"He was good for a fun time, but I'm pretty sure three mil will buy me all the fun times I want. Give him my best though, will you?"

I had considered the possibility that Shelby had actually been the shooter, but never seriously. And I was shocked at how brazen she was. I don't want to say I'd underestimated her, but now I had no doubt that she was indeed coldblooded enough to kill both Kassondra and I, and maybe even her grandpa, if we stood in the way of three million dollars.

"Now, toss me your phones," Shelby said, and Kassondra and I did. "I've got all day," she said, "but it could take a while to find and retrieve the drugs. You'd better get to work."

"You have a plan?" Kassondra asked, looking at me.

I turned my LCSD baseball cap backward and started unbuttoning my sleeves. "Best do what the lady says." I walked over to the folding table and grabbed one of the hardhats, which I handed to Kassondra. Her eyes were desperate and pleading, but I didn't see panic either. I gave her a subtle nod, then reached for the other hat as she grabbed a short-handled shovel.

"I can't believe this is happening," she said.

"I have to admit, it's now how I pictured the morning going either." I grabbed a small bucket and a pick. "After you."

With me giving her a foothold, she crawled up into the tunnel. I was about to follow when suddenly our world exploded in a dazzling burst of light and a cacophony of sound.

Forty-Seven

YEARS ago, in training, I had been subject to a host of unpleasant experiences—being on the receiving end of a choke hold, having pepper spray discharged in my face, and enduring the explosion of a flashbang. I had known then, as now, what was coming, and had learned there was only so much preparation one could make.

My ears ringing and my eyelids feeling as if they had been burned right off my eyes, I quickly turned around. I saw the mayor hunched/fallen against the near wall, and Shelby several steps back closer to the door to the stairs, her left hand over her left ear and her right arm pressed against her right ear with the forearm covering her eyes. That left her pointing the gun into the corner.

On somewhat wobbly feet, I charged, reaching with both hands for the gun and her wrist and using the force of my body to drive her back against the wall. I arrived just a split second before Bill, his department-issued, hooded rain poncho covered in dirt, his service weapon drawn. Together, we raked the gun from Shelby's hand and spun her around against the wall, even as Cheryl descended the steps and came around the door, her gun also drawn.

"I got her," I said, reaching for my cuffs.

"You all right?" Bill asked, I knew only because I could read his lips.

I nodded and then tipped my head toward the mayor. I cuffed Shelby and quickly frisked her to make sure nothing was concealed, while Bill cuffed the mayor and Cheryl hurried over to check on Kassondra. She was trembling, either from fear or the concussive blast, but seemed unharmed other than for some dirt that had fallen from the tunnel into her hair and onto her clothes.

My ears still ringing, I officially placed Shelby under arrest for the murder of Caitlin Thomas and O'Reilly under arrest for conspiracy-after-the-fact, with a host of charges to be added to each of them later. With them both standing by the wall to the stairs and Bill keeping an eye on them just to be sure, I joined Cheryl and the stunned new mayoral frontrunner.

"Kassondra, are you all right?"

"I think so," she said loudly. "You knew all along?"

"Knew is a strong word. Suspected."

She shook her head. "Why was I here?"

"I included you to lead the mayor on into thinking I was on the wrong track. And I wanted you here to see this all play out and to have an impartial witness. Kind of awkward for the sheriff's department to arrest the sitting mayor."

"And you thought his challenger would be impartial?"

"Hmm, fair point. Bill also had a recording device hidden."

"Where *was* Bill?"

"Ninety-nine percent submerged under the dirt," I said.

"And Cheryl?"

"Hidden above the drop ceiling upstairs," she said. "One more muffin yesterday and I wouldn't have fit up there."

Kassondra shook her head. "You really thought Shelby would show up with a gun?"

"I didn't, but I also knew if she did, it could get sticky."

She shook her head some more.

"I'm sorry if this whole thing scared you, but I didn't believe you'd be in any real danger. Bill was monitoring all the while from back there," I said, pointing to where the dirt pile had shifted considerably after he lobbed the flashbang and extricated himself. "You're not going to sue the department, are you?"

"I'll let you know after I consult with my cardiologist."

I grinned.

"So now what?"

"Well, we've got a pair of recorded confessions, he admitted to having saved texts between the middle-man, who I'm guessing was a middle-woman," I said with a look at a defiant Shelby, "and I'm sure between the two of them and Tyrell trying to out-rat the other and the warrants we'll get to search their homes and his office, we'll find plenty of evidence to send them all away for a long time. And . . ." I said, leaning back, "you shouldn't have too much trouble getting elected with only a felon on the ballot to oppose you."

"I don't know," she said with a concealed smirk, "this county voted eighty-five percent for Trump."

"Three times," Bill added with a grin. Then he turned to Cheryl. "Come on, let's get them out of here and processed."

My deputies marched a pair of recalcitrant criminals up the stairs, and Kassondra looked around. "What happens with all this?"

"I think that's a decision for the new mayor."

She shot me a look.

"Seriously, Tyrell did find at least part of the stash. I'm assuming we'll want to extract it for evidence and also to destroy it lest someone else try to recover it. But then this building owner will have a mess on their hands, or maybe it will become the town's issue—or both, I don't know. Seriously, that might fall on your desk next year. Or the acting mayor once one is appointed. Who will probably run and confuse the slate. This will get messy."

"I'll worry about the politics later. Right now, I want to get cleaned up and get to a funeral."

"Yeah," I said. "Being able to tell Pat and Molly we caught Caitlin's killers isn't much, but it's something."

Kassondra shook her head. "It's a lot more than that."

Forty-Eight

SATURDAY night Jessi and I went for a short stroll. The sun had peeked out sometime mid-afternoon, albeit without the heat and humidity that had been present for so long. Summer in Nebraska still had a way to go, but golden hour held a hint that autumn was eventually coming.

The funeral had been hard, for several reasons. The Thomas/Erickson family had already suffered one tragedy this year, and a second seemed to have some of them at the breaking point. The steep cathedral walls of St. Peter's Catholic Church had echoed with wails of grief several times during the visitation and service. It had been full of religion but without any authenticity. It reminded me of a newscaster on one of the local channels who would banter with the sports director about Husker games when it was clear she didn't know a field goal from a first down. Believing in the eternal nature of the soul, of the reality of heaven and hell, it was hard for me to sit and listen to people talking about God in a way that suggested they—and perhaps Caitlin—didn't really *know* God. And it was long, as was the luncheon afterward, and I had a lot of work to do.

Fortunately, Mayor O'Reilly lessened the work by confessing to everything. Wally, Cheryl, and Lake served warrants on O'Reilly's office, his home, Shelby's apartment, and Tyrell's apartment while Bill and I interrogated our three prisoners. They found the communications O'Reilly had mentioned with an intermediary both on his device and on a burn phone hidden at Shelby's apartment. Tyrell's laptop contained a creepy level of research on Caitlin, a profile he had likely used to seduce her. His browsing history linked him to the industrial-strength drill and its purchase, along with a host of other tools and pieces of equipment from the basement beneath Kassondra's old office. His fingerprints were everywhere there, which Lake had recovered late in the afternoon. Bill delivered Shelby's nine-millimeter Glock to the lab in Lincoln to see if it matched the slugs taken from Caitlin's body. Tyrell and Shelby had lawyered up, but the damage had been done by the former mayor (the town council had acted swiftly that morning to remove him) and my initial talks with the attorney general confirmed what I hoped for—all three of them would go away for a long time.

Bill and Cheryl finally sent me home a little after seven, insisting that I needed a decent meal and sleep. Jessi had already eaten, so I grabbed a runza and ate most of it on the way home, only to find I was too wired to sleep. So after changing into something comfortable, I'd talked my pregnant wife into an evening walk.

The farther north you go in Lee, the less the town extends to the west. Our street, 2nd Street, ends at Jefferson Avenue, which itself has a dead-end stub just west of 2nd. The properties across the street from us back up to a field, which wraps around the north side of Jefferson. We walked leisurely toward the corn, practically glowing as the sunlight danced across the tassels. Our pace was slow, Jessi holding my hand a little tighter, it seemed, than normal. When we reached Jefferson, I turned us west, and we walked to the three wooden posts with blue reflectors on them that marked the end of the road. We stood looking at rows of corn, the sun hanging just above them in the northwestern sky. In a way, it felt like things had come full circle since the sun had risen over the corn Monday morning.

"Molly called me this afternoon," Jessi said.

I turned to look at her, the breeze lifting tendrils of hair off a sweatshirt she had thrown on after stepping outside and feeling the evening "chill."

"Oh?"

"She asked me to put the word out that they had enough food to last the month."

I grinned.

"And she said to thank you."

"She thanked me at the funeral," I said. She and Pat both had, he with a firm handshake and teary but steely eyes. It was the lone part of the service that hadn't been depressing, that and seeing a small town's outpouring of love and support on citizens who desperately needed it.

"Well, she said to thank you again."

"It's my job," I said, looking back to the corn.

"That doesn't mean you can't accept gratitude," Jessi said. "Not everyone would have dedicated themselves to justice the way you did, Cash."

"I get it honest."

"I mean it, you're true blue."

I turned to look at her.

"Corny?" she asked.

"Just a little." I leaned over and pecked her on the forehead. Then we watched the sunset for a few minutes.

"I can't believe you had Cheryl hide in the drop ceiling."

"It was that or under a pile of dirt. Easy sell."

"Your deputies need a raise."

"You'll have to take it up with the new mayor."

"When will that be?"

"After the election."

"I mean in the interim."

"Already. Dean Barrow was appointed by the council as Interim Mayor."

"Is he going to run against Kassondra?"

"No idea," I said, looking back at the corn.

"Has this town ever had a Democrat mayor?"

"Some years I'm not sure we've even had a Democrat."

"That'll be interesting."

"She's got spunk at least, I'll give her that," I said, then recapped some of the morning's details I hadn't had time to on the way to the funeral earlier.

Jessi shook her head when I was finished.

"What?"

"What if you had been wrong?"

"About what?"

"Any of it. What if Tyrell had already wiped prints off the truck?"

"Then my trap wouldn't have worked, but I was betting on him not thinking we had even tied him to the truck or it to the murder."

"What if the mayor hadn't had the burn phone on him?"

I shrugged.

"Or what if he hadn't agreed to go with you because he smelled a trap?"

I shrugged.

"Or what if Shelby had seen through your text and known you weren't Tyrell, or sensed a trap, or decided not to come?"

I reached two fingers and gently touched her lips. "Then I would still be at work instead of enjoying this sunset with you."

She nodded. "You got a little lucky, Cash, admit it."

"Luck is the residue of design."

She squinted at me. "Who said that?"

I shrugged again. "Benjamin Franklin? Solomon?"

"I doubt that."

I shrugged one more time.

Jessi shivered.

"You want to go back?"

"Not yet."

I sighed. "Truth is, I played a lot of hunches. This time, they were right."

"Your intuition usually is. You married me."

"Like you said, I got lucky."

The fireball that was the sun sank beneath the nearest tassels of corn. Jessi shivered again.

"Now?"

She nodded, and we turned back. There were still things I didn't know or couldn't explain about the case. Tyrell had taken some long shots, and gotten lucky himself. Bill was right, influencing the timing of the town's road construction and seducing and then murdering a girl as a distraction were indeed drastic steps. But three million dollars could drive men to drastic measures. Tyrell hadn't talked yet, so we didn't know if he had somehow known Tonia would be gone Sunday night or had taken the opportunity when it presented itself, nor how long he'd been planning to use her truck or even why. When and why he'd moved the drugs from the DeBoer barn to his stepmom's grandmother's house, and how he'd done so without attracting attention, apparently sealing them in a wall, was also a mystery. The little unknowns bugged me, the same way writing off Kassondra's apparent connections as coincidences did—even though they were apparently coincidences. But none of them bugged me very much with Tyrell, Shelby, and O'Reilly all behind bars and facing a host of felony charges with evidence to support convictions.

"O'Reilly really tried to bribe you?" Jessi asked when we were almost back to our driveway.

"In not so many words."

"How much?"

"Jess."

"Hey, we have college to think about someday."

"I don't know, maybe not. Maybe Junior will follow in his old man's footsteps and become a policeman."

"That's all I need, worrying about both of you every day."

I put my arm around her shoulders, and she leaned into me. We walked a few paces. Then she looked up. "Besides, I think we may need the money."

"Oh?"

"I've been thinking and . . . when *she* is born, I don't think I want to go back to teaching."

"No?"

"No. I want to be a mom. Period."

I nodded. "That's what I want too."

"Really?"

"I mean . . . for you . . . to be a mom."

"Things may be a little tight on just your salary."

"We'll get by," I said. "And, I kind of did save the future mayor's life, so she ought to lobby for me to get a few percentage points of a raise."

"Saved it by shoving her in a tunnel after bringing her down in the basement to endanger her life to begin with?"

"Besides, what Democrat could say no to a raise when I need it to keep my wife at home, barefoot and pregnant?"

Jessi placed her hand on her abdomen. "Let's survive one—and make sure she survives—before we plan anything else."

"Deal," I said. I gave her a quick squeeze, then dropped my arm and lifted my head to look at a sleepy street lined with trees still catching sunlight in their upper boughs, the blue sky above just starting to fade to darkness. The scent of freshly cut hay drifted in from a nearby field, mingling with burning kerosene from a grill. A dog barked in the distance as a faintly humming lawnmower cut out. An old lady on the other side of the street was sweeping absolutely nothing off her front porch. At the far end of the block, another young couple walked hand-in-hand, their toddler on a tricycle pedaling on ahead of them. I couldn't help but smile as we reached our driveway. The charm of my small, Midwestern town that I had far too often taken for granted felt—with a murder now solved—fresh in my mind and heart again.

Jessi went to check something in her garden, and I crashed on the couch. I closed my eyes, picturing her in the kitchen on a warm summer evening. She was barefoot in a tank top and shorts, her hair piled up on top of her head and falling out in wisps as she tried to find a place for all the vegetables from her garden while also trying to wrangle a brother and sister who were singing and shouting and chasing each other around her. And I would come in from a long shift or one of those odd sheriff duties that took me away at the most inconvenient of times, or maybe from a part-time job to make a little extra money to get us through a tight patch. Our eyes would meet, amidst all the chaos, and I'd ask the non-verbal question that had been on my mind all day, and she'd put a hand on her abdomen and nod with the faintest of smiles.

"Cash?"

I looked over to where she stood at the end of the couch.

"You all right?" she asked.

"Yeah, fine."

"Because you kind of look like a zombie."

"I'm just thinking."

She came and sat down, tucking one foot under her. "About what?"

"Nothing," I said.

Jessi leaned into me, and I put my arm around her.

I took a deep breath. "And everything."

Author's Note

IN 2019, my wife and I took a road trip to Wyoming and back through my "home" state of Nebraska. We visited Chimney Rock and Carhenge, drove through the sandhills, and stopped at The Archway in Kearney. Then, because of road construction on I-80 and a missed turn, we detoured through the small town of Giltner. It was a warm summer evening with long shadows to contrast with bright sunlight on the surrounding fields as little kids walked to T-ball games in the park and grown men drove riding lawnmowers down the street. At the time, it was nothing more than a delay, and we hurried back to the interstate and put Giltner in the rearview mirror. But it refused to stay there.

I can't say exactly when or how the idea for a novel about a murder occurred to me. And it went through a couple iterations before finding its home in fictional Lee County. But with that night in Giltner stuck in my head, *True Blue* ended up being as much an ode to the Midwest as it is a murder mystery. Like my grandpa used to say, "You can take the boy out of Nebraska, but you can't take Nebraska out of the boy."

As usual, I owe thanks to those who helped proof this novel: my wife, Sierra; my parents, Doug and Jean Birr; my sister and brother-in-law, Tiffani and Mark Robinson. I'm sure mistakes remain, but they are mine, not theirs.

Some of those mistakes likely revolve around the particulars of law enforcement, especially in a rural sheriff's department. I have little experience in such matters, and, facing the choice between arduous research and imagination, I went with the latter. Hopefully any inaccuracies won't distract from the story.

And speaking of story, as much as any good novel needs a compelling plot and interesting characters, it also needs a setting that can draw the reader in. That brings me back to that night we accidentally stumbled into a slice of Americana in a little town most people have never heard of. (I won't dare to speak for the fine people of Giltner, but I've always sort of imagined they like it that way.)

www.ingramcontent.com/pod-product-compliance
Lightning Source LLC
LaVergne TN
LVHW090559110826
845146LV00001B/186

* 9 7 9 8 9 9 3 1 3 7 1 1 7 *